A Wolf in

Book Two of
'The Kingdom of Durundal'
series

S.E. Turner

Acknowledgements:

Daisy Jane Turner: illustrator, for the magnificent book covers.

Jeremy Boughtwood for formatting and publishing, without whom the book would still be in its manuscript form.

My friends and family for their enthusiasm and encouragement.

My three daughters who continue to inspire me.

The spirit animal is earned - not taken.

I was a very frightened fourteen year old boy back then; too frightened for my own good by all accounts. My father desperately wanted me to succeed him as a strong king with absolutely no fear of anything or anyone. A tall order back then. He used to tell me stories and I hated them. Because night after night, I had the same recurring nightmare, the same disturbed dream and even now as I speak, it's as real today as it was then.

It is pitch black and my heart is hammering. I can't control my vicious panting. The tunnel closes in and I crouch against the wall. My fingers can feel every crevasse on my shrinking tomb as I slide along the cold, damp, ancient, stones.

And then I feel it. Something cold reaches for me and I instinctively recoil. The thing groans and wails as it claws at my flesh. I manage to break free and start to run; but fettered legs are weak. I am weak. I cannot breath. I cannot move. The creature closes in. A long forked tongue licks along the sweat of the walls and I can feel its icy breath on my neck. I scream and sit bolt upright, trembling in my bed.

His mother ran in and put a candle on the table. She sat down on his bed and stroked his hair.

'It's the same dream every night mother. The same demon in the dark with its monstrous jaws of hell.' Lyall shivered, reliving every moment.

'It's a night terror my love, nothing will hurt you, I promise.'

He clutched her arm and his voice cried panic. 'Will you stay with me?'

'Of course I will. Lay down and close your eyes.' She began to sing quietly.

'The wild wind blows through valleys my love,
The wild wind blows through the trees,
The wild wind blows o'er the rivers my love,
But will n'er get closer to thee.
The wild rain storms through the valleys my love,
The wild rain storms through the trees,
The wild rain storms o'er the rivers my love,
But none will get closer to thee.'

She hummed softly and brushed a wisp of hair from his brow. When she was sure he was settled, she kissed his cheek and quietly left. The maid was hovering nearby, wearing her familiar pained expression. 'Is he all right ma'am? I have been ever so anxious.'

'He is settled now Dansa.'

'I'm worried that his nightmares are becoming more frequent.'

'I appreciate your concern, but rest assured I will speak to the king about it this very night.'

Dansa tilted her head to acknowledge the resolve.

'You get to bed now, the hour is very late,' continued the queen.

'If you are sure that is all ma'am.'

The queen nodded and went to move away, but with foresight she turned. 'Oh Dansa.'

'Yes ma'am?'

'Leave the candle alight in his room.'

'Of course ma'am.'

Dansa curtsied and retired to her quarters.

The queen moved quickly along the corridor, her long skirt skimmed over worn wooden floorboards as candles flickered silently in niches in the walls. She shivered and wrapped her shawl tighter. Sprightly feet ran up one flight of winding stone steps and found the king at his desk in the royal apartments. She swallowed hard as she caught her breath. 'Canagan, please may I talk with you?'

He lifted his head and smiled at the sound of her voice. 'Of course Artemisia what is it?' His own was soft and kind and he set aside a mountain of official papers.

She bit her lip as she found her composure and looked for the compassion in his eyes. 'Canagan please - you must stop telling Lyall about the General and the door and the tunnel and the Seal and what will happen if they get us and...'

'Whoa, whoa, stop there, what's brought this on?' He pushed himself back into his chair as his tone changed.

'It's Lyall my lord, he is only just fourteen years old and you are filling his head with such terrible stories.'

His brow furrowed and his finger tips met as he leaned forward on the table. 'Artemisia, yes he is fourteen years old and is learning to become a king one day. If you treat him like a child, how will he become a man?' He muttered under his breath: 'you and that maid of his,' and let out an exasperated sigh.

The queen found her strong voice. 'All this nonsense about the General and the door, it's too much for him and scaring him. This is the fourth night in a row that I have had to go to him.'

'You should leave him be,' retorted the king indignantly. 'The boy has to face his fears.'

'But he won't settle Canagan, he just won't settle.'

The king stood up and his tone changed. 'Artemisia, it is my duty to tell Lyall about the despicable depths people go to out there. Not everyone is sweet and kind like you. If only they were. Unfortunately we live in a kingdom of demons and devils who will do anything to get power.' He reached for the pendant beneath his shirt. 'This Seal here, the one round my neck, that sits over my heart, this is the holy grail of royalty. It is the key to the Kingdom of Durundal, it is a valuable item, one that many have tried to take and failed. But there is someone out there right now, watching, waiting and ready to vent his evil. This is the monster of all monsters. There is no compassion in his eyes or feeling in his body. He is the General who works for the Emperor of Ataxata, and I have been informed that he is close. He is that close that I can smell him. I can hear his breath in the wind and my skin crawls. I have to protect my family at all costs. Our son has to be told, he has to know everything, but more importantly he has to know the escape route that will take him to safety.'

'But we don't even know if people are still there, we don't know that the tunnel is safe,' persisted the queen rooted to her spot.

'You will have to trust me,' boomed the king as he paced around the room, his hands clenched behind his back. 'I would not send my son from one danger into another, I have been through the tunnel and I have seen them. They are there.'

'You've spoken to them?'

'No, but I saw enough.'

Her face dropped as he continued. 'And yes, the tunnel is dark, I cannot deny that, and yes he will be petrified, I have no doubt. But in the event of an attack, he will be safer in there than he will be in here, you both will.'

He found his soft voice again and unclenched his fingers as he took both her hands and kissed them fondly. 'You are a good mother Artemisia, he knows how much you love him, I love him also, but he must grow and become a man now. Yes he is only fourteen years old, but if that's old enough to shoot arrows then that's old enough to know about the horrors of this kingdom.'

'But...' she tried to intercept.

'No more buts…' he interrupted.

'But he's too young,' she stopped him.

'You are never too young to recognise those whom would harm you.'

Artemisia looked down in defeat. 'You are right Canagan, I'm sorry.'

He embraced her, and with a heavy sigh, spoke softly in her ear. 'No, it is I that am sorry. Sorry that I can not give you a safer place to live and bring up our son.'

'The gods are punishing us for what we did all those years ago aren't they?'

The king startled. 'Of course they are not, we did nothing wrong Artemisia, nothing at all.'

'But I did Canagan... I know I did.' She sobbed into his chest.

He put his hand on her head to comfort her. 'Shhh, no more my queen, it is late and you are tired.'

They gave the silence time to breathe and without another word he led her to the largest window in the room. They could just see the tip of the snow topped mountain bathed in the glorious moonlight. The Giant's Claw had held on to their secrets for a decade and five now and where her nights of a thousand tears were entombed forever.

The weather seemed to change within minutes of them standing there and a rough wind brought clouds the colour of granite with sheets of driving rain, while the pallor of the November sky closed in upon the mountains, cloaking them in mist and obscuring the moon. And for all the tightly secure windows, there must have been a small crack in one of the panes, because every now and again little tears of rain ran down the inside and collected in pools on the edge of the sill.

2

General Domitrius Corbulo reined his panting horse to a halt and turned in his saddle to greet his captains and the thousand mounted soldiers following him into battle. As they approached the eaves of the forest the trees gave way and the land stretched out before them; a patchwork of fields, orchards and herb gardens, where the castle rose out of the ground and stood proud over the royal surroundings. This was the final attack after many years of searching and Corbulo knew the doctrine would yield the greatest prize as he handed it to his Emperor.

The black mare began to strain at the bit and whinny, wet ears swivelled back and forth, nostrils flared and sent out clouds of condensation as she pawed the sodden ground with a frustrated hoof. 'Steady girl, steady, all in good time.' He didn't take his eyes off his goal and gently stroked her smooth velvet neck with a gloved hand. 'We will be home for the winter my beauty, our work is nearly done.' A murderous grin swept across the wicked face as he anticipated the rewards of his brutal endeavours.

The Ataxatan army continued to clatter in rows behind him, restless in their stealth as they reached the summit. Horses bounced their heads and shook their tack, soldiers adjusted their weapons; spears, sickles, axes, all ready to chop and swing, sang the sound of the blade while beating hearts pulsating with anticipation rumbled through the ranks. The dense mass of moving bodies were now ready and the General raised his sword to signal the attack. A flaming arrow was curled into the night sky and a shivering hiss of a thousand blades leaving their scabbards responded to his cue. Hell was unleashed. Arrows curved down from the hillside sending fire balls of oil soaked liniment into the fragile timbers; the impact was brutal as an orange ball of flame exploded across the courtyard scattering the splintered frames of wooden enclosures.

The castle was ablaze and continued to burn as more arrows were fired. Like streams of lava from an erupting volcano the cavalry descended. Arrows flew their course and plunged into the chaos of shrieking people and stricken animals. Servants and maids running for cover were trampled by the invading hoards. Children were crying in their mother's arms. Many were trying to control the fire and others screamed in agony as they became engulfed in flames. Brave men, loyal to the crown ran in to thwart the siege but unforgiving swords hacked into the defenders of the realm. Silver blades and gold tipped daggers sliced through muscle, and a thousand hooves crushed the life out of prostrate wounded bodies.

Amongst the slaughter, a waft of black smoke rose in the air and weaved its way through the empty corridors suffocating everything in its path.

The king and queen had already witnessed the first attack and were preparing for battle. 'Get our boy Artemisia. You must go to the tunnel and I will follow when I can.'

The queen froze as her breath spurted panic. 'Canagan, I can't leave you, I just can't do it.'

The king met her frantic gaze; the words didn't come easily as he knew what lay ahead. 'I will join you when I can but you and our son will surely die if you both stay here.'

She shook her head in despair as her husband tried to reassure her. 'You must take him Artemisia, it is the safest option I promise you. I don't think our forces can cope with this. You must go to the tunnel and that is an order.'

Time was running out, the sound of death was fast approaching and now there were no options. She grabbed the lantern on the desk and chased her thumping heart to the west wing. The terrifying sounds of slaughter compelled her to run faster. People were spinning in all directions, dodging fire tipped arrows and falling debris. She saw Dansa, frantic and confused and shouted out over the chaos.

Dansa didn't notice her. She couldn't hear her. Within seconds a falling beam had ended her life. The queen gasped with shock but there was nothing she could do; she was competing with the devil and got to her son's room first.

'Lyall, Lyall, wake up, quickly.'

The sleeping boy awoke to her trembling voice and rubbed his gritty eyes.

'You remember the secret tunnel that your father has shown you?'

'Yes.' He sat up slowly as the nauseating sound of death filtered into his room.

'We have to go there now.' She felt wretched asking him to do the very thing that he feared the most.

He thought he was dreaming again and whispered a frail response in disbelief. 'Why?'

What kind of mother am I to ask such a thing she thought as she helped him up. 'We are in danger, the castle is under siege and we must go to the tunnel. I will be with you all the way, I promise. I will be right behind you. It's safe in there. Nothing will hurt you. But we must make haste.' The instructions became more hurried.

'Mother, I can't. I would rather die here than go in there.' His voice was thick with fear now. The smoke had reached them and the castle was falling in around them.

'My sweet son, I would do anything to spare you this, but you have to be brave, we all have to be so very brave.'

The flashing lights of fire and the constant stream of wailing terrified him. If he wanted to live then he had to go through the tunnel with his mother and he knew that he didn't really want to die. The queen wrapped her shawl round the young prince and guided him out of his room.

The air was claustrophobic with smoke and shallow pools of debris littered the way like old abandoned toys. Artemisia picked her way through them as carefully as she could, avoiding the six foot long nails that protruded like hideous flags of honour and blocks of black basalt so large that they must have taken a hundred men to hoist them into place. The main tower collapsed behind them and as they ran through the broken masonry, she yelled out all the things that Canagan had just told her; things that would reassure her son and put his mind at ease, but the gnarled fingers of death grabbed her words before they reached Lyall's ears.

Outside, there still raged screams and crying, running of footsteps, the whinny of petrified horses and the frantic barking of terrified dogs. They were now at the concealed entrance. The door was heavy and already had piles of asphalt blocking its access. She couldn't open it on her own. Despite everything in his head telling him not to, Lyall dropped to his knees and pawed at the fallen masonry with his bare hands.

As it edged open her stricken voice ushered him in. 'Go ahead of me. I will be right behind you. Remember everything I have told you, keep going to the end, don't turn back and run as fast as you can.'

But a figure had entered the room and loomed over him like a grim reaper against the black smoke. The figure grabbed Lyall, pulled his head back with one hand and held a knife to his throat with the other. The scream stuck in Artemisia's mouth, she had seconds to do something before the blade penetrated her son's neck. Lyall had his trembling hands on the man's arms, his eyes frantic, his voice disabled, his body writhing like an eel struggling to get free. He kicked back at his attacker with his bare feet but the soldier laughed and tightened his grip.

'No, please no,' she cried, but only a whisper came out.

The fiend bore into her, and with a cruel stare, nicked a cut in her son's skin.

'No!' she screamed out loud and grabbed a piece of granite from the ground and hurled it against the soldier's head. A trickle of blood ran down from his temple and Lyall was thrown to the floor as the brute turned his attention to the queen.

'Go, go now!' she yelled at her son.

The barbarian launched at her and plunged the knife into her heart as Lyall made his escape. But her cry of pain was lost in the abyss as a ball of fire blasted the door shut and engulfed everything else in the room.

He started to bang on the sealed door, he fumbled frantically to push it open. He called out to his mother again and again. His heart accelerated. His breathing was out of control. He was in total darkness and his whole body began to tremble. But it was futile. He slid down against the solid oak barricade and sobbed. The other side of him his mother lay dead.

As the king and his army faced defeat in the blood spilled massacre, a sinister shadow slipped unnoticed into the bowels of the castle to murderously steal its prize; the legendary Seal of Kings and key to the Kingdom of Durundal.

3

Lyall moaned and trembled uncontrollably. 'This can't be happening! This has to be another terrible dream. It's another nightmare. It will pass, I know it will pass.' His voice was over-loud in the empty catacomb.

But it didn't pass. He found himself hunched in the unforgiving dark, the groans of a dying castle muffled through the door. He put his hands to his ears to block it out. The cut on his neck stung. He touched it, but his salty fingers made him cry out.

'Mother will come, I know she will, she always comes when I am having night terrors; I will wake soon to her voice...' But the familiar sound didn't come... No one came.

The decibels of death filtered away and he was left in silence. Alone in the the knowledge that his parents were laying mutilated on the other side of the barrier and there was nothing he could do. He sobbed into the shawl and his stomach churned. Time had no definition in this vacuous space.

'Perhaps if I pray, that's what Governess Teja always tells me, pray to the gods and they will answer.' So he prayed hard until he could hear the inner voice in his head telling him to get up and follow the tunnel like his mother had told him. 'It's safe, nothing will hurt you, keep going to the end.'

'But it's dark, and I am so scared of the dark,' he argued with the voice inside his head.

The voice persisted though, as endless minutes ticked by, egging him on, forcing him to his feet. He tried to reassure himself as he uncoiled himself and stared into the abyss. With blind eyes and stricken soul, his ears tuned into the piercing chaos. Reaching out wildly, his arms flung out to the sides and the tips of his fingers recoiled instinctively when they touched cold rock. His throat ached as silent tears ran down his cheeks and reluctant feet nervously edged forward; shuffling, creeping, his hands stretched out wide with every step.

The voice was still relentlessly urging him on so he walked a bit faster and then a bit more until the dark was rushing towards him. Deeper into the shrinking cavern he went, grazing his flying arms on the ridges of molten rock, tearing the soles of his feet on the uneven surface but the voice told him to keep going. On and on he went, for miles it seemed, he didn't know how far. There was little air in the passage and soon he felt his lungs burning. It was cold and damp, his heart was pounding but still he ran.

The beaded sweat of fear ran down his back in droves and he knew that he must have covered a fair distance when his chest began to hurt and he found it hard to breathe. He slowed to a trot but tired limbs couldn't steady his balance. Tripping over misplaced legs he stumbled and fell, his hands and buttocks went straight into a mud pool.

The dark was still rushing around him as he sat up, the silent chaos still audible. He cried out pitifully and let the slimy liquid run between his fingers. 'Help me please, someone must be able to hear me, please.'

He sat for what seemed like an eternity in his stagnant pool, until somewhere in his disorientated mind the voice told him that he was sitting in water and water must drain into an outlet. Hope ignited him into action once more. The immersing bruise on his thigh went unnoticed as he slowly hauled himself up and staggered some hundred yards. But his legs were useless now. Torn, gashed and weary, he could run no more. He collapsed again, shivering with shock and fear. His heart was pounding and the only thing he could see was the silvery vapour of his own breath. As his back found a crevasse in his damp dark surroundings he pulled his knees tight against his chest and trembled fearfully.

He must have fallen asleep at some point though. A gentle breeze brushed his face as weary eyes opened to find that his abyss was the mouth of a cave and outside hung grey skies and a hazy sun. He felt his gashed neck and winced. He knew that he was still alive though. He knew it had not been a bad dream. New bruises ached and his wounds began to sting as he stretched out his entwined limbs and crawled slowly to the entrance of his tomb. Though relieved to be out of the dark, the misty morning brought other terrors in this unfamiliar kingdom. He looked fearfully out of the small opening. Spots danced dizzily before his eyes as they adjusted to the light, but when they did, a grass covered expanse of land loomed and the sound of running water sent spasms to his parched mouth. And in the mist he noticed something. A figure, a boy; hope.

He was about the same age as Lyall, certainly the same build and height wearing a tunic that looked like the thick hide of a deer over woollen grey britches. He stood by the river's edge, concealed in the long grass, acutely rigid, poised like a heron, with a spear in his hand and didn't take his eyes off the water. Lyall had never seen anything like it. Indeed he had heard of the savages that lived far away and was forbidden to go outside the castle walls because of them. He always had Lord Tanner with him who would say: 'Stay well within the castle grounds Lyall for there are queer folk out there.'

'What sort of queer folk?' he would ask.

'Savages my boy, hunched ugly savages, with no necks and no hair, who feed on the brains of babies and sacrifice their first born to their gods. They rip the hearts out of live animals and eat them for added strength and cover themselves in demonic tattoos to protect themselves and ward off evil spirits.'

'Where do they live?'

'They live the other side of the river my boy, in huts smeared with the skin and entrails of monstrous creatures and they howl like beasts at night. Unless you want to be a part of their rituals and have your face ripped off, you had best keep well away.'

But this boy looked exactly like him. He had his dark features, his dark hair, he even stood upright like he did. He wasn't hunched and ugly and smeared with animal intestines as he had imagined. How could this boy be a savage? In the distance he heard a young girl call his name.

'Namir, wait for me.'

'They speak my language,' he said out loud in surprise.

The girl was a few inches shorter than he but looked about the same age. She was absolutely beautiful. Lyall had never seen anyone so graceful and serene. Tumbling hair fell over slender shoulders and huge whirlpool eyes fixed on her friend. Lyall couldn't take his eyes off her as she ran up to Namir. Still, the savage didn't take his eyes off the water. He put a finger to his lips to signal her silence. The quiet resumed and he suddenly spiked his prey and pulled out a large silver toned fish. Lyall clung to the side of his cave as he watched the girl take her own spear and under Namir's guidance, waited patiently and quietly before spearing her own healthy trout.

He thought about his own skill with a bow and arrow, having target practice most days with Lord Tanner where carefully placed targets were hung strategically within the castle grounds, on trees, on walls, on wooden tripods, and of course he enjoyed it, he was extremely good at it. But he had to be honest, this looked so much more fun.

He craned from his vantage point to view a spread of unusual living accommodations. Small flat roof barns were scattered amongst a range of different sized wattle and daub roundhouses with conical thatched roofs. For a moment he saw his parents there. The fire was roaring and a hog was roasting on the spit. With arms stretched out wide and huge grins across loving faces, they welcomed him into their new home. He tried to scramble up before the image faded. He called out desperately, but his stricken voice was blocked at the back of his throat again.

He crawled back and watched the village come to life instead. People stretched out of their cramped homes. Dogs were barking, children were shouting, a baby cried. And as the mist gave way to a tranquil dawn, the November sun lit up the morning dew and this strange new kingdom opened up before him.

He could see open meadows of grazing livestock and numerous fields yielding produce. Flared eyes rested on an arrangement of huge stones standing in a wide circle. The carefully placed tombs clustered under an auspicious rise in the land, their curved altars positioned like a crooked set of teeth; while last night's rain had left them wet and glistening, and the morning sunlight made them look as if they were covered in black oil.

'For their sacrifices,' he winced.

He waited, motionless. The shawl pulled closely round him. Watching, listening, trying to think what he should do next. Against the busy brook he could hear her faint laughter and his playful voice. Birds were singing and the grass gently rustled. He looked back into the cave and shuddered; it was still pitch black in there, it was still damp. No one was coming for him. He looked down at his wounded legs, his ripped pyjama trousers, his bloodied feet, his gashed arms, he could only imagine what his face looked like. What options did he really have?

By the time the two youngsters had begun to gather up their nets and haul, the sun had moved round and a light dusting of mist remained.

'This is it now Lyall,' he said to himself. 'This is your chance, stay strong and don't alarm them.' He felt the frosted grass crunch beneath his feet, and if he looked hard enough, he could see his parents in front of him, ushering him into the arms of salvation.

The young teens meandered along the shore of the river so deeply immersed in conversation that they didn't even hear him approaching.

'Please, can you help me?' His quivering voice spoke out.

Namir turned and instinctively dropped his cargo and aimed his spear. He looked in horror at the figure before him. This boy, this small being covered in blood, must have been mauled by a mountain lion or a snow leopard, or something even worse. How could anyone survive that he thought.

'Who are you?' he growled.

'My name is Lyall.'

'Where have you come from?' he snarled again.

'Through the cave, my home is the other side of the cave.' An outstretched arm gestured to the crevasse in the mountain.

Skyrah crept out from behind Namir's protective stance. 'How is that possible,' she started. 'The cave is full of demons. How did you survive, only someone with evil powers could survive that?'

'I am not evil, I do not have powers, I just ran as fast as I could through the tunnel.'

Skyrah and Namir looked at each other then at him.

'Please, I am desperate. My parents are dead, the people who looked after me are dead. My home is in ruins. I have nowhere to go.' Breathing deeply he tried to relax as his mind hovered between hope and fear. He tried, unsuccessfully, to stifle the tears.

Namir lowered his spear and softened his expression as he sensed the young boy's dilemma.

'You are injured, and you look cold and exhausted. Come, my father will know what to do.'

The two youngsters continued their conversation as they walked ahead of him.

'He is not a demon Skyrah, look at him; he is a boy like me.'

'Yes I know Namir, he speaks our tongue and sheds our tears. But he is not clan, look what he wears and look at his wounds.'

'All the more reason to help him Skyrah, if he was an evil spirit he would have attacked us by now.'

'But maybe he will attack our village and bring

more people to hurt us.'

'Skyrah, we are good people and we must give sanctuary. Our totems will protect us.'

'I know, you are right, we can't leave him. The elders will decide,' she conceded.

Lyall followed the two feral children with his head so low that his chin disappeared into his sternum. He thought it best to keep a safe distance in case they changed their minds and decided to attack him after all.

He focused on what was around him as this strange new kingdom got bigger and closer. The bustle of village life got noisier and he strained to pick out a range of different sounds. The smell of cooked breakfasts reached out to him first and he felt the pit of his stomach growl. He hadn't thought about food very much at all, but now it was top of his list and he began to salivate. The tempting odours led him further into the camp. He was paraded through the clusters of homes where a hive of anxious faces popped out of doorways.

Groups of working peasants looked up from their chores for the first time. Concerned murmurs from adults weaved amongst the trill excitement from children and a pack of boisterous dogs bounded up to him eager to play. Pens with sheep and pigs sat in freshly laid straw, while chickens and geese pecked their way around the camp.

The top of a mound brought them to a halt outside the largest hut in the village. It had spectacular views amid a magnificent setting, though the vision was of little interest to Lyall at that precise moment.

Namir turned to speak to him. 'Wait here with Skyrah while I go in to see my father.'

Lyall nodded and bent down to pat the excited dogs whilst keeping a finely tuned ear on the proceedings inside.

'Good morning father, I hope you are well today. Good morning Zoraster.'

'I am son, I am very well.' His father ushered the medicine man aside as he stood up to embrace his son.

'He needs to rest young Namir; he just won't listen to me.'

Father and son held a knowing look. Zoraster was always telling his father to rest.

'I have been fishing this morning and made a good catch,' Namir continued.

'Yes I can see you have been up with the lark and been out hunting already. You have done well my boy and the gods will be pleased. You must take the haul to the feasting area for the ritual tonight.'

'Of course father,' he paused and then found his voice again. 'Father, there is something else.'

Both the elders looked worried as they read Namir's concerned expression.

'I have brought someone back with me.'

'Really? Who have you brought here son?'

'A boy father; a boy like me. He's lost. He came through the cave. He says his home has been destroyed and he can't go back.'

His father froze for a moment and looked to his aide. 'Let me meet him, bring the boy to me.'

Namir peered outside and ushered Lyall and Skyrah in. The hunger in Lyall's stomach suddenly vanished and he was gripped with fear again. He felt sick. He wanted to stay with the playful dogs.

Outside the leader's home, Skyrah took his hand tenderly and smiled. 'Everything will be all right, really it will.'

They entered the hut together and faced the leader standing between his son and the medicine man. Alarmed eyes fell on Lyall; bloody, dishevelled and baring a wound that would surely scar for the rest of his life. He didn't know where to look. A ghostly pause filled the air and the boy gripped Skyrah's hand even tighter.

The leader sensed Lyall's plight and broke the silence. 'You poor boy, we must thank the gods that you found us. I am Laith, leader of the Clan of the Mountain Lion. My aide is the very powerful medicine man, Zoraster. You have already met my son Namir and his special friend Skyrah.'

Lyall tilted his head awkwardly at each introduction. He tried to say good morning in response but nothing came out. A dry tongue sat uncomfortably in his parched mouth and time ticked anxiously by as he tried to articulate a few words.

Laith spoke again. 'So who are you young man?'

Fear had gripped his soul. All eyes were on him. He let go of Skyrah's hand and wiped his sweaty palms on his ripped trousers. By now he could hear his own heart beat thumping in his chest and willed the voice into the back of his throat. With a firm stance and a big gulp of air he quashed his nauseous nerves and heralded an answer.

'My name is Prince Lyall of Durundal, son of King Canagan and Queen Artemisia. My people have been massacred in an attack on my home, Castle Dru in Durundal.' He felt the panic rise in his voice as he relived the tale. 'My father knew this would happen, he showed me the door that led to a tunnel. He told me what to do; so many times he made sure I knew what to do. I thought he was just trying to frighten me, to toughen me up. Until last night when I knew it was all true. The General, the door, the tunnel. Last night my mother took me there, she said that she would follow me but she couldn't. She fought off a soldier who was trying to kill me.' He took another deep breath as he found the strength to continue. 'I was able to get through, but the huge door shut before she could get in. She told me to follow the tunnel and it led me to you.'

The chieftain stared wide eyed at the tearful youngster. 'Canagan and Artemisia,' he sighed heavily. 'May their souls be free and their final resting place be Hallowed.'

'Did you know them?' asked the bewildered young boy wiping away his tears.

The medicine man looked to the floor and the chieftain looked upwards to some ethereal being. 'Many moons ago I knew your parents Lyall, so many moons ago now.' His tearful gaze met Lyalls' as the young boy spoke again.

'Perhaps they knew you would look after me; that's why they sent me.'

'Perhaps they did,' said the old man thoughtfully. He lingered a moment, feeling the boy's anguish until the medicine man offered a polite cough.

'How do you know they are dead?' Laith's voice was struggling.

'There was so much noise and people screaming. There was fire and smoke with bits of the castle falling everywhere; no one could survive that. I waited for ages by the door and no one came for me. I tried to open it but I couldn't get back in.'

'And the wounds on your body?'

'The soldier cut my neck. And these.' He offered his bloodied arms and legs. 'By running into the tunnel walls in the dark.'

Laith felt the need to bite his bottom lip to stifle his emotion, after which he faced the boy. 'You have acted remarkably strong for one so young. Even grown men would have wept and trembled when faced with so much fear. Your parents would be proud of you.'

'My father always wanted me to show more courage,' said Lyall sniffing at his runny nose. 'I think I have done as he wished now.'

Sadness tinged the swollen hut for a moment until Zoroaster rejoiced: 'Remember that courage is not the absence of fear but the triumph over it. You have been tested by the gods and have shown tremendous bravery this day.'

The words sat proud in Lyall's heart as Laith

concluded. 'Lyall of Durundal, you will join our clan, we will look after you now.'

'Thank you Laith you are most gracious.' A loud sigh accompanied Lyall's sense of relief. 'And thank you Namir, Zoraster, Skyrah, you are all very kind.'

Each one nodded back to him in response.

The old man continued to scrutinize the new clan member and finally turned to his son. 'Namir, we need to take special care of this boy, he will be in shock for some time. Could he stay with you?'

Namir studied the frightened lad; cold, alone and terrified, he could only imagine what he must be going through. 'Of course father, we must always help those in need.'

'You speak with compassion and I am pleased with your answer. Skyrah, will you take Lyall to Namir's hut, tend to his wounds and give him some warmer clothes, he looks like he's going to freeze to death before those wounds fester.'

Lyall felt the leader's eyes on him, mirrored by the medicine man's gaze as he walked out of their vision with his new found friends.

'Are you all right old friend? That's a terrible shock that you have just had.' Zoraster put a hand on the old man's trembling arm.

'I will be Zoraster... I will go and stand by the menhirs for a while and ask the spirits for strength.' Laith's answer was sombre.

'You know it's him don't you?'

'Yes - I know it's him.'

'You must tell him Laith, he has a right to know.'

The leader shook his head despairingly. 'No, not yet, let the dust settle first. We have all had too many shocks already in one day. But I will tell him when the time is right... I promise.'

4

Namir followed his father's instructions and took his haul of fish to the women folk to prepare for the ceremony. Skyrah took Lyall to Namir's hut to bathe his wounds and put the healing unguent of plants on his cuts and bruises. She turned away as he shyly exchanged his sodden ripped pyjama trousers for a simple tunic top. The leaves were left in place to aid recovery on his neck, arms and legs while his feet were bound with warm sheepskin boots to protect them. Finally she fitted him with the fleece from a boar and made a soothing tea to relax him.

'You have been through a terrible ordeal,' she said kindly, putting his mother's shawl over him. 'I am sorry I was so hostile earlier, I feel ashamed now. Please forgive me.'

'There is nothing to forgive,' he assured her.

He sipped slowly from the tea, and as he watched her stir the contents of a cauldron hovering over a small fire, a beautiful voice began to sing.

'The wild wind blows through valleys my love,
The wild wind blows through the trees,

The wild wind blows o'er the rivers my love,
But will n'er get close to thee.
The wild rain storms through the valleys my love,
The wild rain storms through the trees,
The wild rain storms o'er the rivers my love,
But none will get close to thee.'

Lyall's cup remained poised at his chin as he stared at her open mouthed.

She caught his frozen expression and looked alarmed. 'Are you all right Lyall?'

'Where did you learn that?' his tone was hushed with utter bewilderment.

'Laith taught it to us,' she answered. 'We all sing it to soothe those in need and ward off evil spirits.'

'How does Laith know it?' Lyall continued.

'That I do not know, perhaps you should ask him when you are better.'

He couldn't take his eyes off her beautiful face; a graceful long neck that supported a defined jaw, full lips under a straight narrow nose, high cheekbones on a symmetrical face and huge brown eyes framed by deep dark eyebrows that matched her tumbling waves of ebony hair.

She retracted a coy gaze as her eyes met his.

'What is the ceremony tonight?' he struggled to find some words to fill the void, knowing he had made her feel uncomfortable.

'It is our most sacred custom Lyall, when a new

born son has witnessed three new moons he is presented to the gods and we celebrate with the naming ritual.'

'Naming ritual?' he stammered in a soft, tremulous voice.

'Wait and see, it is such a wonderful experience.'

He had heard stories about the savage rituals so didn't push it any further. Instead he changed the topic and pointed to a dyed image at the top of her arm. 'Why do you have the tattoo of a hare on your shoulder?'

'It's a female symbol and represents intuition and regeneration,' she responded proudly. She sat down and offered him a bowl of food. 'It's been said that many years ago, a young disfigured girl sought refuge in the clan. Laith gave her the totem of a hare to protect her. One day she went away; no one knew why, and she was never seen again. But from that day on, Laith continued to give all females of the clan the symbol of a hare to protect them and tattooed the image onto their arm for added protection.'

Lyall looked on mesmerised. 'That's a remarkable story. I wonder what became of the little girl?' He sighed heavily. 'My mother showed me the image of the hare in the moon many times.'

Skyrah looked at him in awe. 'Did she tell you that when the moon is full, you can see the earth hare gazing up at her reflection?'

'She did, she knew a lot about that kind of thing.' He looked at Skyrah and smiled. 'What is Namir's totem tattoo?'

She smiled back. 'The leopard.'

A movement at the entrance halted their conversation as Namir entered the hut. Skyrah got up to pour him a mug of fresh nettle tea and handed him a bowl of the tasty broth.

Lyall immediately noticed the affection in their gaze; the sensitive touch as she brushed past him, the soft welcome in her voice where the years they shared had created a special bond. He had seen the same subtleties between his parents.

'I hope you are feeling better Lyall,' he said kindly.

'Yes I am, and thank you so much for your hospitality. I hope you don't mind me staying here with you.'

'Not at all, it is a simple home and sparsely decorated but it is warm and comfortable.'

'It's just perfect, I consider myself very lucky.'

It was indeed sparse, and certainly could fit no more than three people in comfortably. An assortment of animal hide cushions served as lounging seats whilst layers of animal pelts and woven blankets befitted the sleeping arrangements. There were a few wooden stools and a table with a few provisions and utensils on, but the fire was the focal point which everyone would sit round. A cauldron and a kettle sat continually on the hearth and would be moved outside in the warmer months.

Lyall looked at Namir's totem tattoo and was

fascinated with the meaning. He studied the boy in front of him and wondered how he would have fared in the gripping darkness of the cave. Would Namir have reacted like a frightened mouse? Would he have cried like a baby and nearly given up? He thought not. Namir was fast and strong like a leopard, he wasn't scared of anything. He had probably grown up with fear around him and conquered it, living outside and surviving off the land, hunting and trapping and making his own spears.

No, this was a far cry from his own life where he had been closeted and cushioned, given a life of wealth, privilege and security, never knowing until now what true courage meant. If he was to ever return to Durundal as a man and take his place as king, he would have to demonstrate a different kind of strength and overcome his fears.

He felt the heat of the wound branding into the crease of his neck, defining a mark that would constantly remind him of his failings and how he overcame them. He continued his self-berating and wondered what tattoo he would have been given. The thoughts consumed him while Skyrah and Namir were immersed in conversation.

With the sounds of his new friends comforting him and the homely warmth of the fire, he felt himself drifting off to sleep; at last it was safe to close his eyes.

But not for long though, it seemed only too soon he was being woken up again. Bleary eyes opened to a familiar voice and someone gently nudging him.

'We must go now,' said Namir.

'Go where?' he replied sleepily, trying to stifle his panic. He vividly remembered that being woken from sleep meant something terrible was going to happen.

'The Name Giving ritual.'

5

He must have slept all day he thought as he followed Namir and Skyrah out into the moonlight. He stretched out his aching limbs and decided that the walk would be good for him. All around him an excitement buzzed and he craned his neck to marvel at his new surroundings. The huge circle of standing stones loomed over him creating a humble temple of enormous power, and between the stones the tribe filtered in with heads burrowed low and hands pressed together summoning the giants to do their work.

As the sun bowed out gracefully to the huge frost moon, the clan took their places quietly and waited. There was not a sound, not even a quiver. A subtle gesture from Zoraster invited the mother to move forward and present her new born baby to the gods. Laith waited for the pivotal alignment of the celestial orbs.

The bright full sphere looked as if it would burst when the leader broke the tranquil silence and began the proceedings. 'Comrades, citizens, people of the clan; a new child is born to the Earth Mother Orla and will be welcomed into our community. Her son has witnessed three new moons, the gods and spirits favour him. And now, we welcome the infant with food, love and other offerings of wealth in our stone circles. It is a special time for all of us to renew our own vows with Orla's child as we remember that nature is connected at an unseen level, and how animals, birds, plants and rocks all have lessons to teach and messages to share. These messages are instrumental for us to survive; they have been passed down to us from the gods and our forefathers, providing direction, protection, and healing. Citizens hold your thoughts within these stone circles and pray for this miracle as we feast with the spirits and give this new creation his guide.'

Lyall watched and listened intently as the clan bowed before Laith in recognition of this ancient ritual. A nudge from Namir instructed Lyall to follow protocol with a bow and he continued to concentrate on the events.

As Orla gave her naked child to Laith, he continued. 'Each new born son is given the spirit of a chosen animal by their parents at birth, this will protect and guide the bearer in this life, the next life and throughout eternity. The spirit guide and totem for this child is the Eagle as it exhibits a great strength, it has established a long life, but above all else it demonstrates freedom. The Eagle will serve its bearer well.'

The infant was then given to Kal, his father, to hold securely, and it took a while for Lyall to understand what was going on as events took a sinister turn.

Moonlight silvered the edge of Zoraster's quill as he began to engrave blue dye into the new-born's flesh with a hollowed filed bone. Lyall looked on in horror. 'Where is the brush and paint,' he shouted in his head. 'This can't be real. I must be dreaming again!' He felt the blood drain from his face and was compelled to put his hands over his ears as the child's agonised screams pierced the air and gravitated round the standing stones. The sound was deafening in the silence and cut an octave higher than Orla's wails begging the spirits to give her tiny boy the strength to overcome his pain.

The clan stood watching, mesmerised. Lyall looked at Namir for guidance but he too was entranced. He wanted to run in and put an end to it. 'Please stop!' the voice struggled in his head. He had to prevent himself from shouting it out loud to stop the torture. Panic set in and he started to retch. Had all those stories been founded? Did Skyrah neglect to tell him the truth deliberately? He felt the familiar beaded sweat of fear run down his spine and his stomach churn. Rooted to the spot with terror he asked himself: 'Is the child about to be sacrificed?'

Kal held onto the tiny squirming frame tightly while the bad omens were sent fleeing from the soul as he howled into the sunset.

'The child is named Arran,' continued Laith. 'The gods have welcomed him.'

His fears were unfounded as the healing nectar of a plant was administered to the wound and Orla put her shivering baby to her breast for comfort.

All those tales of sacrificing the first born and drinking their blood were clearly myths. So why did the guards speak of such things? These people were not savages who ripped the hearts out of animals and ate them for added strength; these were humble people living their lives peacefully and with honour. The boy chastised himself for even thinking any one of them was a savage. He stood by one of the enormous stones and looked up to Skyrah's moon.

Namir spotted the thoughtful lad. 'Are you mesmerised?'

'I am Namir, I really am.'

'It's a wonderful experience isn't it Lyall?' trilled Skyrah descending excitedly on the two boys.

'I really wasn't expecting that, I must admit.'

'This ritual ensures strength and courage for the boy,' she clarified. 'The parents know their son will be strong with its animal totem engraved into his skin.'

'Perhaps I should have had one when I was born.' Lyall's smile was thin.

'You are already strong Lyall, you are the son of a king with king's blood.'

'I didn't feel very strong in the tunnel,' he hung his head in shame.

'We all fear the unknown my friend,' said Namir wrapping an arm around the lad's shoulder. 'Fear is in all of us and you have nothing to feel ashamed about. You are stronger than you give yourself credit for. Remember what Zoraster said; you overcame your fears.'

'I know, I must remember that. Thank you Namir.'

'Come, tell us about life in a castle, we know nothing of that,' urged Skyrah changing the subject.

'Well, it's very different to here,' he began, strangely lifted. 'Here, you live side by side with nature where you have no walls or boundaries. Life in a castle is the opposite.'

'How?' she asked.

'Think of endless stone walls rising to the skies and beyond. Where turrets touch the clouds and a creaking wooden drawbridge echoes with the sound of a thousand footsteps. Imagine a fortress full of rich tapestries and fine furniture where each room has a roaring fire to keep out the chill. A vast space is on the lower floors where all the food is brought in and cooked to perfection. And below that, a winding staircase creeps down into the vaults underground where all manner of castle needs are stored, like wine, beer and armoury.'

Namir and Skyrah opened their eyes wider with each description.

'I had a guard that took me out for archery practice, I had a governess who taught me how to read and write and I had a maid who would make sure I didn't miss my archery or my lessons.'

'I can hardly imagine a life like that,' said Namir.

'What about your freedom?' asked Skyrah.

'Freedom?' Lyall lifted his brows into a

question.

'Yes, to run free, to get up with the rising sun, to sleep when the sun goes down, to gain knowledge from the land.'

'What you don't have you do not miss.' He lowered his brows.

'And now that it's all gone, do you miss it?'

'I'm not sure Namir. It's a strange feeling, but I feel that this is my home now.'

'I hope you don't change your mind,' said Namir. 'We will do everything we can to make your life easier for you, won't we Skyrah?'

'Of course we will, we all will, we are a gentle, peaceful clan. Laith has made sure of that.'

He had been convalescing for a few weeks now, the wounds on his legs and arms were healing and he wasn't waking up in the early hours quite so often now, much to the relief of Namir. Though whenever he woke up with his night terrors, he sat up, saw Namir and that put him at ease, he didn't feel alone or vulnerable, he didn't feel scared anymore, he didn't feel the need for protection - until the day he crossed Suma and Targ.

Winter was just round the corner and that meant shorter days and more time in the camp fixing utensils, mending worn huts, forging weapons and practising skills. Namir was an expert with a spear, as were the other boys; they could hit a target at any distance it seemed. He had watched them sitting for hours, chatting with boyish humour, stripping their lances, polishing the shaft and then letting the sharpened metal head glide through the air to its intended destination. He wanted to make a bow so he could sit with them cleaning the rack, searing his arrow tips and keep on with his target practice in these long drawn out winter months.

This day he had ventured further away to the edge of the forest. Most of the leaves had fallen now, all but a few remaining stragglers were hanging on to the branch that fed them. By chance, a good strong branch had fallen from a mahogany tree; this would make a fine bow he thought. He had cut the wood to shape, seared it carefully and was now creating the arch by slowly bending the timber using vessels of water tied at each end of the bow; and by gradually adding water to each vessel, the frame would bend naturally.

This day, he was so engrossed with getting the curve right, he didn't even hear Suma and Targ approach him from behind.

'What you doing there, little lord prince?' Targ goaded.

'Yes outsider, what you doing there?' Suma's voice was cruel and taunting.

It made him jump. 'Nothing,' he replied and span round to face his intruders. 'Just leave me be.'

'Just leave me be,' they both laughed as they mocked him.

'It doesn't look like nothing - what's all this then?'

Lyall stopped what he was doing but Suma

strode in and pushed his buckets of water over - the bow sprang back to its original shape.

'What you do that for?' bellowed Lyall.

'Because I can,' snarled Suma.

Targ then waded in. 'And I can do this.' With that he yanked the wood from its resting place and broke it in two.

'No! no!' And as Lyall's anguished call sent a flight of noisy crows flapping wildly into the air, he sank to his knees and tried to salvage the weapon he had been working on.

'It's broken, like you. You can't fix something that's broken.'

Lyall refused to let them see him waver. He imagined a wolf at his side giving him strength.

'We don't want outsiders here, what good is an outsider to us? I even heard Namir say that he only puts up with you because he has to.'

'That's not true,' cried out Lyall pitifully, still trying to piece together the broken bow.

'Yes it is, none of us want you here.'

'You are lying,' stormed Lyall, trying to stop the quiver in his voice and holding back the tears.

'What - are you crying now outsider?' Targ laughed at him and looked back to his brother.

Lyall suddenly found his strength and with his hackles up he charged at Targ, but Suma grabbed him and pulled his arm sharply behind his back.

'Is this your bad arm little prince?' and he twisted it further.

Lyall pressed his teeth together to avoid screaming out.

'Oh dear, where's your mummy now eh? or Namir or Skyrah, not much good on your own are you?'

'And neither are you.' A familiar voice came charging out of nowhere and pushed Suma off of Lyall. 'What you going to do now eh?' shouted Skyrah. 'Pick on me as well?'

The two bullies were startled. 'He started it,' began Suma.

'No he didn't,' retorted Skyrah. 'We've been watching you from over there.' She pointed yonder to the brow of a hill where Laith, Zoraster and Namir were standing together glowering at them. 'You are all to come with me.'

Lyall and Skyrah led the way and the two older boys followed like whelped dogs with their tails between their legs.

'I will not tolerate this,' bellowed Laith. 'This boy is our family, we have given him sanctuary and a safe place to live because he has nowhere else to go.'

'Sorry Laith, we won't do it again.'

Laith was beside himself with rage and trod a beaten path as he paced up and down in front of them. 'I do not lead a clan to have members behaving like savages.'

'We are so sorry.'

'You are supposed to set an example, to offer compassion and understanding to those who are vulnerable. Do you not know what this boy has been through?' he raged.

The boys remained silent with their heads low.

Laith continued to march up and down, his thoughts were jumbled in his head and he was becoming more agitated. 'Where will it end - tell me that? you might start threatening me or Zoraster, the older women, the younger girls. I have seen this all before. I have witnessed first hand how evil unfolds.'

'We won't be like that. We have made a mistake and learned our lesson.'

'No, I can't risk the consequences.'

Suddenly he stopped in front of them. The whole village had come to a stand still and were tuned in to the proceedings on the hill. The parents of the boys were making their way up to the commotion.

'You are sixteen years old Targ and you are seventeen Suma.'

'Yes that is correct my lord,' answered Suma with his head still low.

'Well then you are old enough to fend on your own. I do not want you in my clan. I want you to leave straight away. I cannot abide such brutality in my tribe. We are peaceful people and if you want to pick fights and behave like savages then I want you to go.'

'No please, please my lord, we cannot leave. We are not savages, please.'

The parents of the brothers came running up and begged Laith to change his mind. The boys cowered behind them. 'Winter is coming Laith, they won't survive, please, have mercy.'

'Did they show any mercy to Lyall?' he bellowed back at them. The ground shook, the two boys were trembling. Again the parents tried, but Laith was having none of it. 'Enough,' he yelled. 'If you want to protect them, then you can leave as well.'

The boys went. The ageing parents stayed. A highly agitated Laith retired to his tent followed by an equally disgusted Zoraster. Namir took Lyall back to their living quarters while Skyrah went home to her mother.

'I was making a bow - and they broke it,' said Lyall in a low voice.

'I know, but you can make another one that is even stronger, even better than the broken one. I will make one with you if you like and we can spend the winter months training together.'

'Thank you, I would like that.' Lyall's spirits were lifted.

Namir smiled. 'You are so strong Lyall, goodness knows what tough stuff you are made of.'

'Forever learning about myself it seems,' replied the melancholy lad.

Namir went over to the hearth. 'Here, the kettle is still warm, let's have some tea.'

The refreshing liquid was poured into two mugs and Namir gave one to Lyall; its comforting aroma reminded him of someone. 'Tell me more about Skyrah.' The words tumbled out of his mouth like a released flock of caged birds.

'She is exceptional Lyall, there is no other like her. She is funny, intelligent, brave, especially when she runs down a hill to protect her friend.'

Lyall threw a thin smile and looked into his mug.

'And she knows all about plants for a source of food when meat is scarce. The nettle tea is her famous recipe, passed down from her mother, and her mother's mother.'

'She sounds amazing.'

'She is amazing, like I said, there is no other like her... in fact I hope to marry her one day.'

Lyall shot a glance his way. 'Really?'

'Yes,' said Namir. 'I love her more than life itself and have done since we were very small. I have rehearsed the proposal so often that the words are engraved in my head.' He laughed softly to himself.

'Does she feel the same way?' Lyall asked, taking a large sip of tea.

'I think so, I hope so; but we are still too young, neither of us is ready to be married and she would probably say no if I asked her anyway.'

'Maybe you should,' suggested Lyall. 'Before someone else does.'

Namir shot him a concerned look. 'I can't even bear to think that she might marry anyone else but me - but no one would ask her - no - everyone knows that she is my intended.'

'You are a very lucky man Namir, very lucky.'

He soon noticed a change in the weather, particularly how the fresh crispness in the air smelled of snow and that meant winter was on its way. The winds howled and the blizzards swirled, even the mountain seemed to swell with the weight of crystallised snow on its peak. The animals were in from the fields, the harvest was complete, the paddocks were turned and if ever he had thought that life in a castle was glacial, he was just about to experience how the severe cold can numb your limbs and turn your blood to ice.

He had watched how Skyrah and the other women had gathered in an abundance of wild food and then preserve the meat and plants for the torturous winter months ahead. There was always work to do in the camp while the temperatures plummeted; string bows, fletch arrows, sharpen spears, gather firewood, milk the goats. And then when all that work was done they would sit in huddles around their fires, weaving baskets, mending mats and fixing draughty huts.

Whilst everyone took on the guise of some hideous monster draped in their heavy winter coats with oversized hats and wore scarves that stuck to their faces and shivered while the snow fell around them; Lyall found himself thinking about Targ and Suma and wondered how they were faring in this freezing weather. Did they have enough clothing, had they stored enough food. Could anyone survive outside in the brutality of the northern hemisphere he wondered? A part of him felt a little sorry for them. How would he cope, even with his imaginary wolf to keep him safe.?

He had to stop thinking. They brought it on themselves he remembered. Laith always made the right decisions. He thought about his own good fortune and how easily that could have been him if he hadn't made it through the cave. Maybe someone had saved them though. Yes, that's what had happened. They were somewhere safe with a roof over their heads in front of a roaring fire with a belly full of food. They were both safe; of course they were safe.

6

Castle Dru covered a hundred times as much ground as the clan's camp with outbuildings so large they could hold an entire community. The stables housed a thousand horses, its granary was the size of twenty huts, its four towers reached up high into the clouds, stairs and corridors went on for miles. But the most cavernous room of all was the Great Hall; with its tapestried walls, ornate ceilings, huge hearths, carved oak doors, pillared surrounds with endless steps up to the royal dais; and to a small child it looked like everything had been built for a giant.

He remembered how the Great Hall was alive with celebrations on his birthday, and that was the most celebrated custom of the year. If he tried hard enough he could conjure up the noise, colour and smells that surrounded him on those special days. His father would hail the finest musicians to play in the Minstrels Gallery and order the best jugglers and acrobats to tumble their way round the room displaying fantastic feats of artistry. Colourful clowns and dazzling illusionists would mesmerize him with their skilful displays and magic tricks. Dancing bears and birds of prey would be brought in to entertain the revellers. Birdcages full of fine specimens trilling out their delightful tunes were placed round the room.

The kitchen cooks and pantry maids would prepare the most exquisite dishes; pulled pork and roasted chestnuts, boiled grouse and blueberries, pit roast pheasant and cranberries, sweet pies, tarts and cakes served on hand engraved silver platters and all washed down with the finest wines in solid silver chalices. There would be banners and flags hanging from the intricately carved oak supports, displaying the king's coat of arms, and thousands of lanterns positioned on the slender marble pillars to mark each day of the prince's entrance into the kingdom.

The king and queen would wear their crimson robes and jewel encrusted golden crowns, and the royal Seal of Kings was displayed ceremoniously over the king's shoulders while his mother wore the Queen's Blue Diamond pendant and the most beautiful smile he had ever seen. And there he sat between them, on the raised dais, at the head of the hall, greeting the guests, the aristocracy, the nobles and the gentry.

The image evaporated into the soft light and brought him back to the present; because now he was part of a clan, and here, ten months after he had first arrived, everyone was preparing for their most celebrated custom of the year: 'The Gathering.'

'It's a tradition we have every year after we have collected in the harvest. We give thanks to the gods for our good fortune, and the women are able to exchange their produce with neighbouring clans.' Skyrah had told him.

'Each clan from far and wide take it in turns to host the Gathering and the boys celebrate it with a day of tournaments and competitions,' continued Namir. 'There will be horse races, boxing matches, competitions in throwing spears, axes and rocks and the favourite competition of all; the famous tug of war.'

'It's good for the clans to meet up,' chipped in Skyrah. 'It helps to keep the peace in a time honoured tradition. The leaders will disappear into the meeting house and discuss tribal news and anything else that seems important.'

'You will make a fine leader when the time comes Namir,' hailed Lyall commandingly. 'You are wise and compassionate with natural leadership skills and you will be known across all the subject kingdoms as Namir, King of the Clans.' He shot his accolade triumphantly into the air and Namir smiled.

'Thank you, Lyall, I hope I will be as good as my father, he has been a fine role model demonstrating a strong sense of duty, leadership, selflessness and honour. He has guided me well, and yet I still have a long way to go.' His pause was sombre. 'But I know it is my destiny.'

'And you will make a fine king,' purred Skyrah. 'That is your destiny. King Lyall of Durundal.'

'I hope so Skyrah, I hope that one day I will be able to reclaim my throne and restore Castle Dru to its former glory. My father also demonstrated those attributes and I too have a long way to go before I reach those admirable heights.'

The memories of a past life had stirred his soul and he felt the castle ache for his return. He had tried so hard to keep the beautiful image alive, but the shattered remains were not far from his mind.

'Of course you will,' he heard Namir say. 'It will be the most spectacular castle of all the kingdoms and we will govern the lands between us.'

'Of course we will,' he heard himself say. 'It goes without question.'

7

Beyond the colony a hundred marquees had been erected beside the river and the clans gathered in their droves to take part in the Gathering. The splendour of it all took Lyall's breath away and he really had no idea it would be on a scale that was so spectacular and unlike anything he had seen before. The brilliant colours, the excitement of the crowds, the tents and banners flapping in the wind, but mostly the sheer amount of people. Many came on foot, some came by boat, several had pack horses loaded up with gifts for the host clan and produce to trade. Fine weaves and materials, freshly ground herbs and spices, exquisite jewellery made from amber and jet, tailored garments made from animal skins, trinkets, utensils and culinary delights. But the most exciting part for everyone, was the competitions; the competitions most of all.

When everyone was present, a loud fanfare heralded the entrance of the host clan. Namir, as the next leader, proudly held aloft the horn from an Aurochs and led the procession of boys who were taking part in the games. Walking either side of him were Skyrah and Lyall scattering fresh petals across their path; a sign of continued peaceful friendships with health and riches in abundance.

At the helm of the procession stood Laith and it was from here that he addressed the people.

'My dearest friends, guests, comrades, partners; it is with open arms that I welcome you to this year's Gathering hosted by the Clan of the Mountain Lion.'

A round of applause rang out and a stream of nodding heads gesticulated to honour the hosts hospitality and splendid array of entertainment.

'Let us pray for all our gods to watch over us and that our totems will be guiding us as we join together for this very special day.'

A few moments of silent homage was paid to the afore mentioned beings. Then Laith concluded. 'This day is for the young people, a day of fun and games before their lives change forever. Many will take leadership, all will make life changing decisions, and everyone will face competition. This Gathering serves as platform to a challenging life. So now, clans, go and enjoy the celebrations.'

A rapturous applause echoed round the grounds, shouting and merriment broke the sound of Laith's trailing voice and the celebrations began.

No one really noticed Laith and the other leaders disappearing into the chieftain's hut for their regular talks. And not one person present on that day could have known that what they had to discuss would affect each and every one of them forever.

'We come with bad news Laith.'

'What has happened?'

'It's the General; he is under orders from the Emperor again.'

'Does this man ever give up? Come fellow leaders, tell me what you know and what we should do.'

Lyall heralded his archery competition in a loud proud booming voice. 'Come on now, don't be shy. I have made lots of white wood bows and arrows for you all to use, and here is a magnificent mahogany bow for the winner; expertly crafted by my own hands, planed for a smooth finish and polished with layers of beeswax for this deep red shine.' He held aloft his precious offering. 'All I ask is that you do not use the girls as a target.' And he looked towards the forest where, under the shade of the dappled autumn colours, the young women displayed their offerings on exquisitely vibrant stalls. He knew they were positioned far enough away though; he had shot a few arrows earlier in the day to make absolutely sure and nodded to Norg who was lining up a range of spears and rocks for his throwing competition.

Namir was the first competitor in the boxing event and Bagwa was holding court. 'Each boy is invited to take on the champion and try and knock him to the ground. Each opponent will have three minutes in the ring and then there will be a two minute break for the next competitor to prepare. If the champion isn't knocked down in that time then he will retain his crown. If he is knocked down, then the waiting boys will be able to take on the new victor until everyone has had a round. Does everyone understand?' Nods and grimaces acknowledged his words so he continued. 'Those of you who want to spar, then make it known to me.'

There was a crowd of boys around the make shift arena, all eager to watch and learn but mainly to have a go. Last year's champion was heralded into the ring amongst uplifting cheers and a riotous applause. Tore was a strong boy and paraded around the roped off circle to the adulation of the crowd. Namir dived under the rope to shake hands with his larger opponent.

'Good luck Tore.'

'Good luck to you too Namir.'

'Keep yourselves fresh for the last game,' Bagwa continued. 'Only Tore will be exempt from that, as well you know.' He tried to keep order as the line of boys increased. 'I know you are excited but please don't push, I only have one pair of hands.'

Namir and Tore were warming up in their corners while Bagwa rang out the rules. 'I will be watching for a fair game; there will be no punches to the groin, no high jumping or kicking, bare fists only. In the event of a tie I will make the final decision. If anyone breaks the rules they will be disqualified. My decision is final. There will be no contesting my authority, is that understood?' He looked around to make sure everyone acknowledged him and when he was satisfied, he exited the ring and gave the signal to start.

Tore and Namir moved from their positions on the outside of the ring and met each other in the middle. They faced each other with stern faces and Tore gave his first bit of advice. 'Remember to think of something you wish to conquer and then feel the power of your totem guiding you.'

The sparring began. At first they moved with exaggerated slowness, creeping on their feet and focusing through raised fists. They didn't want to make any mistakes and needed to read their opponent. An invisible chord held them together as they bobbed and ducked, swerved and retreated, using the space in the ring to build momentum.

Namir was inexperienced and misjudged his first swipe. He came in too close and Tore struck out. Namir recoiled and dodged the strike. A gasp from the audience showed their reaction. Many voiced their own advice in loud blasts. It was an obvious lure by the champion and Namir took time to refocus. Usually he was very quick and agile almost knowing in advance what was to come, but he was a novice and up against a champion this day. Tore was nimble and twice as strong, he could hit Namir easily but he continued to advise him as he danced round the ring.

'Think with your brain Namir and feel with your soul, then you will connect with your totem.'

The crowd swelled and enjoyed the parry, yelling out encouragement to their favourite to win. Namir raised his concentration levels, he tried to think, he tried to feel. The moves got quicker. Jabbing, hooking, striking as they hopped and skipped round the arena. Each yielding nothing, holding perfect concentration and the tension grew.

Grim faces around the perimeter urged them on, which one would concede first and lose the fight? Tore tried a succession of sweeps but Namir blocked with strong arms and protected his head; he responded with a two fist strike but that was also defended well by Tore. They parried round the ring and Tore launched with a full arm thrust. Namir recoiled again and returned with a clean sweep. He caught Tore on the jaw who staggered back and shook the surprise from his swelling face. Namir launched in again with the other fist and Tore only just blocked it in time. They refocused and eyed each other, dancing and jabbing with continual movements. To them nothing else was around except the time ticking by. They didn't even notice the excitable voices getting louder and louder, giving advice, making remarks and spurring them on. Tore was still giddy from the knock but he came back into the game with a swipe that knocked Namir off balance. The invisible chord was still taught but Namir staggered and lost his footing.

This was the opportunity that Tore was waiting for and a full arm forward thrust put Namir on the ground. A roar went up from some, a rumble of discontentment from others. Tore was still champion. He pulled the contender to his feet and embraced him.

'You fight well Namir. You will become a strong warrior as you grow. Develop that aggression and channel that energy. Then you will beat any contender that you face.'

'Thank you my friend.' And he bowed graciously to the winner.

Both boys shook hands and Namir exited the ring, dazed and bruised but in no way a failure. He stayed for a while to watch Tore take on his next few opponents and then went on to support the two lap horse race where Ronu and Clebe were the strongest contenders.

Much merriment abounded that day. Champions were hailed and records were broken and as the autumn shadows began to drift away, the teams began to congregate for the final activity of the games; the boy's tug of war.

'How was the archery?' Namir asked when he found Lyall later.

'It was very entertaining with lots of skilled archers today. Siri from the Giant's Claw was leading the way for a few rounds and then our Hali found his rhythm and beat him to second place.'

'So who won it?'

'Lace, from the Marshland Tribe. With absolutely incredible skills she took the contest with three targets in a row.'

'I didn't think girls entered the competitions?' Namir's tone was puzzled.

'Neither did I, but she had her hair scraped back in a tight ponytail and wore boy's britches, so no one knew until the end when she told us.' He watched

Namir digest the information. 'So how did your boxing go?'

'Well I'm still standing, put it that way, and Tore is still champion; but Dainn from the Hill Fort Tribe is the one to watch, Tore will have his crown taken next year, you mark my words.'

'Hmm, interesting. Tore and Lace from the Marshland Tribe and Dainn from the Hill Fort. Let's hope they're not in the tug of war together.'

Namir laughed. 'Come on, we had better get to our positions. Silva will be getting everyone ready.'

He put an arm round Lyall's shoulder as they strode off to discuss strategies that would put their team in the best position possible.

'You hold the rope with an underhand grip like this.' Silva was demonstrating the procedure with the rope. 'It's not about pulling, it's about pushing with your legs. The deeper you push with your legs against the ground, the more energy you will save.' All the boys got into position as Silva continued. 'When moving, take small steps back otherwise you might slip. It's only when we have control that we can take larger steps, and we must all do the same movement at the same time.'

'How will we do that?'

'I will call out commands so we get into a rhythm and that will keep us focused, we don't want anyone slipping and falling, otherwise the whole team is at risk.'

'Understood.' Hass replied.

'Let's have a warm up, but not for too long, we need to conserve our energy.'

'We've got a good team,' said Namir proudly.

'We certainly have, we have a lot of strong boys here.'

As the traders and other demonstrations closed down their stalls, people slowly moved towards the centre field and took their viewing positions around the perimeter. The teams were preparing, getting focused and limbering up.

After several quick rounds, there were two clear winners; the boys from the Marshland tribe and the Clan of the Mountain Lion.

'Let's show 'em what we're really made of,' heralded Namir.

'Come on now boys,' Lyall urged. 'Stay focused, stay strong and let's smash this contest.'

A chorus of excited voices trailed off into the distance and sat perched on the crest of the Giant's Claw to view the unfolding final.

The teams took hold of the rope. Namir was at the front with his feet firmly in the ploughed up soil, his legs were in the squatting position, his arms were out straight.

'Follow Namir's stance,' Silva called out from the back.

'Take positions,' came the call from Lyall to start.

'Ready boys, take the strain, dig deep with those

legs and push hard into the ground,' shouted out Silva.

The rope snatched tight. The Marshland Tribe were strong. Their boys began pulling and shouting. Froth and spit burst from bellowing mouths. Sweat poured down straining faces. Snot and phlegm mixed in quantities as veins popped out of developing muscles charged with energy.

'Stay focused,' Clebe called out. 'Let them tire first, keep a grip, dig deep with your legs, they are pulling with their arms and will tire quickly. Hold on boys, dig deep. Keep pushing into the ground.'

Their feet stood firm in the soil while the Marshlanders used up their energy with a pulling action. They seemed to be in a stale mate for ages with the red centre of the rope hovering over the line. Lyall's arms were burning just by keeping it taught - he was not used to such strenuous activity on this scale; his comrades were more muscular and had more strength. The team began to gradually feel the tension of the rope edging their way as the Marshlanders grew weary. Their bare bloodied hands were losing the grip and Ronu heralded his response to the thrown gauntlet.

'Boys pull now.'

They pulled.

'Boys dig deep take small steps back.'

They took small steps back in unison.

'Stay focused! Do not look up from the rope!'

They stayed focused.

'And heave!'

More steps back. The tension was coming their

way. They had control.

'Stay focused boys! Stay focused - dig those legs in firm - lean back - and - heave.'

They heaved with all the strength they had, having gained the advantage over the fatigued team. Low sitting thighs skimmed the soil with the exertion. Defined triangular calf muscles took the weight.

'Now big steps - move with the rope - keep momentum - and pull - and pull.'

They responded to his roars with their own deep guttural growls. Rivers of sweat poured down straining bodies, focused eyes squinted and teeth clenched hard, young hands were shredded and raw.

With a final surge of exertion they strode back with giant strides and pulled the failing Marshlanders off their feet. They tumbled on top of each other; a sweating, heaving mass of testosterone with arms of useless jelly. Exhilaration voided the exhaustion and they celebrated together, jumping and cheering and punching the air. The girls danced with joy beyond the perimeter and the youngsters applauded them. Silva, Hass, Bagwa and Clebe held Namir high on their shoulders while Hali, Wyn, Norg and Ronu lifted Lyall.

'Well done boys,' they shouted together. 'Well done all.'

'And now we have a year to prepare ourselves for the stag hunt.'Namir reminded Lyall. And they marched off arm in arm to stuff themselves silly and get drunk on weak beer.

In the distance, two men smiled as the boys ran off; but the air of sweet camaraderie was blanched with a sour reminder.

'You still haven't told him have you and I am deeply concerned. I see that you have aged with the burden and the worry.'

'I know, my whole body aches with the torment. It never seems the right time because it's not just him who it affects; and on top of that we have worrying news of the General. So help me Zoraster - what do I tell them first?'

8

The air of contentment in the pause between autumn and winter did little to conceal the harshest of snowfall that would follow that year. It was four months since the celebrations and the full brutality of the unforgiving northern hemisphere was under way as the biting east wind was once again preparing its gusts of icy blasts. By day the sky was a shimmering blue gauze that sprawled out over the horizon. By night the sky was full of grey swollen clouds, and a polished drizzle scattered over the surface of the ground making most areas impassable and dangerous. Life stood still in these torturous winter months; everything had to conserve its energy until the spring brought the welcomed thaw.

The tribe were ready for the chill by stocking up with their regular supply of meat, fish, eggs, berries, nuts and vegetables. The orchard trees had been stripped of their fruit, ready to be made into wines. The herds had been brought down from the summer pastures; the best animals were put into shelter, the rest had been slaughtered. Their meat had been dried and salted and wrapped in layers of animal hide. Some families kept a few sheep and goats in their huts for added warmth, even using their droppings as a heat catalyst on the open fires. The mighty aurochs with their thick hide and woolly coats were undaunted by the biting winds and gathered in groups when the temperature plummeted where their breath loomed in clouds; hovering, momentarily suspended in the freezing air.

The first heavy flurries of snow meant regular inspections of the livestock in the barns; breaking the ice in the water troughs, giving them food, as well as checking the clan's supplies.

On that crisp bitter morning Lyall left his hut to check on the animals and the supply of wood. Clouds of smoke hung in plumes above the thatched roofs and frigid icicles clung like daggers of steel from every eave and crevasse. He could feel the ice cold flakes land softly on his face while the crystalizing snow and frozen ice crunched beneath his feet. The biting air chaffed against his skin so he pulled his aurochs robe tighter and tilted a fur hat over his eyes. Round a corner a ghostly shadow approached him and through a haze of misty condensation he could tell who it was immediately.

'Lyall, I am so glad I have bumped into you, I didn't fancy trawling round for hours in this cold.' Namir breathed warm air into his cupped hands.

'I was just going to check on the supplies Namir, make sure we all have enough timber.' Lyall began to wave his arms and slap his shoulders in a futile effort to keep his body warm.

'Good idea, and I'll give you a hand with it later, but right now my father wants to see us urgently. He seems quite agitated about something.'

The snow was falling heavily now and the bitter north east wind stabbed and slashed at their skin like sharp silver swords. They needed a heavy shield to protect them from this force, but without such a device they gripped onto each other and carefully tackled the frozen ground. When the two boys found Laith, he was in his hut with the thick hide from an aurochs wrapped around his body and hunched over a low simmering fire with a pan of boiling water balanced on a triangle of molten lead. 'Anyone for a brew?' he asked.

'Yes please,' they said together, eager to fight off the bitter cold.

The piping hot nettle tea was dispensed into three mugs which were grasped with thawing fingers. Laith looked at the boys under untamed eyebrows and a creased forehead which gave away his ageing years. 'You are still so young and yet will be treated as men by this time next year.'

'Yes we are practising our skills. Ronu and Clebe take us out most days as they made their kill last year.'

'Goodness me, are they seventeen already? How time flies. They have grown into fine young men who will make fine husbands soon. They will guide you alongside your totems and keep you safe.' His words of praise were sucked into the chilled air as he returned to sipping on his tea.

'Is there anything wrong father?' asked Namir alerted by his father's heaviness. 'You look deeply troubled.'

'I am son, I am very concerned and I don't know ` where to start.' He finished his tea while the silence grew heavy and the two boys waited patiently for the leader to find his words.

'I had a meeting with the other leaders four months ago at the games.'

'Yes father, you always do that, it is a custom.'

'But this time grave news was discussed.'

Namir and Lyall felt uneasy.

'There is a General who goes by the name of Domitrius Corbulo, he works for the Emperor Gnaeus of Ataxata and he is the most evil creature you will ever meet.'

The two boys looked at each other uneasily as those words chilled the air even further.

'He calls himself the angel of the gods, that he is a tool for cleansing the kingdoms of unwanted savages and parasites.'

'So what does he want with us?'

'We have been told that the Emperor and the General have devised a scheme to entertain his guests over several weeks in the summer; they call it the Killing Games.'

'What? I don't understand,' Namir's tone was beyond shocked.

'The Emperor is in possession of a stolen heirloom, an important piece of the realm that has given him even more power than he had before. With this legacy he has propelled himself to even greater heights. He displays that authority by kidnapping clan boys to fight in his new arena. He considers everyone outside his kingdom a savage and a parasite, and must be disposed of.'

The boys slowly digested the enormity of this revelation.

'He will send his General to come after us. He considers us scum, unworthy individuals that are only fit for his entertainment.'

'What? He really thinks he can do that?' A shiver went through their spines at the same time.

'In the wrong hands, power does evil things.' Laith's words cut like ice. 'The games have already begun. Boys have already been taken and never seen again. I and my contemporaries have reason to believe that this is the same General who murdered your family and ripped the Seal of Kings from your dead father's neck for the Emperor.'

Lyall felt the vomit rise up into the back of his throat and the colour drain from his face. The tea didn't seem quite so appetising now and he dropped the mug to his feet. 'My father told me about this man. That's why he told me about the seal and the tunnel,' he shuddered at the memory. 'So many times he told me but I didn't want to believe him. I was so scared. I had nightmares for months. I believed it was flesh eating monsters that wanted to hurt us, not people.'

'Oh believe me, it's the living that you have to

be fearful of, not the monsters in your head. And just when you think you have met the most depraved human being, there will always be one more who is even worse.' Laith's voice was grim as he spoke from memory.

Namir put an arm round the lad as his father continued.

'You are safe for now, the General doesn't travel in the winter months, it requires too many resources and leaves little light to track down clans. But when the thaw begins we have to be vigilant, we have to be prepared, so that means lots of training for any attack and taking extra care.'

He drained the final drops of tea and studied the bottom of his vessel. 'An important reminder for you both as you train to hunt the stag; make sure you acquire the skills to be the hunter and not the hunted.'

The chill in the air almost froze over as Laith delivered those fateful words.

'We must pray to the gods and ask our totems for help during these dark times. I will be informing the others in due course, but I wanted to tell you both now.'

'Lyall hasn't been given a totem father, perhaps he should have one to protect him given the circumstances.'

'Yes, of course Namir you are right.' He looked at Lyall. 'What animal serves you best young man?'

This was something he had thought about ever since Skyrah had told him about Namir's leopard tattoo and why it was his guardian, and then after the incident with Targ and Suma, he knew what animal would protect him. He had often heard the wolf cry out its haunting howl under the cover of darkness and wondered why this beautiful animal did that. Perhaps it was like the hare and had a connection with the moon; perhaps like the moon gazing hare it was reaching out to its ancestors for strength and guidance. Persecuted and hunted, just like his family had been, this wolf had survived and had come back fighting. Now he understood the anguish in the call. Strong and resourceful, brave and fierce; this beast was a true legend of the forest. He would like the wolf to be his totem guide and voiced his decision. 'The wolf works well in a pack, he is protective and strong, he is a good hunter and a good provider, I believe this animal would serve me best.'

'I think that is a fine totem for you.'

Zoraster entered the room to administer his healing potions to the ageing leader. He knew by the anxious look that hung on the boy's faces that they had been informed of some disturbing news.

'Have you told them?' He asked inquisitively, busying himself around the leader and setting out his utensils in perfect alignment.

'I have.'

'About time too, they should have been told a long time ago.'

'I know.'

'Yes I was wondering why you didn't tell us sooner father,' interjected Namir. 'You have known about this for some time.'

'I kept telling him Namir, I really did,' interrupted Zoraster massaging a pulp of warm birch bark onto the leader's swollen knee. 'He was always saying that the time wasn't right.'

'Yes, yes, I should have told you before now, I'm sorry. I have had a lot on my mind.' The old man stammered.

'Well, we know now,' answered Namir.

'And Lyall, are you all right? I mean with what you've discovered; what a revelation for you,' Zoraster continued.

'Yes, it was a shock I can't deny it, but I'm all right,' replied the boy.

Laith suddenly twitched his leg and moved it out of the way. 'Careful Zoraster, you might be doing more damage than you realise there.'

Zoraster stopped what he was doing instantly and looked up at Laith. From the old man's fearful expression he knew that he hadn't told the boys everything and lowered his gaze in disappointment. 'I'm glad you're all right Lyall,' his voice softened. 'You are stronger than you think.' He put a cloth over the dressing and stood up. 'Is there anything else you wish me to do today?'

'Yes there is actually,' said a weary Laith. 'It has been decided that Lyall should have his own totem tattoo, could you do that for us now?'

'Of course I can, what is it to be?'

The response was unanimous. 'The Wolf.'

9

The winter finally released its frozen grip and the last icy breaths that covered the land were exhaled; fresh ripe buds on the trees heralded the spring awakening and the pulse of the earth quickened as life started to pump through the soil once again. New shoots and a variety of colours patch-worked the contours of barren grey moors while the sun made a welcome appearance and beat off the blistering attack of winter. Rivers thawed and ran freely. Shivering transparent icicles slowly dripped away. Evergreens pumped up their sagging branches; shaking off their top hats of moulded snow. Mythical plants robbed of their identity were exposed once again, and bushes that had been concealed for months reappeared. The animals were back in the meadows and a spring cleaning ritual began in the huts.

Many hands made light work as they swept out the stagnant stale straw, the old embers and the animal hairs. The chimney was brushed. The floor was scrubbed. The eating area was cleaned. All the coverings used for keeping out the driving rain and bitter cold were hung out and beaten rigorously to get rid of the accumulating mould and the stench of confined animals. Doors were left open to welcome in the new season and the fresh air burst in.

The clan boys had been hunting in the frozen woods as much as they could, but tracking was almost impossible. Instead they spent most of their days forging weapons, repairing worn fences and preparing the camp for an attack as Laith had requested.

The great man approached Namir and Lyall a few days into the thaw. 'Pack a few provisions to keep you going, we are going on a little trip this morning.'

'How long for father?' asked Namir.

'Just for the day, we will be back by dusk.'

Lyall raised an eyebrow, Namir furrowed his, both obeyed the orders.

Namir packed some dried meat mixed with clean rendered fat and dried fruit all wrapped in greased animal skin. He didn't know if the opportunity would arise to hunt, better to have something wholesome and nutritious to eat on the way. Lyall carried the treated gut of a boar, it served as a serviceable water container that was duly filled. Their weapons had been seared and lathed for practice sessions, now they were ready to go.

It was mid morning by the time they left the enclosure and headed towards the mountains. Laith was steadying ancient shaking legs with a well-used gnarled walking stick as he took each intrepid step. They trooped down the wooded flanks of the foothills and reached the plains while the sun was still rising. By noon they were tracking a narrow canyon following the path of boulders and jagged rock faces. An hour later the view opened up and the trio stood at the edge of a spectacular precipice with humps of bearded moss clinging on to its surface; where tendrils of green germinated from the growth and entwined itself beneath a veil of blue spray cascading over the edge and into the water below. Estuaries were flanked by paths and glades, and the green of the land was splashed with a rainbow of mouth-watering colours topped by the hazy hue of the skies. Herds of grazing animals roamed freely and gliding birds drifted effortlessly across the pale horizon carried along by the rising pockets of air.

Laith breathed in deeply. 'There is nothing like returning to a place that remains unchanged to find the ways in which you have changed yourself.'

'What is this place father?'

'This is sanctuary Namir, a very special place which I shared with your mother.'

Lyall's face fell to the floor looking awkward and uncomfortable as he tucked into his snack.

'We would come here often, no one else knew about it, we were totally alone.'

Namir smiled.

'It was a haven in a sea of tranquility.

Lyall felt even more uncomfortable and tried to concentrate on the scenery.

'It was many years ago that we fell in love. By the time we were eighteen, we were betrothed to be married. Of course we did wrong by consummating before the ceremony, but we loved each other so very much and this place overpowered us; it seemed so natural.' He stalled as those precious moments flooded his mind again.

'On the eve of the wedding our settlement was attacked. It was a different place to where we are now and I was taken prisoner.'

'Who by?' asked his son, hanging onto his every word.

'Emperor Gnaeus of Ataxata, he wanted to know where the Seal of Kings was.'

'How would you know that father?' The anguish in Namir's voice was clear.

'Because my father was a king and on his death bed the seal was given to his eldest son, my brother. Your mother lived in the castle with us, she was the daughter of one of the ladies in waiting - my brother and I both loved her. When my brother became king, your mother and I left to start our own lives in a clan. We had always yearned the freedom of living off the land and we had planned it for so long. Zoraster and a few others came with us and the rest is history so to speak.'

'And the Emperor wanted you to divulge his whereabouts?'

'Yes Namir, an informant told him that a clan member was the brother of a king, he didn't know which king or where his castle was, but I was of use to the Emperor. But I kept to my story that I was a penniless nomad and that the informant was misinformed. How could I put a death sentence on my own brother where the consequences would have been catastrophic?'

Lyall began to listen in on the story, his chin wrinkled and his brows furrowed as he tried to make sense of the unfolding saga.

'The General wasn't there then, he would have undoubtedly killed me. Instead, the Emperor imprisoned me for two years in the deepest dungeon in the Palace of Ataxata. I spoke to no one, I had no contact with anyone except the guards who threw a daily ration of bread and water into my cramped cell.'

'How did you survive that?'

'A belief in the protection of my totem, a hunger to live, the thought of your mother and my unborn child. All of those things. But every day the guard asked me if I wanted to talk to the Emperor, and every day I said I had nothing to say.'

'What about mother, what did she do?'

'She thought I was dead, she thought I had been killed or drowned or something equally grotesque; and for a long time after I wished that the Emperor had killed me. I had lost everything. I thought that the gods had punished me for consummating before my marriage.'

'So what did she do?' Namir persisted.

'She was expecting a baby. The camp was a decimated ruin. The people that survived the attack were trying to salvage what little they had. She was alone and scared, so she went to my brother, the king.'

'Did he take her in?'

'Yes he did, he had always loved her. We had both loved her. She was beautiful, charming, witty, clever, all those things.... but she chose me. She loved my nomadic ways and the freedom I craved back then.'

'And he was happy to bring up another man's son?'

'It was his brother's son, and he loved her, he was a good and decent man.'

'So how come I am with you then father?'

'Because when I was released I knew what she would have done. I went to my brother to see her. I wanted her to come back with me. But she had a new life; she was married, she was a queen now, she didn't want to bring dishonour to herself or my brother. He had taken her in when she was carrying my child, she owed him so much.' He looked deep in reverie at the memory. 'I asked if I could take my son back with me - which she allowed.'

'She gave me up?' choked a startled Namir.

'She did my boy, she gave you to me, because she loved me and wanted me to have something that was ours. She couldn't take everything from me and leave me with nothing.'

He saw the tears well up in Namir's eyes. Then the old man looked at Lyall. 'But she didn't have just one son... she had twin boys...and she kept you Lyall...the first born by a few minutes... so that you would be the next king.'

The earth suddenly stopped moving, time stood still, the spectacular scenery froze in an instant. Namir was visibly shocked as he digested the revelation. Lyall looked at him in disbelief and a nourished mouth went dry. He had listened intently but hadn't even imagined that it was the same castle, the same seal, the same king and queen as his own.

The old man took a pendant from his pocket and opened it for Lyall to see.

'It's my mother,' his voice was barely a whisper.

Namir peered at it. He had seen it many times before. As a child he always wanted to see the beautiful lady he knew as mother. An exquisite miniature painting of an enchanting woman with ruby red lips, long dark hair and the most captivating smile that would melt the ice off the highest peaks. 'This is my mother too.'

'You are twin brothers and by an incredible twist of fate you have been reunited and I have at last been able to look after you both.'

The boys looked at each other, then they looked at their father. The crushing pause that followed was unbearable. Lyall's initial impulse was to run into Laith's arms and sob with joy; the man who had saved him and had given him salvation, who had given him strength and hope, who had protected him vehemently from Suma and Targ. He loved him dearly. But he already had a father who had loved him and nurtured him, and for the past year and a half he had been mourning his death.

Now he wanted to run away. But apart from scaling the mountain in front of him, all he could see were swaying trees and waterfalls that forged down into winding streams. Beyond that was nothing; a vast open space where he would be lost, alone and vulnerable again. He remembered that feeling. That crushing avalanche of absolute terror that would never leave his soul. Every single day he had thanked the gods for his good fortune, how he had been given a new family, the strong relationships he had made, the skills he had learned, and all that was because of Namir and Laith. He should be rejoicing because they were his family. But he couldn't. He was confused. Why hadn't Laith told him sooner. All that time he knew so why didn't he say anything? The thoughts spiralled round his head until he was quite dizzy. Nothing made any sense. Eventually the words erupted like an awakened volcano.

'Why didn't you tell me?'

'Yes father, why?' echoed an equally confounded Namir.

'Please listen, please try and understand.' Laith took a breath to compose himself. 'When you arrived here, shocked, frightened and very scared; you had been through a terrifying ordeal. You had just lost both your parents. I had lost my dear brother and the woman I had loved for all my life; and yes, I hadn't seen them for years - so many years - but I knew where they were - I knew they were alive - but now...' He choked backed the swallow.

Lyall felt his pain. He was dealing with his own. He gave the silence time to breathe.

'....it was just never the right time.' Laith shook his head.

The two boys looked at each other then at Laith.

'Please understand Lyall, I did it to protect you.' Laith sniffed back the emotion.

Lyall kicked a stone and followed it to its resting place. Namir remained silent.

'Why didn't you stay in the castle with us?' Lyall chastised himself immediately for asking such a juvenile question. But Laith answered him anyway.

'How could I live alongside the woman I loved, watching her live her life with another man? How would Canagan have felt with my eyes on them at every turn, knowing that I was your real father and not him? No, I had to go back. Besides, the call of the wild beckons me. I live off the land, I hunt by the spear, I live by the sun and the moon, I respond to nature. Your mother was like that once.' He paused at the memory. 'My brother Canagan had a responsibility to the crown and he honoured that position. He was a good man and an exemplary king.'

'But we could have kept in contact. I had a brother and a mother there,' said Namir, following the line of each stone that Lyall threw with his own.

His father saw the agony. 'I know, it was such a hard decision to make, but for the same reasons I couldn't stay; those are the same reasons we couldn't keep in contact. But there was the safety aspect as well by then. Someone had told the Emperor about me, someone had committed treason against the crown. You must remember that not everyone is good and honourable, happy with the simple things in life and just content with what they have been given. There are so many that will go to sadistic and brutal lengths for recognition and status.' His thoughts turned to the monsters, who, in his lifetime had caused the misery of so many. 'I had already witnessed the horrors of the Emperor's rule and we couldn't risk it again. We needed to keep the Seal safe with Canagan. I moved the clan to where we are now, to be nearer to the cave; but if anyone had seen us going in and out of there, word could have spread and we would all have been put in danger.'

'So that's why the horror stories of cave dwellers were told to us as children,' said Namir.

'Yes, so no one would ever go in there.'

'The Emperor found out about the castle though didn't he, and massacred everyone in it.'

'I know son, like I say, it's difficult to trust everyone.'

They both looked at Lyall.

'How did the tunnel get there in the first place?' Lyall was still firing stones into the abyss.

'Long ago the fortress of the castle had been undermined and a tunnel ran beneath its foundations. It led to the entrance of a cave by the river, which you both know. It was built as a safe passage for the king and his heirs. When we said our goodbyes, we swore it would only be used in the case of extreme danger. That's why they sent you to me.'

Lyall wiped at the sting in his eyes and swallowed the lump in his throat as a song played in his head. 'The lullaby,' he murmured. 'That's why Skyrah sang it and said it was passed down from you.'

'Oh yes the lullaby.' Laith drew a thin smile on a melancholy face. 'Artemisia's mother sang it to her, it's so beautiful.' The boys could see him reminiscing. 'So beautiful.'

Silence resumed as the boys digested this information and Laith eased a heavy heart. They were all immersed in their own thoughts. The boys stopped firing stones.

'Forgive me for keeping you two apart and keeping your true parentage a secret for all these years. At the time we all thought it was the best thing to do. I am not sure it was now.'

The Giant's Claw loomed over them, its body aching with the weight of a thousand tales as it stretched high into the sky pushing to release its secrets. Below, a frail old man was trying to do the same. 'Only Zoraster knows about this, now that my brother and Artemisia have gone.'

A shiver of snow cried down the mountain side. An eagle came into view and the sun reflected on its seraph wings.

'Of course. Zoraster. That time in your hut. He thought you had told us about this, and not the General,' said Namir trying to stifle the irony of it. 'No wonder he suddenly went quiet.'

'Yes I remember the awkward silence that day; I thought he had hurt your leg,' recalled Lyall.

Laith looked to the ground. 'I know. I'm sorry - forgive me.'

The eagle floated by them and was joined by another. They swooped and soared together; they owned the skies. This was their domain.

'There is nothing to forgive,' hailed Namir. 'You are my father, and I respect you. You have always chosen the right path. I cannot sit here and judge you; I am still a boy with much to learn in your eyes and I know you were protecting me. I have always been proud of you and still am.' Then he turned to Lyall. 'And I am so proud that you are my brother Lyall. On the day we found you, I said to Skyrah that you were like me; little did I know then how true that statement was. To share the same parentage as one as strong and as fearless as you is an honour.'

The old man tilted his head in appreciation. Lyall wiped away a tear.

'I am shocked, not angry.' Lyall stifled his quiver and let out a sigh. He was totally moved by Namir's words. 'Just now I wanted to run away. I couldn't understand why you kept it from me. All this time you knew, my mother knew and never told me either. But you both have always made the right decisions and I have to respect that. When Namir found me, the first thing he said was that you would know what to do - and you did. You took me in and gave me a new life with new friends and protected me when I was threatened by Suma and Targ. I have to accept that you were protecting me with this revelation.' He looked towards Namir. 'We have the same parents Namir, but I had grown to love you as a brother long ago. I had always felt there was something special between us, a connection, a bond, call it what you will, and I always wished you were my brother, and now, I couldn't be happier.'

A gentle breeze lifted the smiles and words of affection as Laith spoke again. 'Thank you boys, thank you for your understanding and maturity beyond your years. We are truly blessed.' He pondered as he digested the vista. 'Life is full of challenges you know, like climbing a mountain, some parts of the mountain are treacherous and unforgiving while other parts are smooth and allow you to stand a while to breathe. Just like this mountain range before you; the Giant's Claw.' The brothers followed his gaze. 'It holds so many memories and secrets, but more importantly it represents one's life. These are your mountains boys. These are your challenges. Your lives are amongst these glaciers. Be more like the wolf and the leopard, listen to the mountains, listen to your heart, then you will make the right decisions.'

Namir and Lyall listened with a numb respect, totally moved by the triumphant speech.

With this accolade, Laith found his strong voice again. 'I believe that the gods are working together now. There will be dark times ahead; times when you will face death and defeat, but never give in boys, never give in.' He paused as he thought about the fallen comrades that had gone before him and continued. 'I have one last request from you both my sons.'

'Anything father, name your request.'

'Avenge Canagan and Artemisia's death and cut the heart from the man who murdered them.'

The boys looked at each other and raising their hands together to seal the pact declared.

'We promise.'

10

'Your mother went through the cave when she was with child?'

'Yes she did, twice,' answered Namir. 'The first time Laith took her through when they left the castle, and a second time when she had to go back.'

Skyrah embraced the courage with a respectful gasp and shook her head in disbelief.

'Amazing what you can do when you have to,' Lyall responded to Skyrah's reaction. 'She kept telling me that it was safe and that nothing would hurt me; because she knew, she had been through there herself.'

'A truly remarkable woman,' sighed Namir.

'And you are twin brothers, I just cannot get my head round that one,' continued Skyrah. Her expression hovering between various stages of astonishment. 'I know there are many coincidences but I never thought you could actually be long lost twin brothers. I mean twin brothers!'

'I know, it took us by surprise I can tell you,' exclaimed Namir.

'A good surprise though brother,' said Lyall. 'Just when I thought I had lost my entire family, I am given a new one - and it doesn't get much better than that.'

Laith had eased a heavy heart and the trench lines seemed to fade miraculously from his face. Zoraster hailed to the skies and thanked the gods for finally giving Laith the strength to tell his boys the truth. And several days later, Ronu and Clebe finally came to get the brothers back on track.

'Come on you two,' said Ronu, eager to get the practice sessions started again. 'Your stag hunt is just round the corner; and as brothers, you will doing it together. But you must accomplish the penultimate ritual before we can let you lose with a stag.'

'I know, we have to kill a boar.'

'Not just kill a boar Namir, it has to done quickly and honourably. These animals are giving their life for you. They must be blessed and prayed for so they can give you their spirit.'

'We will be quick,' Lyall assured him.

'This will be a real test for you both. You have to be swift and know what each other is thinking. There is no time for hesitation.'

'Ronu is right,' said Clebe. 'Only the most accurate hunter will be acknowledged by the gods.'

'We will honour the gods and the chosen animal,' said Namir humbly. 'We will be focused and vigilant.'

'Good luck brothers,' called out Skyrah. 'Wish I could come with you.' And she watched Namir and Lyall disappear into the forest with their guides as she headed off to her botany lessons with her mother.

How tedious that was she had often thought;

hunting with the boys would be so much more fun. She knew that they had been taught the strokes of the blade and made to throw the spear for many months; killing small game and practising on birds in flight. But now they would be tracking a boar to slaughter and execute the perfect kill. The spear, she knew, had to be placed deeply in the beast's chest, followed by a dagger into the neck. The animals they tracked had thrice the strength of a man let alone a boy, and only when the boy had succeeded in the final ritual, could he be initiated as a man.

'A boar can kill you in an instant if you are not prepared,' Ronu had told them sharply. 'He can rip you open and tear out your heart if you don't spear his chest in time; and if you don't penetrate the chest you have to go in with a dagger or an arrow.'

'Call on your adult totem, a yearling will be clumsy and make mistakes,' advised Clebe before they departed.

They had tracked a male boar. Remembering everything they had been taught Namir threw his spear with precision and caught it full on in the chest. Unfortunately there was insufficient force and the beast was able to charge towards them. Its small eyes were wild and it was as angry as a whelped child. The smell from it was overpowering and the bristling hairs covered cracked skin and dried ground in faeces. Namir then aimed his arrow and fired it quickly into the boar's throat. Still it came roaring and scrambling with the two weapons protruding.

Namir had no weapons now and the beast was upon them both in no time. Without a second thought, Lyall ran in to drive his dagger through the thick hide of its neck. It was not a clean thrust and the pointed blade merely punctured its skin. The aggravated boar knocked Lyall to the ground, snorting and roaring as it tried to grip the boy's throat, but the lithe youngster wriggled out from beneath him, grabbed the protruding spear and rammed it down the hog's gullet.

This time the boar squealed as weak legs scrambled feebly. The boys then threw the full force of their weight onto the animal and heard the life rasping out of it. The hunt was over. The kill was done. The brothers tumbled off the carcass exhausted but exhilarated. Covered in blood and sweat they blessed the animal and hugged each other.

'You did well there,' said Namir when he had got his breath back.

'That's what brothers are for, we are a team.' Lyall returned the compliment and lay there contemplating his good fortune; that they really were brothers, and they really were a team, and nothing could get in the way of that, nothing at all.

11

Another summer had been and gone. This year's Gathering hosted by the Marshland Tribe had been another success and the Clan of the Mountain Lion had retained their tug of war champions status. A new contender had pushed Lace to second place in the archery competition and Hali had come in third; and Dainn from the Hill Fort Tribe had taken Tore's crown in the boxing ring. Ronu, at eighteen years of age had married a girl from a neighbouring clan and Clebe had married her sister. Bagwa had become a father for the first time. All was quiet from any threats and no one had heard about the General at this most recent Gathering. Many thought he had been killed in battle, or that the Emperor had died. Either would have been welcome news.

But now it was the rutting season and time for the brothers to take the greatest prize of all in clan life. - the final ritual - the celebrated Stag Hunt.

'Today is the day brother,' exclaimed Namir excitedly. 'Everything we have ever learnt and worked for has all been for this moment.'

'We will succeed because we work as a team Namir, I have your back and you have mine.'

They clasped hands and prayed to the gods for guidance.

'You are good hunters,' championed Ronu. 'You will do well.'

'Listen to your inner voice,' advised Clebe. 'It is your greatest friend.'

'Look out for each other boys,' shouted out Skyrah.

The two men embraced, and through an archway of well wishers throwing good luck charms across their path, they set off for their task.

As they entered the forest on this cool morning, a mist hung heavily over the thicket, twisting itself in spirals through the dense wood, losing itself in crevasses and gnarled roots. The sun's rays lined their path as they edged slowly through cackling leaves and creaking branches.

Namir followed a set of tracks which he knew to be fresh, the pointed end of the almond shaped prints were leading him further into the brush. Recently devoured foliage from overhead branches and low lying bushes also signalled the presence of a target. They crouched by an old oak tree and Lyall plied fresh droppings between his fingers. The temperature and aroma told him how recently the stag had passed through there. The stools were still warm and the pungent smell of digested vegetation was ripe. The target was very close. But they had to remain calm. They had to relax.

Ronu and Clebe had made them rehearse the call of the deer, thus drawing the stag into the kill. They practised until they could mimic the sound of a doe and the roar of a buck, and in the rutting season this was an excellent ploy. This time though they didn't need to make the call.

'Listen to the forest, Lyall, it is our friend; smell the air that makes you strong, listen to the breeze against the leaves, touch the trees that empower you, wait for the sun's light to guide you. Forget you are a man, think only of your spirit totem, and let the wolf become your eyes.' Namir's outer shell seemed to close as he switched on his senses and intuition. 'Feel the magic of the forest and it will make you strong and invincible like the wolf.'

Those words became a mantra that filled Lyall's soul. He chanted softly. 'Keep focused and he will come...'

The forest added its own harmonious vibrations to the sounds of the dark overgrown kingdom, and as they lay in wait, crouched in the undergrowth, Lyall felt the image of his wolf tattoo with his hand and then ran a finger along the scar on his neck; both made him invincible.

Pores of sunlight were beginning to pierce through the glade. Namir gripped the handle of his spear as the palms of his hands moistened with anticipation. Lyall held his dagger close, he was ready, he dared not breathe. The forest was alive now.

In the silence a branch fell and a twig snapped.

A gentle rustling of leaves underfoot announced an intruder. A cloud of condensation from flared nostrils filled the space in front of them. A grunting cough followed the cloud. The stag trod carefully. He owned the forest. He was the King. The brothers knew that. They respected him and would honour him, for this was not a hunt for fun, this was not a trophy killing; this was a hunt to show their coming of age.

The stag stopped. Still. Motionless. Black eyes looked around. Tufted ears swivelled and rotated for sound. The impressive antlers swayed with the weight. He billowed and he snorted. He sniffed the air and puffed out his chest. The long neck was gracefully curved and something of a mane adorned his powerful front. He bellowed out a guttural, deep throated roar pushed out from his lungs in blasts as his breath steamed in the chill air.

As the stag stood impressively tall surveying his forest, a burst of sunlight broke free and lit up the beast through the shadows of the trees. Instinctively and intuitively, Namir sprang out of his camouflaged position and took aim with coordinated weapon and target. The beast heard the movement. The forest had alerted him. The leaves had sounded out their alarm. The twigs had signalled a warning. The wind began to spiral in a uncontrollable frenzy and the sun's ray's slid away like a scolded child.

Hunter and prey locked eyes. Both breathed heavily. Both raised their hackles and prepared to move. Fear induced drool hung in chords from the stag's jaw. Beads of sweat dripped from the man. The beast turned to locate his route and averted his eyes. He stumbled in panic. The hunted had no chance. This time Namir's spear had a force that rendered the stag immobile. This was Lyall's cue and he ran in to sever the jugular with his dagger for a quick kill. He leapt onto the stricken beast's back and with a swift movement the deed was done. The Emperor slumped onto his forelegs. Lyall jumped off so he was not crushed in the fall. Namir's arrow was ready but not needed. A roar rumbled through the air and a squadron of stricken crows took flight in response. He fell onto his side. Dust and foliage made way for his final resting place. One last breath left his lungs. Blood trickled from the open wounds, and brown lids closed over the blackened eyes to signify death.

Namir smiled with pride, he was waiting for his pumping heart to calm down and for his dry mouth to moisten again. The hairs on his neck were still raised from the anticipation. Lyall wiped away the sweat from his brow and kissed his dagger. They both stared at the kill before moving closer to the animal where Namir retrieved his spear. Without cleaning the weapon, he knelt down and paid homage to the spirits for leading them safely to the target. Lyall then placed his hand on the animal and thanked the beast for its life.

'We work well together brother,' Namir said proudly. He ran his finger along the wet glistening red blade and painted two strips of stag's blood either side of Lyall's face.

'We are men now and the stag has witnessed that.' Lyall held his dagger to the catch the sun's rays and offered the same ritual.

With the acknowledgement from the great beast they used all their strength to haul the mighty animal onto a plinth of timbers and twine. The carcass was secured tightly and they pulled it back to the camp, reliving the hunt and the kill with every slow step.

The stag's body not only elevated the boy's position to men - the antlers indicated a man's forthcoming nuptials and would be worn as a ceremonial crown on the eve of his wedding.

There would be enough skin to cover a small coracle, or make a tunic and shoes. The fat and hoof oil would light a lamp, the stomach, bladder and intestine would make good water carrying vessels. Bones were used for flint work, needles, tooth picks and harpoons. The gut and sinew was used as cordage to make fishing nets as well as the meat that could feed a family for three weeks. The heart would be buried at the head of the stone circles and the blood would penetrate Namir and Lyall's hut to keep them safe - a sign that the spirit of the stag would always look down on them and give them strength.

That same evening the beast's carcass was blessed in a ritual before the megalithic monument. Everyone attended; men, women and children, all witnessing the birth of a new era in the brother's lives. Wild dancing and singing accompanied the chanting and rhythmic beating of drums. Howling and wailing summoned the gods and spirits; for they too had witnessed the transformation and bravery of the brothers. Namir and Lyall stood together in the centre of the circle dressed in the ceremonial robes with painted marks on their faces. Namir held the blood stained spear in both hands as high as he could towards the sky to please the gods and Lyall walked round the congregation displaying the bloodied dagger.

Zoraster eventually stood up and waved his hands to order quiet and indicate that the spirits were present. He took Lyall's blade to make another incision in the stag's vein where the blood was collected in a metal drum. The belly was then slit from the anus to the chest and opened to expose the liver, heart and other organs which were ceremoniously removed.

He approached the boys. 'The stag has brought you together as hunters and as men, he will keep you together and nothing will ever part you as brothers.' He stood in front of them holding the smooth blood red liver and cut it in two. A piece was handed to the men who bowed low on receipt of the offering.

'This is for you Lyall, we are united forever.' Namir consumed his piece in one go.

'This is for you Namir, the gods are our witness.' Lyall devoured his piece with pride.

The liver was smooth and warm; it seemed to be still alive as it glistened, saturated in the stag's blood. Lyall knew this was the most important organ in the body, and to eat it right after the kill was somehow even more powerful and meaningful. He didn't flinch at all and consumed it in one go. Unlike the name giving ritual where he felt sickened to the core and was retching on the side lines. He was a part of these people and nothing affected him now. He would never fear again, he would never recoil from adversity. He would lay down his life for his comrades. And as the two men and the other members of the clan followed in drinking from the goblet of life, the medicine man administered the final tattoo onto Namir's and Lyall's arm - the mark of the stag.

Laith was restless though, he could sense a change in the air. He filled his lungs and closed his eyes. The breeze began to whip his face in chaotic movements and he sensed the fear.

And now he could hear the breath of a devil approaching. He reached to the skies and summoned the totems. When he had finished the tattoo, Zoraster lay down his instrument. He too was aware and reached to the skies. The clan stood in the centre of the stones with a wind circling them, round and round it went carrying the voices of a thousand totems, whispering to them, caressing them, breathing courage into their veins, giving them strength, trying to protect them.

The clan knew, the brothers knew. They all knew it was time.

Out on the horizon a caravan was edging up the hill. Four horse drawn wagons which carried the cages full of slaves, the rations for the men and the provisions for the horses, teetered on the brow of hell. They were tired now and far from home for this had been their most arduous journey yet. They had been marching north for two months and were finally going to attack the Clan of the Mountain Lion. Some people thought the General had left this tribe to last because he was afraid of the savages there, but the soldiers dismissed that. General Domitrius Corbulo was afraid of nothing; even death was scared to face him.

The black horse began to strain at the bit and whinny, her ears swivelled back and forth, her nostrils flared. She pawed the ground with a frustrated hoof.

'Steady girl, steady, all in good time.' He didn't take his eyes off his goal and gently stroked her smooth velvet neck with a gloved hand. 'We will be home for the winter my beauty, our work is nearly done.' A murderous grin swept across the wicked face as he anticipated the rewards of his brutal endeavours.

The monumental cavalry concertinaed to a halt. The boys in the cages tried to cry out a warning to those below but were butted in the ribs with torturous bayonets. Unforgiving chains were pulled tighter. Strangled voices were carried away by the teeth of a gale, and the haunting sounds of the howling wolves were swallowed up by tumultuous clouds.

As the boys waited anxiously and pitifully in their prisons, the rest of the party waited for the command from their General.

12

General Domitrius Corbulo waited silently watching the celebrating party below him. 'Let them enjoy these last few minutes together,' he lamented to his captains and neatly arranged his white gloves around his fingers.

The breeze quickened its speed, circling and growing in strength as it howled and raged through the branches of the trees. It tried to push the General and his army off course, it blew hard with all its force but the General stood firm. The wagons rattled. The cages shook. The wolves were on the move. The horses were scared and whinnied. But the General stood defiantly still, unperturbed by the frenzied supernatural events around him. Eventually the wind died down as abruptly as it had started and dropped to a deathly silence.

This was Corbulo's cue; he had waited long enough and signalled to his captains. They in turn sent the force of the cavalry storming down the hill to the unsuspecting victims.

The clan were prepared but not ready for this assault. They had been celebrating the spiritual journey of two brothers and were now about to witness how wretched a fellow man could be.

Namir rang out his orders. 'Men look out! They are here! Quickly to your positions! This is not a drill! This is the real thing!'

Norg and Bagwa sprinted over to their long line of traps and waited for the command from Ronu. Namir jumped onto his waiting stallion and created a dust screen as the animal pounded up and down the banks of the river; this allowed precious time for the women and the children to take a safe path into the refuge of the cave. The women were crying and babies were whimpering; a generation of inquisitive children had been told about the monsters in the cave to stop them going in there; and so now, as the wind picked up speed, the echoes of a deadly predator became real again.

'We must hurry, there is such little time, you will be safe in the cave, Lyall has been all the way through and there are no monsters we promise,' chanted Zoraster.

Namir was still creating a diversion. Lyall was assisting Laith and Zoraster. 'We must make haste, the cave will be your sanctuary for the time being.'

'We will be all right, we will be safe I know that,' said Laith. 'But I fear for you and your brother.'

'This is no ordinary man Lyall, this is a devil, you must be careful,' echoed Zoraster.

'We will be fine, don't worry, either of you.'

Orla called out to him. 'You need to speak to the clan Lyall. See how scared they are.'

Lyall ran ahead to ease the panic. 'Please do not

be afraid, you will be perfectly safe in the cave, I have been all the way through and there is nothing in there, I promise.'

'But it's dark,' cried a young girl.

'You have to be brave little one, sing the lullaby that Laith taught you, the one your mother sings when you are scared. But I have to go now and help my comrades. Be brave little one and summon your totems, we all have to be so very brave.'

He looked over to Hali who had grabbed his mahogany bow and was stacking his platoon of arrows in front of him. A proud smile had time to reveal itself as he saw that Silva had made one too and both boys were a squadron to be reckoned with. He darted to get his own bow from its hiding place, lined up his own ranks and sent them pulsing through the air.

Clebe ran into the supplies hut to grab as much as he could. Sling shots, arrows, rocks, spears; all sharpened and lathed for this most treacherous of assaults. 'Hass, Wyn, come with me; you will need to line up the weapons for me. Be quick on your feet lads.'

The two boys skidded ahead of Clebe for their lives depended on it. The other men of the village formed an impregnable barrier and got into position with their weapons.

As the cavalry advanced, Ronu shouted out the order to Bagwa and Norg. They cut the heavy rope holding the long line of batons down and on release a deadly spiked trap flew in the air unseating the riders.

The horses screamed in terror. The men shouted to retreat, but as they did so Bagwa and Norg ran alongside them to unleash a second trap. As the General's horses were turned about they found their route of escape blocked by the impassable rows of murderous batons. Many of the horses stumbled and fell which allowed Bagwa and Norg to drag the soldiers from their saddles and render them immobile from where they lay. Namir and Ronu ran in to aid the attack. The General stared at the unfolding bloodbath and sent down more troops. More men and boys ran in to them, the clashing of metal on metal and shields on shields was deafening.

The General cocked a half grin and spoke to his captains without taking his eyes off the field. 'You see that down there, that is what the Emperor wants to see; desperation, survival, working as a team.'

The captains all nodded in agreement.

'You would be wise to watch and learn my comrades; this is why the Emperor seeks teenage boys for his entertainment. They have no fear, only the determination to survive. It makes spectacular viewing don't you think?'

He sent another line of archers in, all the while watching from his elevated position. These troops were met with spears and arrows as weapons were continually replaced by the youngest boys. None of them gave in or waned. But it was like a game to the General, he never once thought about his own tired men who had travelled for months and were now being slaughtered down there. But it was getting late and he wanted to be on the road before it got too dark.

'There has to be a weak spot in this force,' he said to himself. 'It's just a matter of finding it.' His eyes scanned in a panoramic gaze, searching for the one thing that had gone unnoticed - the one element in the battle strategies that the boys hadn't prepared for.

'It has to be here, they are savages and too inexperienced to have thought of everything.' He rose up higher in his saddle; his mare snorted and shifted the weight beneath her. The General extended his neck and jutted out his chin, squinted eyes followed the tip of his nose as he focused slowly and carefully. His gaze took him to the perimeters of the battle ground and he saw what he wanted; a young girl crouched behind some bushes. 'Now who is she looking out for I wonder?' He put a gloved hand up as an order for his captains to remain in position. He nudged his obliging mare into a slow trot and silently crossed the plain to ambush the unsuspecting victim.

Skyrah had been there all the time, watching unnoticed while her friends fought for their lives. Her dagger was fixed firmly in her belt and she was poised ready to run in and help if they floundered. She was hoping for a chance to shine with a heroic act in which she could rescue them all. Right now, she didn't really know how she could execute this plan, or when would be the right moment, so she just waited silently and rigidly for the opportunity. She was so focused on her clan that she didn't hear the mounted General approach her. He reached down and grabbed her from behind; she screamed out loud as he threw her in front of him. Immediately the gloved hand wrapped itself around the piercing cry. 'If you want to live young lady, then you had better keep that mouth of yours shut.' He then curled his sinister face closer to hers and whispered in her ear. 'Now let's go and see how brave your friends really are.'

Skyrah knew who this man was. The black mare, the gloved hands, she knew straight away this was the General who would cut out her heart if she struggled. In fear for her life she dared not move a muscle.

The General didn't have to say a word. As soon as he entered into the battleground with Skyrah astride in front of him, the fighting stopped. Even his own soldiers retreated in front of him. His horse fidgeted underneath him as he addressed his audience.

'Well that's better,' he said cruelly. 'But I was rather looking forward to squeezing this smooth white neck in front of you. But then again,' and he smelled her through deep nostrils. 'She seems far too good to waste.'

The clan men and boys instantly threw down their weapons. A soldier snapped Hali's precious bow in two over his trunk of a thigh, threw it on the mounting heap and set fire to it. A tear ran down Hali's cheek.

Lyall recognised the man on the charger at once, and he reached up to feel the scar on his neck. He trembled and felt the rage burn in his stomach. He looked straight at the ogre and felt his whole body stiffen. The memory flashed before his eyes so vividly that he could almost smell the torched buildings and hear his mother's screams. He saw the cruel eyes that had watched his home burn to the ground. This was his enemy. This was the one he had sworn to destroy. And ` now here he sat, smugly with Skyrah at his side. The beast didn't even know who he was. But one day he would, most definitely he would.

A deathly hush resumed in the hostile landscape as the General continued. 'All I wanted was a little chat and you respond like this. But thank you for the entertainment, it has shown me what a delightful time we are in for.' He looked around the village. 'I see you have moved the rest of your clan, but that is of little consequence to me, I am only interested in the young men, and I have just seen ten of the bravest souls it has been my pleasure to witness. And on top of all that I have a little extra something for me.' He roughly turned Skyrah's face round and licked it. 'I am sure the Emperor will allow me this little treat.'

Skyrah nearly vomited over him. Namir looked up with the guise of a vexed man. Why didn't she go with the others as instructed? This one time she should have done as she was asked - she would have been safe in the cave.

'I will leave my dead men for your elders to clear up; after all, where you are going, we will be clearing up your corpses.' The sinister smile spread across his face. He turned his fidgeting horse and cantered back up the hill with Skyrah in front of him.

His troops gathered up the captives and led them to their fate. The last empty cage was waiting for them. Ten bruised, battered and fearful boys were now slaves of the Emperor of Ataxata.

13

The immense caravan rolled across the land in a south westerly direction, through the subject kingdoms and onto the border territories. Fragile faces hung low, too tired to speak, too drained to think, but all in dread of what lay ahead. The wheels of the cages creaked and groaned as they sank into the deep ruts on the road, while the dispirited horses plodded sullenly to the whip of the driver.

For days they were engulfed by damp weather and relentless flying assassins eager to feed on their blood. Swatting and smacking these creatures only encouraged more squadrons to enter their domain to feast and gorge, while dusk brought even more menacing creatures. But even worse, was the meagre rations of stale bread and rancid water which did little to relieve their hunger and thirst, and for many it made them violently ill.

The General's supplies were thinning now. He knew he had to get back before the weather turned, or he lost some boys before the games had begun; so he pressed on arduously, not resting until darkness fell and resuming the journey at first light.

Namir had been thinking for days, there had to

be a way out. There is always a solution, always an answer, and for the first time he saw a light at the end of the tunnel.

'Don't worry comrades,' he whispered. 'Wherever we're being taken, will have walls with doors and the locks will have keys. Skyrah will help us. We will escape.'

'If the General doesn't kill her first,' sighed Silva with a heavy breath.

Namir raised his eyebrows, aghast at the supposition. 'He would have done that back there if he had wanted to punish her or us. No, she will be safe, I know she will.'

'I admire your tenacity Namir, but we are dealing with evil here and who knows what that monster will do?' Ronu's voice was grim.

'If we give up hope now then we might as well be dead, we have to rely on our totems - and Skyrah.'

The boys looked up at Namir's defiant expression. Hali and Silva had already found a strength from Namir's words. The boys he grew up with, got drunk with on his birthdays, the ones who pulled together to win the tug of war two years in succession, who had tried so desperately to win this battle; they had to remain strong.

'And then we will gather an army to get rid of the devil,' seethed Lyall between clenched teeth.

'Of course we will Lyall, we will get our revenge.'

After several days the barren landscape morphed into a road with tatty ravaged meadows on either side. Farmers could be seen in the fields tending to livestock, then they would pass a few travellers on foot followed by a couple of horse drawn traps. Civilisation was getting closer now. Sparse living accommodation and small neat gardens patch-worked between the pastures gradually turned into rows of large handsome houses made of timber and clay with sweeping frontage enclosing well stocked outbuildings and steep roofs that hung almost to the ground. Heads began to pop out of windows as they heard the rumble of the goods train, and recoil just as quickly when they saw the cartloads of savages.

The first sign that they were approaching a city was the noise, followed by an array of disproportionate buildings and finally a mass of people vying for a glimpse of the new prisoners. Jostling and pushing, yelling and screaming; a tidal wave of abuse was hurled at them as wretched dirty fingers poked and throaty venomous spit splattered. The bars were a useless defence in this instance.

They were on the road to hell, and wide flared eyes searched round this alien kingdom, for none of them had seen such constructions, heard so much noise and been faced with such enormity. The younger boys withdrew to the corners of their cages; petrified, sobbing, yearning for the safe arms of their mothers again. Most were smeared with the blood of soldiers trying to defend themselves. They certainly didn't look human anymore. The berating crowd was eventually beaten back by the captors with copious amounts of venom. The boys didn't look at them; they didn't want to give them the satisfaction of witnessing their tortured souls.

They passed street advertisements and panel painted frescos of boys fighting. Whole porticos were covered in life size murals of young adult males in full protective dress armed for combat. These were the boys that Laith spoke of. These were the crowd pullers that the Emperor dreamed of. This would be them one day.

An avenue of overly laden stalls swallowed them up, with its artefacts begging for attention. Sculptures, figurines, lamps, glasses, engravings bearing mono prints of fight scenes. They passed a stall selling babies utensils and each one was stamped with a boy's head, imbibing certain fortitude and courage. There were pictures of fights with demonic creatures, disfigured wolves, creatures that were half man and half beast. Were these the creations from an artist's imagination or did they really exist? Many boys shook with fear and the stench of urine slowly covered the base of the cages.

They continued to make their way out of the city and as the roads got wider they entered a staggeringly rich and opulent area. Building after building was bigger and more impressive than the previous one; tinged in various shades of pink and clad in grand ornate gold pillars where the domes of coloured mosaics towered high into the air, scattering a prism of every colour imaginable onto the streets below. Bathed in the rainbow of hues were the entrails of the summer's creeping jasmine, and the remains of honeysuckle vines entwined round magnificent heralding fountains. Noticeably, every few yards there was a shaved errand boy clearing away the dead leaves and discarded petals that landed near the gentry's path.

The women wore fine dresses that skimmed the gleaming pavements and portly men brushed past with an over-indulged swagger. There wasn't a tunic or woollen cape between them, just silk gossamer, rich damask and everything exquisitely embroidered and luxurious.

The boy's torturous journey continued, eventually turning in to the wide entrance of a walled palace. Those who still had their eyes open noticed a colossal marble statue, to which everyone bowed as they filed past. This had to be the Emperor; the epitome of ruthlessness and avarice; the instigator of fear.

Their transporter carried on along the wide driveway flanked by rows of laburnum trees and aconitum bushes that veered right and then channelled around to the back of the palace. The Emperor's pavilion was huge, bigger than any castle Lyall had ever seen. Painted white, with oval windows clad in pillars of gold, surrounded by a well-kept terrace and immaculate lawns, while bright lamps burned in windows in preparation for dusk. And as they took the final curve round the building, they saw the maids sweeping the autumn debris from the outdoor terrace.

Tired, beleaguered faces went from orange to green to purple under the glow of the lamps and as the noise from the city began to fade away, they saw it. There, in the distance, on its own, stark and forbidding; the huge arena, cruelly cleaved into the hillside. An open wound disfigured and maimed by a thousand slaves which cried its own tears of blood and reached out to them with misshapen crooked arms. And to the left of them with its door facing away from the arena, protruding from the earth like an unwelcome parasite, was another place that reeked of unbearable suffering; a cold slab of shale, blotting the violated landscape.

The General made a left turn at the centre of the causeway with Skyrah still firmly fixed in front of him, to inform the Emperor of their arrival. The convoy proceeded to the arena where the grim-faced boys were ushered out of the cages. Some fell and had to be supported, others looked about in disbelief, most just stood quietly, looking blankly ahead. Once the captives had tumbled out, the caravan continued round and veering to the left of the palace went out of sight. The General could be seen discussing terms with a huge man. This had to be the Emperor for there was a resemblance to the marble statue that they had just passed. He pointed to Skyrah who was taken inside by a guard - she would have to wait to discover her fate. The black mare was led away by a cowering stable lad and the Emperor walked towards the arena with the General.

Both men wore their hair long and tied into a pony tail. By definition, it seemed the longer the pony tail, the more authority one had. The Emperor's spindly grey hair was pulled back off his plump ageing face. He wore a red cloak over knee length britches and a white shirt while his hands were concealed inside gold coloured gloves.

'You see my lord, I have brought you a fine selection of savages this time.'

'You have done well Corbulo, you will be greatly rewarded.' A nod reinforced a job well done.

The General tilted his head at the accolade.

'Here is a list of their ages as you required.'

'Thank you Corbulo.' The Emperor took ownership of the list and studied it carefully while stroking the jowls on his wrinkled chin.

'It makes for such good entertainment when savages like these are locked up together.' The General drooled as he leaned into his master and shared the delight.

'Yes, just like last time Corbulo; they will go mad, they will fight and they will kill each other.'

Corbulo stifled a pertinent cough. 'Have you spoken to the other two savages. If you get my meaning sire?'

'Our two spies you mean?' The Emperor curled one side of his mouth and his eyes narrowed into a cruel slant. 'They have been given their instructions and will pass on the details of who we should put in the arena first; and yes I am fully aware of what happened last time, so they have been warned.'

The two men sniggered at the thought and exchanged a glance that validated their similar thinking. Then the Emperor scanned the paperwork one last time before handing the parchment back into the possession of the General. He walked slowly up the line of boys, feeling their arms, looking inside their mouths and inspecting their teeth; then recoiling in disgust at being in such close proximity and wiped his soiled gloves on their shoulders. He took note of their tattoos.

'What is this mark on your arm?' he asked with a frown.

'It is my totem, it is a wolf,' replied a galant Lyall.

'And this one, what is your totem?'

'It's a leopard.'

'And yours, what is this?'

'A bear,' said Norg.

'And how old are you to have a bear on your arm?'

'I am seventeen.' Norg stood tall to enhance his age.

'You are a seventeen year old fool.' The Emperor's venom knocked him back. 'You are all fools; depraved, unruly savages that rely on the marks of animals to give you strength.' He snorted from the back of his nose and turned his back on them.

'It is our custom; we are not depraved, we are not savages and we certainly are not fools,' shouted out Bagwa.

The General punched him hard in the stomach

with a cruel fist. Instantly Bagwa folded like a scythed ear of corn and the General followed into his agonised posture and seethed at his crumpled face. 'Forget about your customs, forget about your clans; forget about everything you have ever known before. Here you are savages and will be treated as such.' He wiped the spittle with the back of his hand and lowered his tone as he stepped back to address the Emperor. 'They may be savages with ridiculous marks all over them but they fight extremely well my lord; I have already witnessed a range of animal like hostilities and pack behaviour.'

'So maybe the marks do work for them,' the Emperor sneered again. 'That all sounds very promising indeed.' He raised an untidy eyebrow as he relished on the information with his gaze still resting on the boys. 'Animals always tear each other to shreds if provoked enough.' He turned to face his accomplice. 'You may retire Corbulo; your work is done here for now, go and enjoy yourself with that wench of yours.'

The General was dismissed with a wink from the Emperor.

Namir felt his blood rise but there was nothing he could do. He was flanked by two burley guards who could crush him with one blow. One was particularly pugnacious with a furrowed scowl and the other bore deep pitted pox marks across his face.

'Welcome savages, welcome to your new home.' He jutted out his chin pointing to the accommodation behind them. 'This is far better than the mud huts you are accustomed to.' His grin was sickening. 'And this is my new arena where you will train hard, and in the summer you will entertain the nobility.'

The boys turned to see the ravaged face of the quarry and observed the sombre grey walls of the dormitory.

'But you will have to do something in return for my generosity. You get nothing for free in this life.' He paused while the boys digested his words. 'I am not an unreasonable man, I know that the daylight hours will be short now, I know that we cannot accomplish very much in these dark months. But you will still train and you will learn how to use weapons. And as the daylight hours increase you will train even more and work even harder for your comfortable accommodation,' he paused to sniff the air. 'We have games in the months of June where you will fight each other. Everyone is treated the same regardless of age and health concerns. There will be winners and there will be losers. Life is like that. Freedom comes to those who fight well for two years. And for those who don't,' he paused to inspect his manicured fingernails. 'Well, you will see...'

'What if we don't want to fight, what if we want to go home?' cried out a piteous voice.

The scowling guard stepped forward and punched Silva in the face with a brutal fist. He fell instantly; almost unconscious, he lay there dazed, his head throbbing, blood running from the wound.

'You don't get choices here,' the Emperor bellowed. 'You are my slaves now and you do what you are told.' As he turned, the billowing cape swirled and his pony tail sashayed and he strode back up the causeway into his pavilion leaving those final orders to settle.

The two repulsive guards unlocked the doors to the dormitory and let the boys in. No words were exchanged. Namir helped Silva to his feet. The guards left without a word and locked the heavy doors behind them. They followed the Emperor to their positions outside the palace and faced the dormitory. They would only move again to protect their master or bludgeon escapees.

The boys now faced a room with one large wooden table and several chairs arranged on a cold stone floor. A huge recess allowed for a fire around which was a display of worn cooking utensils. There were no knives or sharp implements. In an adjacent room was the store room where food rations would be left on a daily basis. A pump brought water up from the indoor well and a rusty tin tub was provided as a bath. Sombre faces matched their pitiful surroundings and their freedom seemed a lifetime ago.

Suddenly, a voice sounded out over the gloom.

'Well seeing as we are going to spend some time together I should introduce myself and my clan. I am Dainn from the Hill Fort Tribe. This little lad is Rufus, ` and four more boys from my clan are Storm, Durg, Malik and Tay.' He gestured to them as they were introduced and grim faces responded to the introduction. 'But I remember many of you from the Gatherings.'

'Yes,' said Namir. 'You beat the champion Tore in the boxing this year.'

'I certainly did, and still bare the scars to prove it.'

Namir and the others immediately shook his hand as nodding heads and gestures of recognition tripped round the dormitory.

'I am Siri from the Giant's Claw, this is my little brother Zeno, and for two years in row I have been beaten by a woman in the archery event at the Gatherings. I don't think I can ever live that down.'

Hali laughed. 'Lace gave me her prize winning bow two years ago, and I still can't match her skills. Came second again this year to another woman.' He shrugged.

Dainn smiled knowingly.

'Well it's better than me,' complimented Siri with a raised brow. 'I came third. I think I'm getting too old now and have lost my edge!'

Zeno clung on to his brother's hand.

Hali smiled at his friends misfortune but was tinged with his own sadness. 'That bastard trashed the bow she gave me.'

'I saw him do that Hali,' said Siri. 'But remember, he may have broken the weapon but nothing can break the skill; nothing can take that away from you.'

'How come it's just the two of you that were captured?' asked Storm under the guise of uncertainty. 'There are six of us and ten of the other clan - I'm just baffled - if you don't mind me asking?'

Siri looked ashen as his younger brother gripped his hand tighter. 'In all honesty - we were totally outnumbered and unprepared; we were weak amongst the Emperor's men. Many of our clan fell; it was only my brother and myself that were of use to the General in the end. I will never forget the smells or the sounds as the wagon was pulled away. I am not even sure if our leader, the great Thorn, will survive.'

Dainn put a strong arm around him. 'Have faith Siri; your strength saved you and your brother, and that courage will get back to your clan again.'

'All of us have been tested these past few days,' said Namir. 'All of us have witnessed unimaginable brutality, but we must not weaken, we have to stay strong.

Those words sat proud with Siri and he found his valour again, while around him old acquaintances found familiar faces and began to introduce themselves. Smiles replaced forlorn guises, jokes were exchanged, banter and playful boyish behaviour broke out. A happier time brought back so many good memories and for a while the reality of why they were there in the first place seemed to escape them.

'Oh yes, such happy joyful times,' sneered an unfamiliar gruff from out of sight. 'So glad that you were all so happy.'

'Because it ain't gonna last now you are in here,' mocked an equally distasteful tone.

Slowly and systematically each group of new

friends turned and sought out where the taunting was coming from. The voices came from another room where twenty frames were arranged. Underneath each bed was a commode and on top of a thin mattress was a pile of clothes, one grey sheet and a sack filled with straw for a pillow. A small table offered a candle and a solitary book about the 'Rules of Ataxata by Emperor Gnaeus.'

Sitting together on one of the beds, wearing only lightweight exercise trousers, were two severely undernourished boys with shaved hair and red eyes that stared out from dark grey sockets. Their heads looked far too large on their thin, twisted, hunched bodies with barrel chests that bore deep scars, while snarled callous fingers gripped on to the edge of the frame and white veins ran down their arms.

'Suma? Targ?' Namir barely recognised the two gaunt faces behind their death like veil. He was visibly shocked at their appearance, though the memory of their exile had not escaped him.

Targ looked at Namir, then at Lyall. Suma followed his gaze. Both savages began to piece together a detailed map of loathing as the hideous memory unfolded. Their faces turned to hatred while their fists curled tighter onto the frame. Namir sensed the unease and Lyall steadied himself ready to protect himself. He was bigger now, he had faced a lot since he last encountered these two brutes, he was prepared this time. Suma stood up and making his way across the room, unravelled himself against Lyall. 'I remember you small prince,' he growled menacingly. 'I've been praying for this day ever since I was thrown out of the clan because of you.'

'You are mistaken Suma,' corrected Namir. 'With all this time away you have forgotten the true events.'

Suma span round to face Namir. 'Because of him your father banished us.'

'My father banished you both because you threatened his son.'

'His son. What are you talking about. The prince of darkness has stolen your father as well?'

'That's right,' said Namir. 'This is my true brother, and Laith is his father as well as mine.'

The hatred in Suma suddenly gave him strength, he found a voice that had been dormant for many months and he began pacing around like a prowling carnivore. Everyone backed away as he advanced. 'And now we all meet again to finally thrash it out.'

The smaller boys looked terrified; these two looked like ogres now and capable of anything.

'Leave it, you are frightening the younger boys,' urged Namir.

'We are frightening them?' Suma laughed out loud. 'Just wait until the games of death start; we are like puppies compared to the Emperor and his entourage.'

'That's enough!' Dainn's tone was low.

'What - are you scared big man?' Targ goaded. 'Are you frightened that someone might hurt that pretty face of yours? Hey Suma, do you remember the pretty boys who fled the arena in terror but were hunted down and killed by the guards?'

'Of course I do, that was really exciting,' came the chilling reply from his brother.

Dainn squared up to him at nearly twice his size and bellowed. 'I said that's enough!'

Ronu then exploded. 'You are the depraved, foolish savages that the General likened us to earlier. Have you not learned anything during your time in captivity?' he raged in disgust at the vagrants before him.

Responding to the nefarious blood being pumped round his grey veins Targ threw himself across the room and landed within a finger's width of Ronu. 'I remember you. Pretending to be the great hunter when actually you favoured boys over girls. That's why I always had an excuse not to go trapping with you, just you snared me and kept me for yourself. Will we all be safe from you in here I wonder?'

Ronu launched at him, knocking him backwards into the large wooden table and grabbing his head started ramming it against the timbers. 'I'll rip your head off right here and now, by the name of the gods I will kill you.'

Clebe rushed in to pull him off.

'Leave him brother, he's not worth it. Vengeance will be yours another time.'

Ronu was led away with Clebe, his tense anger unable to settle.

Targ sat up feeling the back of his bloodied

head. 'Yes, you are all going to die anyway, so let's wait until we get into the arena where we can fight it out with swords, axes and other implements that will decapitate.'

'And I thought the General was the only barbarian here,' said Lyall with a withering look.

'Once a savage, always a savage, it's people like you that give the rest of us a bad name. It's little wonder that the General and the Emperor believe we are the scum of the earth, only deemed fit for fighting and throttling each other to the death,' seethed Dainn.

'I'm sorry Dainn,' said Ronu. 'I should have known better.'

'It's not you Ronu, it's them. Look at them, goading, threatening, playing right into the Emperor's hands, doing exactly what he wants by instilling hatred and fear amongst us. But I'm telling you two right now, while there's breath in my body and a will in my heart, I believe that we will all get out of here alive, and you two are not going to jeopardise that for any of us. Do you hear me?'

'You are not going to tell us what to do big man, no one tells us what to do.'

'You really are an unsavoury pair, no wonder you were banished by a clan leader,' Dainn seethed coldly.

'Yes we were banished, a heavy price to pay for something so insignificant.'

Lyall rolled his eyes hardly able to stop himself blurting out. Dainn held out an arm to stop any more attacks as Suma continued.

'We were walking for days. Foraging, doing a bit of hunting and fishing, trying to keep warm, stocking up for the winter; you know, survival and all that.' A sarcastic tone accompanied the satirical words. 'We managed to build a makeshift den, we had collected a lot of firewood to keep us warm, but that must have alerted the soldiers. Because after a few weeks we were approached by Scowler and Poxface, the two guards that you have already met.' The savages glanced at each other as they recalled the events. 'They offered us shelter, food, warmth, clothing, everything to keep us safe, so of course we went with them. Our supplies would have run out very quickly. You know how difficult the winter is; even with lots of men, women and children helping, we have to stock up for months before.' Suma slowed to a stop as the horrors flooded back.

'But we were really their prisoners with eighteen other boys,' continued Targ, still rubbing his head. 'Just like you are now, and we were made to fight to the death, just like you will have to.'

'We are the two survivors from last year's games,' said Suma. 'We took the powerful stimulants they offered to give us strength. If you survive two years combat then you win your freedom.'

'What stimulants are you talking about?' asked Dainn.

'Stimulants; moon mushrooms, white reed grass, that's what we were told by one of the guards. They

126

make you go crazy and stuff.'

'Yeah, crazy, like mad, with froth coming out of your mouth and blood seeping from your eyes and...'

'That's enough Targ,' butted in Dainn. 'I think we get the picture.'

'Yeah, that's all it is right now, a picture that you don't have to look at. But the reality is when that picture comes to life and you've got nowhere to hide.'

'And that is what we are going to do this year, take the stimulants again, go crazy and get our revenge.' Targ's hateful eyes flickered between Lyall, Namir, Ronu and Clebe.

'We will see about that,' muttered Clebe. 'The gods will decide, that's what is certain. For now though, we have to remain as civil as possible.'

'Ha,' retorted Targ. 'Just watch your backs that's all I can say.'

The boys looked at each other. They were all thinking the same thing; wouldn't it be simpler just to finish them off now? It would be so easy, there were eighteen boys much stronger than these two malnourished misfits. I mean where would they go to and what depths would they sink to if they got out of there? Roaming the mountains, living in caves, destroying everything and everyone in their paths. Collecting vagrants from the depths of humanity as they trailed their path breeding further hostility and hatred.

Suma sensed the unrest creeping amongst the clans and spoke out. 'Brother, stop, we must try and get along with our comrades.'

'What?' came the shocked reply, but a look from the older brother told Targ what could happen if they disobeyed orders.

'Yes, you are right Suma. We must all try to get along.'

But Lyall didn't trust them, he noticed the subtle nods and facial gestures that conveyed other meanings. 'Yes we must all get on, but watch your backs,' he muttered to himself.

And with the renewed declaration Suma delivered the next process. 'We will have to shave your heads now, it's all part of the arrangements. It shows that we are beneath them, even the guards are allowed to have some hair.'

With this declared truce, Dainn responded to them again. 'How come the two of you were allowed to survive the games?'

'Perhaps the General and the Emperor see something in us,' responded Targ. 'They like people with no morals. We've already been allowed to shave your hair.'

'Why don't you attack a guard with the shaving instrument if you've got no morals?' queried Lyall scathingly. 'Get yourselves out of here.'

'Because that would be stupid. We quite like it here, killing people.'

Suma threw a deathly glare to his out of control brother while Namir had to hold his sibling back.

'I won't be able to control myself much longer,'

snarled Lyall. 'I can finish them both off right now, look how scrawny they are, and that gobby one who can't keep his mouth shut already has a deep gash to the head thanks to Ronu.'

'Leave it brother, like Clebe says, this isn't the place right here and now with so many little ones. They are scared half to death as it is. We must set an example remember.'

While the other boys were getting their heads shaved with the bluntest cruellest blade imaginable they tried to come to terms with their plight. Lyall returned to peer out of the bars at the towering white building ahead of him, he was sure he could see the glint of a telescope from a high oval window. 'Evil barbarians,' he thought to himself.

The sun had set and the first star had appeared far off and bright in the southern sky; it was the only light source in this cold, brutal place. He stood there for a long time watching the illumination and his thoughts turned to Skyrah.

14

She had sat quietly in front of the General the whole journey, hardly daring to move. Initially she chastised herself for being so stupid and shrouded herself in misery. What would Namir think of her? What would they all think of her? She had ruined their triumph over the General and his army; no wonder girls weren't allowed to hunt or take part in the clan's games. She berated herself constantly and felt she had let them all down, while here she sat, with their arch enemy breathing down her neck and constantly nibbling at her ears. She couldn't stand it and tried to blank it out. That murderous self-important General, with a girly pony tail and pure white gloves.

'What purpose do they serve?' she thought to herself. 'Hide his blood stained hands.' She clarified her own question.

When they stopped for rest at night he had sat her so she couldn't see her friends. He could keep her under control that way. She had managed to sleep a little and had been given better food than the boys, but still she kept her eyes down and never once looked at him. As the days rolled by her initial thoughts of failure turned to something a little more positive. If she could somehow get the trust of the General and somehow find her way around wherever they were going, she just might be able to help the captives more than she had realised. She could turn this hopeless scenario around. So with that in mind she didn't jerk her neck away when he breathed down her neck and she didn't pull aside when he nibbled her ears. As revolting as it was, it was the start of her redemption and proving herself to the boys. She was the only one who could help them escape.

When the General had taken her into the palace she was met with a place she had never imagined. Even in her wildest dreams splendour like this didn't exist. The walls were made from precious polychrome marbles, with frescoed ceilings enriched with gold glass paste and lapis lazuli. There were water features that gleamed bright orange from the well-stocked carp. Fountains, whirlpools, deep wells made entirely from mosaics. One ornamental statue was so exquisitely carved it looked like a flock of white birds hovering in flight in a fountain with their wings beating fast against the rapids - but it was the work of an expert who had created the illusion.

Every wall and ceiling and pillar was inlaid with gold, ivory and mother of pearl. There were sunken gardens inside vast rooms, complete with exotic ornaments adorned with playful golden cherubs. Two more rooms full of art depicted magnificent epic scenes and the most celebrated artists of the day were commissioned to display their fine works for the

Emperor. She saw the enormous dining room that had a revolving domed ceiling that constantly moved day and night like the heavens. When the Emperor was entertaining, the ceiling would expose the effect of a rotating celestial sky complete with stars, moons and planets and he would release hundreds of rose petals and lashings of perfume to the unsuspecting guests below.

Treading lightly on the carved staircase and along the corridor to her room, she past vast guest rooms with magnificent marble bathrooms, painted ceilings and jewel encrusted chandeliers. The east wing looked out to a lake that was surrounded by ornate buildings, vineyards, pastures and woods. The west wing looked out to the stable block that housed the horses, wagons and cages.

'The Emperor has been very gracious and has said you can have this room,' he mused.

She looked ahead at the magnificent arched window, framed with pale blue curtains that matched the colour of the deep pile carpet. She scrunched her toes into the warm wool that peeped through and separated each appendage as she played with it.

'Exquisite isn't it? It overlooks the arena, so when the games begin you can watch your savage friends perform.' He then hissed into her neck. 'Remember you are my property now, and I am right down the hallway; so don't try anything foolish.' He stood behind her and ran his fingers through her hair.

She shuddered as he reached her shoulders

fearing what he would do next. He lightly skimmed the top of her spine with a finger nail and breathed heavily onto her skin. 'For a savage you are incredibly beautiful.' A pause held her rigid with fear. He stopped as abruptly as he had started and moved towards the door. 'Shame you are a clan girl.'

She still had her back to him and closed her eyes with relief as a sigh escaped from her lips and she could breathe once again. But her ordeal still wasn't over.

'I will send for you when I am ready.' With that he turned and left.

A clatter of locks and latches sounded and the door closed her in. She looked wildly about her huge, overly grand room. How was she going to orchestrate this, how on earth could she help her friends? The guards were everywhere, her captor was a stone's throw away and he had now locked her in.

To her left was a huge bed complete with a canopy on posts and blue and yellow damask silk covers. Opposite the bed was a dressing table and large ornate gilt edged mirror. A beautifully carved mahogany chair slid nicely under the vanity unit. Along the same wall stood a chaise longue covered in identical dusty blue and primrose yellow material. Beside the door was a wardrobe on one side and a chest of drawers on the other. She looked out of the window and faced a carefully laid out central garden full of shrubs and herbaceous borders. There were bird statues everywhere. Narrow paved paths winding around flowerbeds and miniature ornamental trees with dangling bird cages led down to another terrace. And beyond that was the arena and the dormitory.

'They must be in there now,' she thought. She tried to open the window to make herself known to her friends, but that too was locked and shut tight. She gasped, shocked. Her task was an impossible one. She fell on to the bed, buried her head in the pillows and sobbed.

She awoke much later with the tears dried to her face. First of all she didn't recognise the room. She nervously looked around in her sleep induced state. The ceiling was too high, the walls were too far away and the light wasn't from the sun. The smell was different and there was furniture in the room.

But from somewhere down below came the sounds of vibrant jaunty melodies and fiddles accompanied by the sweet lament of pipes. A coral of harmonies vibrated up the stairs and filtered into her room and she found herself smiling. She had never heard anything so beautiful. The engaging sounds encouraged her to sit upright on the bed where she found fresh clothes hanging on the wardrobe, and a plate of neatly cut sandwiches and a fresh glass of milk was placed atop the chest of drawers. A porcelain bowl of water sat waiting on the dressing table accessorised with a light blue flannel and a light blue towel. The flickering lamp by her bedside concealed the fact that the curtains were closed and it was now night time.

Suddenly she remembered where she was, but

worse than that, she remembered her captor. 'Had he been in?' she frantically thought to herself. 'Oh no, what had he done to her while she was asleep?' Instantly she discarded her old clothes and washed herself almost raw with the warm soapy water. She took ages wiping away his breath from her neck, scrubbing her hair where his fingers had touched, polishing her ear lobes where his tongue had licked. There was not one part of her body that was left unclean and only then did she put on the freshly laundered garments.

She looked at the food on the tray for a long time. The hunger pangs in her stomach started to grumble and saliva drooled around a starving mouth. She just couldn't be sure that he hadn't put something in the food to drug her, to render her unconscious. If she was his captive that meant that he was capable of anything.

Then there was a knock outside her room that instantly took her famished appetite away. She froze with terror. A key in the lock turned. The door edged open. A hand curled round the frame and a shadowy figure entered.

'Did you not like the food I gave you?'

And as Skyrah's eyes fell on the young girl, she found her appetite again and the answer to her plight.

15

The boys heard the music too, the huge double doors that led out to the terraces also filtered the delightful sounds into their prison. They had shared the stale remains of the courtesan's food, swallowing it down with mugs of freezing cold water from the well, then crowded round the barred windows to get closer to the carolling songs. While their ears gorged on the music, their eyes fell on the glows from the palace. The soft lamp light split a rainbow of colours across the terrace and the glass windows shone like jewels. As they looked closer they could also see the green and blue embroidery of peacocks strutting rhythmically with wide fanned tails while albino peahens looked like mythical white goddesses as they glided around the manicured lawns.

'The Emperor arranges that twice a week,' said Suma. 'He likes to surround himself with music, instruments and choristers.'

'To drown out the screams of boys in his nightmares,' suggested Dainn.

'Perhaps it is,' agreed Suma. 'It's happened every week since we arrived.'

'There is nothing more satisfying to the troubled

soul than music and dance,' lamented Bagwa.

'And the birds?' asked Hali.

'He seems to like birds as well,' answered Targ. 'They represent the freedom he yearns for I expect; cooped up in that palace all day, no wonder he has gone mad. A bit like us really.'

Those words hung heavily amongst the cold grey walls. Most of the captured boys secretly wished that Ronu had been left to finish the savage off, and that Lyall would have attacked the other one. And in thinking that, they were already horrified at what they were turning into.

'I suggest we get an early night, I am sure the guards will get us up at the crack of dawn for our first practice session,' Clebe said warily.

'We will share one bed,' said Suma looking at his brother.

'And we will share another,' said Namir nodding at Lyall.

'Yes, I'll watch your back and you watch mine eh brother,' warned Lyall.

Rufus fell on his bed sobbing; he was way too young to be here, wrenched from the loving heart of his family at such a young age. Dainn sat with him, trying to comfort him, trying to make him strong. 'Do you remember saying to me, 'never give up,' the day I lost the boxing match, and then you said: 'Dainn you have to come back and fight next year.'

Rufus nodded his head.

'And I came back the next year and I won it.

137

Because you made me strong and you made me win. You made me believe in myself - and that's what you've got to do now. You've got to be strong and never give up. Because if you do, you will never know what you are capable of.'

The youngster spoke between sobs. 'Will I die?'

'No Rufus, you will not die. I promise you that. I will get you safely back to your mother and your father and Ajeya and Hagen and Jena and you can tell them how strong and brave you were. Despite feeling so very frightened and thinking that you might die; but you rose above it and you never gave in to the monsters.'

Dainn lay on the bed and held him close, and wondered how on earth he was going to keep his promise.

*

'You don't know how pleased I am to see you,' she said to the young maid. 'My name is Skyrah.'

'Hello Skyrah, I am Roma and my instructions are to look after you. My master is the General, he is even more fearsome than the Emperor.' And then she whispered very quietly against a raised hand. 'We girls love it when he is away and dread it when he comes back.'

'Why, what does he do?' asked a stricken Skyrah.

'Oh nothing improper, he just has no patience with us girls and treats us like savages.' The maid blushed awkwardly at her reference.'

'I am not a savage, but I can understand why you think I am.' Skyrah remembered how Lyall thought they were a pack of wild animals at first.

'He thinks you are beneath him. But he won't hurt you, he just wants to dance with you.'

'What!' exclaimed Skyrah.

'That's all he wants you for. He might smell you and taste your feminine sweat, but he won't hurt you. His kingdom is so brutal as it is, he just likes to dance with a beautiful girl.'

'Why doesn't he dance with you? you are pretty.'

'Yes I am pretty, but not beautiful like you or the last girl that was here.'

'What girl?' her anxious words were cut short as the General burst in.

'Did I tell you to come in here and have a cosy little chat?' he boomed so ferociously everything around him seemed to rattle.

'No sir, I am sorry sir, it won't happen again sir.' The maid scurried out with her head held low.

'Come with me!'

A huge hand took hold of Skyrah's own and dragged her out of the room past a disgraced Roma and left a gust of disturbance in its wake. He pulled her downstairs into the ballroom from where the music was coming from. She stopped in her tracks as all manner of birds flew in and out of the open double doors to the tune of the harmonies. Pink flamingos, white doves, blue peacocks, turquoise kingfishers, yellow canaries, green parrots; there were so many exquisite varieties; she couldn't believe such beauty existed.

'Dance with me!' he barked; forcing her to look at him and away from the incredible menagerie.

'What?' she implored.

'Don't ask what, just do it!'

He pulled her close to him and began to move her around the floor in time to the music. He closed his eyes the whole time; he didn't look at her, just breathed deeply through his wide nostrils. This soldier, this tyrant, this destroyer of lives; liked to dance. It was all too surreal.

But it changed him. He was no longer the General with an army of soldiers at his command, now he was Domitrius Corbulo who loved music and waltzing. She could feel him relax. She felt his love for the dance and the movement flowing through his body. He was totally absorbed. She copied his stance and closed her eyes. She imagined she was free like the wind, her heart was pounding, her cheeks were flushed and yet she felt enormous power. She moved her feet lightly and rhythmically in time to the music, she began to hum the same tune sweetly to herself, keeping her movements fluid with the drumbeat and the strings. She arched her back and pointed her toes as she was twirled through the air by her partner. She felt like one of the birds she had just seen with all their beauty, grace and majesty. The General was surprised. He moved and she moved with him, she was a natural.

'You see, savages can dance as well,' he

whispered into her ear.

He could feel her beating heart against him and the vibrations from her vocal chords as she hummed quietly. That made him feel good. He smelled her hair and licked the sweat from her glowing brow. Nothing else existed but them and the music.

'What a strange man you are,' she thought to herself. 'Why don't you just find a nice wife and settle down instead of trawling the lands instilling fear at the very mention of your name. Surely even you must have a core of decency and are capable of changing.'

He was actually a very handsome man. His long ponytail somehow suited his tall muscular frame as it hung half way down his back. His dark eyes were enhanced by symmetrical almost manicured eyebrows and his features sat proud on a healthy dark skin. She studied the colours around him; he exuded mostly yellow which promoted self-absorption and arrogance, it also showed that he didn't suffer fools and that he didn't mind his solitary life. Around that was a red hue which was to be expected with his strong body and mind, the adventurer in him and the leadership in him, though he was quick to anger and would easily lose his temper. But most worryingly was the wide aura of black that surrounded all those colours and slowly filtered into the whole of his body like a poison; for that indicated hatred, death and a burning negativity towards anything good and pure. She shook herself free from analysing him, she was worried that he would feel her tension and fear so she focused on her steps and concentrated on the dance. Eventually the music began to slow, her thoughts and humming muted to a stop. He held her small white hand gracefully, and with a gaze that held her own, he bowed to her. She felt the need to curtsey before him and lowered her face as she did so. He didn't say any words. Without letting go of her hand he led her back up to her room. Only his eyes thanked her as she bid him good night. Even though it could have been so much worse, he could have demanded so much more, things that only lovers did and wedded couples engaged in. But now she was deeply troubled by the beautiful dancing partner who preceded her.

16

The next morning at day break, Scowler and Poxface unlocked the doors and ushered the boys out. They were filed unceremoniously into the chilled morning air wearing thin grey trousers and even thinner vest tops. Despite the cold, many of them were beginning to sweat with fear and a tense silence amplified the arena as they watched ten well insulated guards setting up an arrangement of weapons and targets around them. When they were done, an officious looking man with the regulation pony tail signalled to get back in line. His billowing black gown covered a white shirt and black britches, while behind his back his hand was flexing the rod of a stiff cane. Everyone shifted to his command.

'I am the Teacher and this is the Emperor's new arena, and you had better get used to the size and shape of it, because the more familiar you become, the better you will fight.'

The boys looked around them and set their eyes on the arrangement of weapons.

'You will begin to train in here and alternate with days of basic weapon training; throwing spears, swinging maces, thrusting swords. For the latter, we do not use sharpened blades for practice; we don't want to lose a boy before the Emperor has seen him fight, so we use a Palus.

'Here catch this.' He threw the weapon right at Lyall, his unprepared weak body buckled forward with the weight of the thing. It was amusing to the Teacher who threw back his head and laughed out loud. 'That, boy, is twice the weight of the sword used in the fighting arena. And that's why you have to train and be prepared. By practising with this heavier weight, you will become stronger, more developed and more agile in the fighting arena.'

Lyall closed his hands around the leather bound grips and swung it around in the air.

'Remember that a sword is an extension of its master,' continued the Teacher. 'And there is nothing like the element of surprise.' He left Lyall getting used to the weapon as he paced about ringing out his instructions.

'You will have to practise manoeuvres such as thrusting, cutting and slicing without injuring your opponent too much in the practice school. We also have a range of weapons such as these.' He pointed to the cross bows and sling shots. 'And you will use this.'

He took them over to a gruesome swinging rotating device. It resembled a monster with eight moving limbs. The novice had to use his skill and strength to avoid the rotating arms with angry blades as well as strike and aim at the heavy sandbags that came round.

'You will train in pairs; you will become elite fighting machines. And if you survive, you will come back again the next year, and if you survive that, you will be given your freedom.'

'I will be gone before that day,' thought Namir. 'Then I will return with an army of vengeful warriors and raze this place to the ground!'

The Teacher led them back to the centre of the arena. 'Every day you will train, in the summer you will fight; we will then see who is the strongest. The strong survive, the weak will die, it's as simple as that.' He looked at the line-up in front of him and threw another heavy wooden sword at Namir. 'Fight,' he demanded.

The only boys holding a weapon at that moment were Lyall and Namir.

'You two - fight. I want to see what you can do.'

'But we're not trained yet,' muttered Lyall indignantly.

The Teacher strode menacingly close to Lyall's face, spiting and frothing at the mouth as he bellowed.

'You do not answer me back, do you hear me savage?'

Namir felt Lyall shiver into stillness, his whole body tensing for a strike.

Lyall nodded meekly in response.

'Good! Now fight!'

The other boys hung their heads low in case they were chosen for something worse. A sickening gush went through everyone except the guards. The brothers faced each other.

'It's just a game Lyall, just a game, we have done this loads of times,' Namir tried to ease the deadly situation. 'It's what you feel and how you think remember.' He breathed deeply pressing the panic into an invisible ball at the pit of his stomach.

He swung his sword into the starting position, his focus encouraged Lyall to do the same. With a twist of both wrists he brought his weapon down on Lyall's defensive cut back swing. Namir retreated and bounced on the balls of his feet just like he did in the boxing ring against Tore. Lyall pressed forward and tried to knock his brother off balance. Namir managed to block again but the weight of the sword dragged him over. Lyall lunged forward forcing Namir to stop an overhead blow. They stood together, swords attached.

'Do your best Lyall, for your life depends on it,' he whispered through the locked hilts.

Both boys retreated. They had an audience now. Even Scowler and Poxface were showing interest. This should be a good match. But the Teacher had other ideas.

'Stop playing around. You're like kittens playing with a ball. You do it like this.'

The audience shuddered. No surely not. The Teacher threw down his cane, grabbed Namir's sword and launched in with an attack that split Lyall's cheek over the bone. He crumpled down onto all fours, stunned, dazed and totally confused. He looked up at the Teacher and shook his head like a dog, splattering blood all over his white shirt.

'Element of surprise, yes I must do better,' he seethed. He was fired up now. 'Fight me,' he snarled between bared teeth.

'Don't be a fool savage,' grimaced the Teacher.

'What are you afraid of?' He focused on the monster, his eyes narrowing and burning bright blue like the wolf inside him.

'Lyall please,' urged Namir.

'Let me do this brother, I couldn't fight you because I don't hate you.' He glared at the blood splattered Teacher. 'But - he is different.'

He dug his palus into the ground and hauled himself up, never once taking his eyes of his prey. The Teacher took his gown off and handed it to Poxface. The hairs on Lyall's neck stood upright as his back hunched and his spine curved, his toes curled into the sand and the fight was launched. The heavy sounds of wood on wood chilled the morning mist while sparks of Lyall's hate crucified the air. His left arm steadied him while he got used to the movements and found his balance.

He was still reeling from the forceful blow as they danced and shuffled, jabbing and swiping, attempting to unsettle each other with each missed shot. The Teacher was relying on the hunger and evil in his body as his main focus of attack. He managed to catch Lyall's supporting arm and the crack echoed round the arena. The blood from his face wound was spilling onto his thin vest. The Teacher smelt the blood and began to jump towards him. Lyall held out the wounded limb for balance. The Teacher caught him again on the balancing arm. Lyall groaned in pain; then he howled. Like a wolf he shook himself free from his human body.

'Give up now savage.'

'Never!'

The Teacher taunted him and jibed at him; he was deliberately disfiguring his facial expressions to scare him and mouthing obscenities to distract him. But he didn't know the monsters that Lyall had already encountered and the strength that he had got from those demons.

Remembering his parent's death, the terrifying ordeal in the cave, being brave in the face of what he thought were savages, and now here he was, surrounded by demonic devils disguised as guards and hierarchy. Laith was right, the only monsters that prowled the kingdoms were demons pretending to be human.

Channelling that hateful aggression, he focused his energy on this ogre in front of him. Lyall moved about lightly and got into his rhythm and roared. He stabbed at the Teacher's torso and caught his shirt.

'Very close savage, too close in fact,' the Teacher teased looking at the frayed material.

As the challenger looked down, Lyall swiped his face and blood oozed from the gash in his cheek. The Teacher stumbled back as surprise took over and reached up to the wound with his fingers. They parried as the wooden swords orchestrated together in a sinister musical rendition. Lyall advanced nimbly swiping the Teacher's other cheek and drew more blood.

'Good, good,' taunted the Teacher, wiping the blood from his other cheek.

That goaded Lyall even more and he rushed in screaming, bellowing and shouting. The Teacher retreated quickly. Lyall pushed him further back with each invading step. He jabbed forward and the blow brought bright red blood streaming from the Teacher's nose. The challenger staggered and tripped over his entwined feet and he crashed to the ground. He looked up smiling. This was the chance Lyall had been waiting for.

'Go on savage, do it, get angry, hate me, kill me!'

Lyall looked at the Teacher, his pumping heart full of rage, full of hate. He was panting with fury, he was bellowing his lungs out, his face was smeared with sweat and blood, his hands were shaking now. He held the sword above his head ready to strike the monster, searing determination and force into the final blow. Scowler and Poxface were poised ready, they had never seen anything like this before. Guts and grit from one so young was seldom seen. The Teacher held up his hand to hold them back. He tilted his head to catch his breath.

Lyall stopped in his tracks. He could so easily have smashed the monster's skull. But at what cost? The safety of the other boys would be in jeopardy. That would be stupid. He lowered the weapon and stepped back allowing the devil some room. He threw down the palus and retreated back in line with the other boys. Scowler and Poxface rushed in to help the Teacher stand up and he brushed himself down. He wiped the blood from his face and glared at the terrified boys.

'Now, that's real fighting. That's hate and aggression. That's what I'm talking about, that's spirit. Channel that fire into your battles and that will keep you alive in the arena.'

*

Roma came into Skyrah's room with her breakfast, she put the tray down on the chest of drawers and pulled open the curtains to let in the early autumn sun.

'Good morning Skyrah, did you sleep well?'

'Yes I did thank you,' Skyrah replied smoothing the sleep wrinkles from her garments as she sat up. She swung her legs out of the bed and slipped into the robe over her bedside chair.

'And how was the General?' continued Roma.

'Everything you said he would be.'

'That will happen three times a week.'

'And the rest of the time?'

'You stay in here.'

Skyrah nearly choked on her hard boiled egg. 'What! I do nothing, not even go for a walk outside?'

'I am sorry but no, the girl before you was allowed to go out for walks but she got away. A guard's family was burned to death in one of the cages as a punishment. We are all terrified now.'

'She got past the guards?' asked a shocked Skyrah.

'Yes, she completely out smart everyone. So with you, as her replacement, any form of freedom is forbidden.'

Skyrah had to be clever now, she couldn't let on that she was contemplating an escape - Roma would tell the General. Besides, Skyrah was going to take the boys with her. Too risky to get someone else involved. No, she couldn't let on; instead she had to act as if she was perfectly fine with the arrangement but use the time wisely to conduct her plan. She had a plan; a fool proof plan. It would take months to get Roma to trust her - but it would work.

'Well, if I am to stay here indefinitely, perhaps you could bring me some flowers each morning and I will ask the General if I can have some paper and colours so I can paint for him, I think he would like that.'

'I think he would be most agreeable Skyrah; that would please him immensely.'

Long cold dark days were spent cultivating and hatching, planning and orchestrating. Often she would look out of her window to find a face that she recognised, to give someone a sign, to give them hope. But the cold frosted glass of winter allowed no such passage of communication.

17

The new year came in an abundance of celebrations and the palace concubines were attended by courtiers all dressed in their fine silks and jewels, and fanned themselves between sets of games, dancing, gourmet food and music. Exhausted cooks prepared a range of braised meats, game pies, sweet pastries and fancy cakes, while harassed maids rushed between the kitchens and storerooms to keep the palace running smoothly. Young boys kept the log fires burning continually through the day and night, and worked tirelessly to ensure the waves of aromatic steam rising from the sunken pool, infused with cinnamon and ginger, were warmed from the pipes below.

Housemaids had decorated the indoor ornamental gardens and fountains with gold and silver coins, and the tiled mosaic floor and trestle tables were festooned with a range of winter grasses and exotic plants. The Emperor had instructed that the marble pillars were adorned with his own bunting and banners to herald the rewards of another successful year. And to top all the ostentatious extravagance, by chance, an impressive meteor shower lit up the sky that night and the General was typically pleased to explain to all the ladies what a meteor was.

'They are the sparks from the golden chariot of the gods being pulled by the fastest stallions in the whole of the empyrean above and it brings you tremendous luck if you catch a falling nugget.' He wove the story in such fastidious detail, dancing around them with delicious intricacies and delicacies that his captivated audience were spellbound and hanging on his every word.

Though apart from the brief meteor shower, outside was dull and boring grey; there was a thick layer of deadly dirty ice over everything. Lyall's face was healing now, the bruise fading into dull browns and yellows. The boys struggled to keep their accommodation warm with the few logs they had left. They had even thought about burning a few of the wooden beds to toast their chilled bones, but they didn't have the strength to break them up. Their well had frozen over and massive icicles hung like murderous crystal swords and wicked daggers from the rim. Forgotten by the attendants who were now consumed with the preparations at the palace, they had to smash into the well for water and make rations of stale bread go round equally. Without adequate food or logs, their shivering bodies found it difficult to stay awake and they went to bed early to dream of distant shores.

The next morning Scowler and Poxface came crashing in and forced the prisoners from their frozen slumber. It was still glacial outside and the boys awoke in the numbed shapes they had fallen asleep in.

Crooked necks shot daggers of pain through stiff contorted skeletons. Parched dry mouths, desperate for warm food and fluid, couldn't move at all. Cold limbs and muscles tried to penetrate life through iced veins by straightening out into a stretch.

'Get up now!' screeched Poxface and began to hit their feet with a biting rod.

Recoiling instantly, the frozen disorientated figures forced apart congealed eyelids and breathed out billowing wafts of condensation. Scowler began to beat a torturous baton in the palm of his hand; rhythmically, systematically, spoiling for a fight. They stumbled out of bed and kept their blankets tightly around them; their toes curled automatically and tried to avoid contact with the frigid stone floor.

'The Emperor wants some entertainment on this grey morning,' Scowler growled amid his thumping.

The boys tried to focus as their eyes squinted and their bodies swayed to keep warm.

'There is food and clothes in your dining area. Eat now, get changed and in one hour you will be the amusement for some of the guests. Don't keep us waiting. Be ready in your teams for a tug of war.'

The door was locked with a clang and a grating of keys while the thumping sound still reverberated in their ears.

'What the hell is going on now?' asked Lyall who was now blue with cold.

'I have no idea, but at least we get some food,' said Dainn.

Ignoring the warmer clothes, the boys fell on the feast; the left overs from the night before were far more inviting. Unbelievably, there was enough to feed a small army, so they decided to save a lot of it for the coming weeks.

'Better late than never,' said Clebe as he stuffed a whole venison pie into his famished mouth.

'Too right,' said Bagwa, swallowing thick spongey cakes.

'Don't mind doing a little tug of war for the old man if we get this first,' said Ronu.

The other boys laughed out loud, their food and spittle sprayed everywhere.

'I think I'm beginning to thaw,' said Siri. 'I can actually feel my fingers now.'

'My belly is swollen,' said Hass looking worse for wear. 'I literally can't move.'

'What a great feeling though,' and Hali belched into the air.

That started a cacophony of burping, all the boys wanting to outdo each other. At last they could laugh out loud. Smiling faces joked and messed about. Now they could celebrate the new year; albeit a little delayed.

With the added strength from the food, they broke up one of the beds and got a fire going. They were then able to heat up some water. Bagwa suggested taking some the meat from the pies to make a warm broth for the evening. The only good thing about the freezing weather was that food wouldn't deteriorate so quickly and there were no flies and wasps to bother them. It was cold enough in their dormitory to freeze anything but the boys wrapped the left-over food in the cloth it had come in and put it on top of the frozen ice in the well.

They could see an arrangement of chairs being set out for the Emperor's guests, so they climbed into their jerkins and breeches and the group split into four teams of five. Dainn decided to take the two smaller boys - Rufus and Zeno with Siri and Storm; that left his three comrades to team up with Suma and Targ. The Clan of the mountain lion then split into two further teams; Namir, Lyall, Ronu, Clebe and Wyn were in one; and Bagwa, Silva, Hali, Hass and Norg were in the other.

Outside they marched into the raw January day to entertain the Emperor and his guests. Their breaths created clouds of condensation and the swollen grey sky looked as if it was going to burst with snow. They would all compete together and the two finalists would then battle it out. The game wouldn't take long; the Emperor wouldn't want his guests out for hours, even though they were covered in layers of furs while skeletal maids stood shivering to death delivering mugs of hot soup for the dignitaries.

Each lad was given a role by the team leader and each one listened intently to their instructions; though so engrossed were they in their activity that they didn't notice Scowler preparing to remove a huge cover from the centre of the arena. It had a diameter of five foot and a depth of the same. But the grinding noise of the monstrous mouth being dragged from its resting place filtered through the air. Piercing abrasive sounds filled the arena where each boy in turn stopped and gawped at its origination. Determined faces, glowing and warmed from the good food and outdoor excursion now froze in terror as the blood drained quickly from their young complexions. What on earth was inside the pit?

'Snakes,' yelled out the Emperor in response to their shocked expressions. 'Huge venomous snakes.'

'Snakes kill, right?' whispered Lyall to Namir.

'Yes they do.'

'But they are dormant now,' hissed the Emperor. 'They are sleeping.' Then he carved a cruel smile. 'They were fed well in the last games.'

The audience of overly indulged men allowed their contemptuous arrogant smirks to emerge through swollen red cheeks and their excited commentaries hissed like their counter parts concealed in the stone cold tomb.

'In your summer games they will wake again, they will become active and they will be very hungry.' The Emperor smiled at his audience, relishing in his knowledge and the boys fear. 'They will bite and kill you, then they will feast on your pitiful bodies. But for now this is just a little game for you and a little entertainment for us.' He settled back into the folds of his ageing chin and signalled for the tug of war to begin.

The boys had lost their gaiety now. Was the Emperor telling the truth, were the snakes really dormant, doesn't everything need food in the winter months? It suddenly became a game of life and death and no one wanted to be pulled into the pit. The first team was put into position. The rope hovered menacingly over the unmoving hibernaculum. The boys didn't want to make too much noise for fear of waking them. The sweat of fear hung like frigid icicles on their sunken cheeks. Scowler whipped Rufus on the legs to get things moving. He screamed in pain and yanked at the rope in a reflex action. Suma and Targ's team responded and pulled back in response.

'Dig deep,' came a cry from Tay at the back. 'Use your legs, not your arms.'

Both teams pulled, both teams sat low on their haunches, thighs skimming the ground. The observing teams could only watch, they couldn't find the cheer or encouragement. They were as silent as the snakes in the pit.

'Pull boys, pull,' Tay continued.

Extreme tests of strength and endurance were now pitched. Some of the gorged boys felt sick with the exertion. They shouldn't have eaten so much, they should have been sensible, they should have waited. Cramp hit others. Indigestion set in and severe abdominal pain attacked both teams. Siri threw up his breakfast. Zeno skidded on it. Rufus lost his balance and clutched on to Dainn. The whole team lost their focus and fell into the pit. The snakes moved. They started to hiss. The younger boys screamed. Storm leapt out quickly, followed by Siri and pulled the others out by the arms. The snakes were warmer now.

'Next teams,' called Poxface, delirious with excitement. 'Quickly, we don't want them getting too cold.'

'Which snakes are you talking about?' sneered Lyall.

'Good luck men,' called out Namir.

There was nothing much they could do. Their stomachs were already full. They could see a few of the other boys on the perimeter vomiting; others were writhing in agony on the floor. The rest just stood clutching their sides.

'Dig deep,' cried out Lyall. 'Remember our strategy in the clan games.'

But it was useless; no amount of instruction and expertise could overpower the deteriorating performance of the body in these conditions.

'Don't you even think about giving up,' yelled out Namir.

The Emperor looked impressed, the dignitaries lightly applauded and cocked a grin. Namir's team pulled with all their might and resisted the poisonous pit. Their winning team helped the others out. The snakes began to move a bit more. No one had been bitten. But the pit was awake. They were less lethargic with the warmth from the sweaty bodies and vomit. It could be dangerous now.

Two maids suddenly appeared, crouched under

flimsy mop caps, carrying a tray of piping hot beverages and handed them to Scowler. Their thin tunics and soft slippers did little to protect them from the freezing cold, so they bowed quickly before scurrying back to the kitchens.

'The final will resume in a few minutes after the Emperor has taken a rest.' Poxface called out the farcical instructions as Scowler passed around the hot broth amongst the overly portly grotesque men. Jovial comments were exchanged as they expressed their dismay if the Emperor was telling the truth about the hibernating snakes. The Emperor had begun to look chilled under all his furs. He knocked back the last few drops of broth and signalled to Poxface.

'Savages, into position!' the throaty snarl was delivered through two missing teeth.

The teams dragged themselves up. Most were covered in sick, the rest were consumed with pain.

'This is for you mother and father,' seethed Lyall. 'I won't ever let an evil wretch get the better of me.'

The onlookers waited for a response from the Emperor.

'Savage language,' he mused. 'They don't know what they are saying most of the time... continue.' And he circled his hand to speed up the entertainment.

'Come on now men,' Lyall urged. 'Stay focused, stay strong.'

Namir was at the front with his feet firmly in the sand. His legs were in the squatting position. His arms were out straight.

'Follow Namir's stance,' he called out.

'Ready boys, take the strain, dig deep with those legs and push hard into the ground.'

The rope snatched tight. The other team were still strong despite having thrown up the entire contents of their stomachs. They began pulling and shouting. Froth and vomit burst from bellowing mouths. Sweat poured down agonised faces.

'Stay focused,' Lyall called out. 'Dig deep. Keep pushing into the ground.'

The tension of the rope edged towards Namir's team as the opponents grew weary. Their puke drenched hands were losing the grip. Still Lyall wouldn't give up. 'Come on Ronu, dig deep Clebe, don't let Wyn fall in the pit.'

The smug look on the Emperor gave him all the strength that he needed. His team responded to his roars with their own deep guttural growls. Goodness knows where they found the strength from but Lyall pulled as if he was pulling his mother to safety.

'Don't give up now, don't you dare give up, one more pull, come on, come on.'

With one last pull Suma and Targ's team toppled into the pit. The other two teams had to come and get them out. The two finalists were spent. No energy left. Only Durg and Malik got hit by the irritated end of a viper's tail. But that was all, no bites, and certainly no deaths. The cover was hauled back on and the snakes returned to their comatose state.

'Bravo! Bravo! I look forward to the summer games!' The Emperor's jubilation wobbled on his chins and he ushered his entourage away from the arena and back into the warmth of the palace.

Lyall watched him leave. 'One day I will get my revenge you evil wretch; and it will be oh so sweet.'

18

Roma came to see her at the same time each day. Duties in the palace ran on a tight schedule, and so Skyrah worked tirelessly during her hours of free time. Gradually she won the trust of the girl and would speak to her often about her family, her life in the palace and her hopes for the future. Skyrah had asked about the layout of the building.

'It's a new year gift for the Emperor,' she said. 'A thank you gift for treating me so well.'

'He will like that,' assured the maid.

Fortunately, with an abundance of time at her disposal, she was able to draw out a perfectly scaled drawing of the palace, while the young maid was particularly helpful as she rambled on about herself and obligingly conversed at length about everything and anything.

'It's nice to talk to you Skyrah, not many people have the time to.'

'Do you have any friends Roma?'

'The stable boys and grooms are very nice, they come from the village, so I know most of them, but the guards are not so pleasant.'

'Why, what do they do?'

'They think they are far too important so don't speak to any of us. I don't know where they come from either. They complained to the General that their breakfast was too late, so now we have to make it in the evening and have it ready at first light. It means our day is very long now.'

'More power, higher expectations.'

'Yes, you are right Skyrah.'

The clan girl conversed daily about the maid's life in the palace and built up a detailed picture in her mind. To everyone concerned she was just being friendly. Even if the General was listening outside, he would never have known that a plan was taking shape. Skyrah was being the dutiful dancing partner to him at dusk and a listening partner to Roma in the day, but all the while working on her exit strategy.

Three times a week she would spend the evening dancing with the General and she did her very best to please him, making sure she looked her finest and that she smelled divine. She didn't even flinch when he got too close or stroked her silky raven hair now. He supplied her with the most beautiful gowns to wear; rich silks and taffetas enhanced with layers of organza and lace, decorated with trimmings of exquisite precious stones. They were always off the shoulder or scooped low at the back so he could smell her tender young skin and feel the warmth of her touch.

The General had summoned her to dance with him at the new-year celebrations and provided a very sleek and flowing silk organza dress that felt cool on her body and brushed against the floor like a wind's whisper. The concubines had flirted and fluttered around the charismatic General, but he only had eyes for his regular dancing partner.

The bass of a drum beat began the sequence, then the string quartet strummed in with its delicate chords, followed by the fine reeds of the wind instruments. Skyrah showed great excitement at this accolade and thanked him continually as she span round on the tips of her ivory satin slippers enjoying the swirl of her silk dress as it flared and settled around her body.

At first she would follow his lead but now with so many sessions she could almost do another dance alongside him as he twirled her around. Now, as they both looked at each other, she didn't see the blood thirsty General and he didn't see a savage. Now, they didn't avert their eyes; instead, they held the gaze. The enchanting tune took them to another place, another dimension in time where they forgot about why they were together in the first place and let themselves move gracefully to the music. Like an eagle with its wings spread wide she felt like she could fly high in the sky and do anything she wanted. She responded freely to his touch and he was entranced by her.

But being locked in her room for the rest of the time brought her back down to earth and she remembered that she was his captive; a frightened little bird in a cage that he could discard at any moment.

19

Skyrah had waited patiently for the onset of spring. The cold winter months had gone on for too long. Everything had been crystallised with frost or snow, even the animals darted quickly in and out of their warm nests. But now she could smell the richness of the air around her as the gentle wind blew in the pulse of new growth. Wild herbs and trees full of blossom were stretching out their stems to the skies. Small shrubs exposed themselves revealing a patchwork of fragile posies and fauna. Flowers appeared heralding the onset of milder temperatures and an abundance of brightly coloured blooms offered themselves to the insects for a reward of nectar and pollen. It was a beautiful sight and a perfect setting, because now, her desired plants were surfacing.

The General had allowed Skyrah to paint as requested and Roma was permitted to bring in fresh winter blooms; snow drops, crocuses, holly, ivy, ferns. She spent the days painting and getting Roma familiar with the range of flowers she particularly desired. Once a week she would present the General with a small painting of one of the flowers as a thank you gift for his kindness and one was given to Roma once a month.

She also spent her time sewing. She used the lining of the curtains, the lining of her dresses, the under sheet on her bed. She carefully picked away at the threads to re-use, and then painstakingly made needles from the stiff brushes she was given for her painting and began to make clothes for the boys. She had moved the chest of drawers and pulled back the carpet. This exposed the wooden floorboards and made an excellent hiding place. She had managed to free a few panels with the provided cutlery and stuffed the garments inside. They would have to blend in with the villagers. For if they escaped as they were, they would be recognised straight away. The hairless stable boys and grooms all wore baggy white shirts and brown coloured britches; she watched them daily, and took detailed notes of the size and style. She dyed the britches with the colours from the red poppies and purple aconitum flowers that she was given, and the shirts were loose that slipped over the head.

Eventually she requested laburnum and azalea blooms; she used a lot of them and soaked the petals in a bowl of water she had stowed away. They would take a long time to ferment; the petals of the laburnum tree were especially temperamental. She had fresh flowers everywhere in her room so the pungent smell didn't raise suspicion from Roma or the General. She just had to wait until the petals were ready. Impatience would mean failure.

In the dormitories the boys were down to ten beds and all of them were sharing now, top to toe and dreaded the setting sun; for it meant another unsettled night of disturbing dreams and another day closer to the games and certain death.

Every evening Lyall looked out of the window up to the palace. 'What are you doing up there Skyrah? Hurry, please hurry and save us, we don't have much time left.'

And every evening Namir looked to the hare in the moon to give Skyrah the strength she needed.

The boys had trained hard for months now. But rather than be well developed with muscled physiques, they were actually skeletal with malnourished bodies. Inadequate food had carved out that failing. Hope had gone as well. Many had thought they would have escaped by now; been lucky enough to outwit a guard and make a brave get away, or run off to the hills when no one was looking; but they weren't strong enough, and besides, the guards were too well trained or too scared themselves to let anything like that happen. Most of the captives surmized that Skyrah had been disposed of and ruled out any chance of escape with her aid. So for many, it really was hopeless. In reality, the only way out was to survive the games.

20

June arrived and deep cushioned chairs were placed on the terraces leading up to the arena. Yards of gauze was secured to a twelve foot square rail that served to separate the stage from the viewing gallery. Futile in its construction, it was a pathetic attempt to obscure the reality. The deception of disguise was abhorrently obvious.

Huge displays of bountiful flowers had been arranged in rows alongside the seating arrangement. The fountains on the lawns were set to gushing heights and exuded a range of vibrant colours. Musicians and singers began to practise in the arena; their conductor, fastidious for the perfect pitch, brought tears to the eyes of those in attendance. The cooks and chefs were busy creating mountains of mouth-watering temptations for the many guests that would attend that afternoon, and all the while, in the dormitory, all but two prisoners were at breaking point.

'I told you that you wouldn't escape,' said Targ gloating. 'It's too late now, the games will start tomorrow and you will all start to die.'

'Shut up Targ, nothing but vile excrement comes out of your mouth,' Ronu vented.

Targ only smirked this time. 'Vengeance will be mine and you will be the one excreting vile excrement.'

Ronu walked away. Targ continued to smirk. The others were at a loss.

'The only thing any of us can do is to seek strength from our totems and our loved ones,' said Dainn looking over at Rufus.

'He's right,' said Siri.

'I still live in hope,' said a subdued Lyall. 'I just cannot see myself killing anyone here.' He looked over at the two misfits and whispered behind his breath. 'Not even those two.'

'The stimulants do that for you,' snarled Suma. 'You will be amazed what you are capable of.'

'Shut up!' cried out the captives in unison.

Suma and Targ crept off like a couple of conniving hyenas and kept themselves out of the way for the duration.

The rest of the boys spent an agonising night together; it was difficult to speak, there was no comradeship, no fellowship. They didn't know what to say to each other. How could you offer words of support to the boy who might be trying to kill you the next day? Those who managed to close their eyes wore the hideous face of fear in their sleep. Those who couldn't drift off easily lay wide awake, their haunted eyes focused on the ceiling above but seeing nothing. The thought of the unknown consumed them and plagued their ravaged dreams. Each one prayed to their own god, their totem, their spirit guide. These were boys who had given up hope and were waiting like terrified animals in a slaughterhouse. Lyall kept his vigil by the window; his eyes drawn to the glowing light which never went out and Namir prayed to the hare in the moon.

The next morning Namir stood by a basin, trailing his hand through the water. The movement was soothing. He didn't know how long he had been up. It felt like minutes but it was probably longer. As he cupped his hands and bent forward to splash his face, there was a hard click from the solid inner workings of the lock followed by a harsh grating sound from the hinges. The door was thrown open and the light suddenly changed in the room as the dreaded voice of Poxface snarled. 'Today is day one of the games and General Domitrius Corbulo has made a request.'

'Oh no,' they synchronized together. 'What has this monster prepared for us now?'

'He wants the boy called Namir and the boy called Lyall to start the games.'

Namir turned, feeling the water trickling away between his fingers.

'What?' called out Lyall.

He dodged the sharp edged fist that was thrown his way.

'I'm going to die today anyway, what's the point in attacking me?'

'Hmm,' Poxface sneered. 'Come with me!'

Namir and Lyall walked out of the dormitory for the last time and left the other boys bewildered in their thoughts. They were obviously glad that they would live another day, but absolutely crushed for their good friends who had been so optimistic for all these months. The other boys from their clan couldn't look. Dainn put a comforting arm around Rufus. The remainder slumped down where they stood.

It was only Targ and Suma who looked jubilant.

Lyall remembered the last time he was part of a royal pageant. He pictured a boulevard of lemon groves filled with lines of drummers and trumpeters playing the king's own Royal Anthem. The ranks were dressed in their blue and gold colours; stern, sombre and totally focused on the auspicious occasion. There were rows upon rows of soldiers carrying their own weapons with ceremonial gilt edge swords fixed rigidly at their sides. The King's Guards on horseback would carry flags and banners waving proudly in the breeze; a figure head, a monument of honour. Ahead of the royal party would come the king's own personal guard on a magnificent black stallion carrying The Royal Standard that displayed the imposing Durundal Coat of Arms. The majestic throng followed the Royal Standard and finally lantern carriers brought up the rear. The crowd would bow and curtsey and throw flowers to their beautiful queen, dressed in her most regal gown and wearing the Royal Diadem of pearls, diamonds, rubies and emeralds. The king wore the ceremonial robes of office and gold crown that had been in the family for generations and Lyall would wear his uniform and a small bronze coronet. They paraded along to the joyous shouts of 'long live the king' which echoed through the kingdoms for miles and trailed in the wind for hours. What an experience for a young boy, Lyall thought to himself. And now here he was, heir to that crown, fighting for his life and entertaining the man who ordered his parents death and ended that life for so many. He looked to the skies for his father's blessing and touched the totem for his guide's help.

Namir and Lyall had to be marched past the Emperor's celebrations before any of the guests arrived. Then they were led round to the back of the arena where a jug of liquid waited for them.

'You would be wise to drink this,' they were told. 'It will give you added strength.'

The boys looked at the jug, then at each other. They both saw exhaustion and fear.

'I don't need this,' said Lyall.

'Neither do I,' agreed Namir.

'As you wish,' and Poxface took his sentry position a few feet away from them.

The boys sat. They had waited in their barracks tormented and anguished for so many months now, a few hours on their own was ironically the only comforting respite in this continual nightmare.

'Make it quick Namir, just do it quickly.'

'What are you talking about brother?'

'Just kill me quickly, that's all I ask.'

Namir was thinking, he was always thinking, waiting for an answer, a sign, anything that would end the horror.

Lyall hugged him, he wiped away a tear, he didn't want his life to end like this. This life had only just begun. His new family, his home. He felt his wolf tattoo and smoothed the scar on his neck, somehow that gave him strength. Namir looked straight ahead.

After a few hours they were led away to be dressed. They could hear the assembly taking their seats, they could hear the General and the Emperor, they knew those voices. The boys shuddered, fearful now, clutching each other like frightened infants going into the unknown.

Lyall tried to find his inner voice to comfort him and give him strength, but even that had abandoned him. The few patchy strands of new hair were shaved off again with the cruel edge of a knife; the guard didn't care about the blood that flowed with each cut. Their tunics were replaced with a yarn that went round them like a loin cloth and green slime was rubbed into their bodies. It smelled revolting and made them retch. Their necks disappeared into their hunched frames as the whites of their eyes glared out through camouflaged faces.

'You look like a savage now,' said Lyall dismally.

'I think that's the desired effect,' replied Namir looking at his unrecognisable twin.

'Good luck dear brother, I am so glad I found you, albeit for a short while.'

'Good luck to you too Lyall, you are a

courageous sibling and it's my one regret that I didn't know you for longer.'

They stood in the centre of the arena, focused, poised, their hearts beating frantically in unison. The sweet music stopped playing and the shrill excited voices stopped chattering. The sound of drums and trumpets announced the start of the games. The gauze was pulled to either side of the packed arena and the two brothers faced their audience.

Finely dressed women adorned themselves in the finest weaves and threads which billowed to the floor. They coiffured candy floss creations on their heads and arranged elegant jewellery upon their whitened skin. They looked straight ahead at what stood before them. Wide eyes peered through colourful faces. Spectacles on long sticks enhanced the vision before them and shocked hands flew up to wide open mouths. The men wore oversized coloured shirts with embroidered waistcoats and long ponytails hung down their backs. Tight fitting crimson britches covered white stocking calves and shiny black shoes completed the ensemble. The boys would have looked like naked reptiles to the overly attired spectators.

A gasp went up from the crowd. Some of the women screamed. The General smirked. The Teacher nodded to the General. Namir put a hand out to stop Lyall. The Emperor stood up.

'Welcome, welcome, my honoured guests and people of the realm. It's that time of year where we celebrate our good fortune by being entertained by those who are not so fortunate as us.'

A staccato of fake titters followed his introduction.

'These boys have been training for months so that you will be entertained, and today you will be delighted with what the General has in store for you.'

Swivelling faces looked joyous at the mention of the General's involvement.

'So without further ado, let us witness together the General's auspicious surprise.'

The brothers looked shocked, what on earth did he mean?

'Boys select your weapons. Guests stay well back for your own safety,' came the order from the guard.

Heavy gates at the side of them nervously edged open. The boys hadn't been prepared for this. The misfits Suma and Targ hadn't mentioned this before. The brothers looked at each other and recoiled as a shadow emerged.

'What in the name of the gods is this?' yelled out Lyall.

'Just stay calm brother, do not panic, do not show your fear.'

The monstrous gates were fully dilated now and revealed a creature from their depths; a creation that had been concealed from them and the awaiting crowd. The sun's shadow quickly drained away like a scared feline slithering out of view.

Namir tried to settle Lyall's terror. 'Do not fear

brother, we will conquer this challenger.'

'But it's the Baal Namir.'

'What's the Baal?' Namir said, feeling a bead of sweat escaping down his temple.

The boys quickly selected their weapons and backed away slowly, not taking their eyes off the monster.

'It's the devils servant, I have seen pictures of it, I didn't think it really existed, I thought it was folklore. Namir, we are going to die!'

The sight of the demon dragging itself from beyond the heavy gates made the crowd gasp. Even they hadn't seen anything like this before. The pictures on the street walls were nothing compared to what was emerging from the depths. The General managed a misshapen grimace and the Emperor and honorary guests started to fidget nervously in their seats. At that moment the boys felt the assembly suddenly on their side. They felt their compassion and support, all those pompous eyes, fuelled with disgust and prejudice, gradually changed to pity. The fear of the boys saturated the warm summer air and the crowd gasped as Lyall took aim with a feeble bow and arrow.

'We are not going to die Lyall, there are two of us. It is folklore, it is only your fear that will cast doubt. We will conquer this.' Namir's strength was admirable.

Lyall glanced at his brother. Was he was actually going to try and fight this thing? Wasn't he going to run away like the others and be hunted by the soldiers and the guards and make another game out of this theatre?

The sweat from his palms made it difficult for him to grasp the weapon. A taste of vomit came from deep within his core and lingered like an unsavoury dish in his dry mouth as even more adrenaline was pumped around his stricken body. He fixed on the Baal which resembled half beast and half human and was of a monstrous size, goodness knows where they found it, and who on earth could have even captured a devil such as this? It must be old, he thought, it must be injured. There was no other explanation. But then his thoughts quickly evaporated as the beast hurled itself forward towards his brother.

Namir shook the sweat of terror from his brow and quickly sprang into defence stance as he held up his two swords, one above his head and one protectively across his chest. 'Remember brother; engage with care for accuracy is more vital than power.'

The Baal lurched, strings of mucus spewed out of its nostrils like entrails, sweat ran down its disfigured face, its claws gripped onto a grotesque spiked ball of iron as it wielded it around its head with Namir's skull in its sight. Lyall fired the first arrow which unbalanced the creature and Namir dodged the launched weapon. He ran in to the mutant, slicing its leg while it was still unbalanced from the motion of oscillating. The savage tried to impale Namir with its axe but Lyall catapulted a rock from his sling shot which smashed into its skull. Lyall ran to the other side of the arena and picked up another boulder. Sounds of horror and anguish from the crowd echoed around the dome. The guests recoiled and looked to the boys to save them from this creature.

Again the fiend advanced with the spiked monstrosity shredding Namir on the arm. A brief paralyses prevailed as he instinctively gripped the limb in pain. Red fluid oozed between his fingers, congealing with the oil and sweat that his body was excreting. The ogre salivated with desire at the sight of blood and lumbered round the arena shrieking and howling like a possessed being. Lyall aimed with the bow again and sank an arrow into the beast's eye; warm liquid spurted from the wound, the crowd winced and could only look between fanned fingers.

This gave Namir another chance and he ignored the pain in his arm. He wiped his saturated hands on his legs and refocused. He dug his sword into the ground and pulled himself upright. His eyes fixed on the target and his grip tightened on the weapons. He lowered his head as he took several deep breaths while the beast displayed its misshapen form in front of the shocked audience. With a surge of acceleration he charged towards the parading monster. He launched in with a double blow from the swords, slicing it across the abdomen with one stroke and as he jumped over his assailants arm, swung round to plunge the other sword into its exposed back. The creature shrieked in pain and sent Namir's sword flying into the air as it doubled over. Two arrows fired from Lyall protruded from the creature's back haunches and it was left immobile. The crowd shuddered. Namir took his opportunity and punctured the creature with full force again in the back. An axe was thrown at the human skull and missed by a hair. The beast had only one weapon now and began to circle it high above its head gaining force and momentum, and with a last exultation of energy, threw it to crush Lyall's crown, but Namir propelled his sword into the air and knocked the ball off course.

The crowd were standing on their feet now, urging the boys to victory, swiping the air with clenched fists. Namir was fired up and withdrew two daggers from his boots; he threw one to Lyall who ran round to the back of the creature. Namir rushed towards the staggering body and with precision, threw his dagger at the mutant's heart. Lyall took a long run up from behind, executed a tremendous burst of power and leapt on the fiends back and with one swift movement slit its throat. With a flash it was over, the jugular was severed with one blade and the nucleus ruptured with the other. The Baal fell with a tremendous thud and the place erupted with thundering cheers and a rapturous applause of satisfaction and admiration. Namir strode around the corpse like a leopard with its prey eventually standing proudly with one foot on its rump to receive his adulation. Lyall paraded round the arena howling like a wolf before he ran up to Namir and lifted him by the waist to another accolade.

'What a team,' Namir said triumphantly, championing a fist into the air.

'We killed the Baal, we killed a devil,' shrieked Lyall, and looked to face the General. 'That's what we will do to you one day you monster, enjoy the time you have left, for your days are numbered.'

The General didn't hear the words but saw the venom in Lyall's eyes and turned to leave with the Emperor. The audience were still on their feet as the curtains bowed them out. The two boys dropped their heads respectively low in response to the support.

'That wasn't supposed to happen Corbulo,' raged the Emperor.

'I know sire, I am as baffled as you are.'

'Make sure tomorrow's event goes more to plan.'

'Yes Gnaeus, it has already been arranged.'

'Good, now, let's make it look like we are as pleased with the result as our audience is.'

'Yes, we will have to.'

The two statesmen slid around sharing pleasantries with the guests, and the two brothers strode back to their rooms.

'What! How on earth are you both alive?' rejoiced Ronu.

'I think the General's plan backfired,' answered Lyall stoically.

'Tell us how you did it,' urged Clebe.

'You imagine the devil in front of you, all your fears and nightmares in one form and then you find courage from within,' answered Namir. 'You reach inside yourself, to your totem, to your instincts and focus hard. But most importantly you have to believe.'

'When you feel that you have all the strength of your totem to suck the energy from your enemy, its pumping blood and its breathing heart, then you can finally take the life from it,' continued Lyall focusing his venom on Targ and Suma. 'And it helps if you have an amazing brother; the one who has your back.'

Namir smiled at the tribute and embraced his twin.

The captured boys rejoiced at the unity and found strength in their solidarity. This gave them a platform, this raised their spirits. For Namir and Lyall they could now relax a little. For the others, the General's depravation had reached another level.

21

The long hours of wakefulness gritted their eyes after another sleepless night of worry, and the heat of the day was already seeping through the rafters and pressing on their skin like a heavy wet blanket. The clatter of keys announced the arrival of the guards, who were met with a row of tortured souls awaiting their instructions.

'Targ and Suma, Clebe and Ronu, come with us.'

Shaking legs wracked with despair tried to support the frames of Clebe and Ronu; whilst Targ and Suma stood up tall and eager for battle.

'I told you we would kill you all,' snarled Targ.

That's all that was needed to fire up Ronu and he found his strength again. 'I have waited a long time for this you pathetic wretch, you have made this all too easy for me.'

'Come brother,' said Clebe. 'This day, revenge is ours.'

Outside in the open air, the two excitable vagrants laughed and ran ahead. Ronu and Clebe remained stoic with a dignified walk. Inside the dormitory Namir retreated to his bed; he lay back with his hands behind his head, staring up at the ceiling, trying to find an answer from somewhere in the vaults above him. Lyall filled a bucket from the well and washed himself. The bruises from the previous day had now emerged and the freezing water was soothing them. He didn't remember being struck by the creature but in the frantic chaos he must have been. He ducked his head fully in the bucket to drown out the sounds going on around him and then returned to his look out post behind the barred window.

'You two stay here, you two come with me,' churned the orders from the guards.

Ronu and Clebe remained at the back of the arena, while Suma and Targ were led round to the stable block. Now separated, Ronu and Clebe took their seats behind the gauze curtain and waited for the unknown. They spoke quietly, they talked of a distant time, they shared their hopes and dreams, and then they turned to the present.

'We have prayed for this moment brother; Suma and Targ brought disgrace to our clan and now the gods will decide their fate. We have been chosen to seek retribution, so we have to put faith in our totems and only then will vengeance be ours,' Ronu's words were solemn.

Clebe nodded his head in agreement. 'You are right; our totems will guide us, but we have to keep our guard up, we have to stay focused and strong, and then we just might walk out of here alive.'

It seemed like time had abandoned them until their

ordeal was worsened with the identity ritual. Their masks were adorned and the stimulant was offered. The astonishment on their devilled faces was only superseded by the arrival of a beast pulled by two black destriers.

'What is this?'

'I don't know, hopefully someone will tell us.'

'Guaranteed it will be something gruesome though.'

'Silence you two!' bellowed the guard. 'If you want to survive then pay attention.'

The young men looked straight ahead, suddenly filled with fear again.

'Choose your weapons wisely and decide who is going to steer and who is going to fight. This is a race to the death.'

Another guard brought an assortment of armaments and dropped them at their feet while a wry smile creased the corner of his mouth.

'Do you want to steer the chariot, while I use these?' Clebe asked as he lifted a crossbow and a catapult. 'I can cause a nasty injury with these.'

'That's fine with me but I will still take one of these.' Ronu took the largest sword and held it up high. The sun caught the edge of the blade and sent spectrums across the cavernous pit. 'I might just need this.'

The horses were checked over before making their way to the start line, and hearing an excited crowd taking their seats, the animals began to nicker.

Eventually the ghostly gauze was pulled back to reveal the identities of the overly dressed dignitaries and they in turn looked horrified at their scantily camouflaged entertainers. Once again the General smirked and the Emperor grinned with sickening pleasure at his menagerie of horrors. There was no sign of the competitors and the crowd was getting very impatient with low rumbles of discontent beginning to vibrate around the arena. The animals were restless and tried to free themselves from their constrictive breast-straps.

'This is a deliberate tactic,' said Ronu with flared eyes. 'I might have known they would do something like this.'

'We shouldn't have expected anything else,' and Clebe jumped down from the platform to settle the horses. He stroked their velvet muzzles and smoothed their muscular necks while whispering to them gently. The anxious clock was ticking in their heads as the minutes dragged by. Shadows appeared and silently slid away with the moving clouds overhead and a gentle breeze caused temperamental sandstorms around them.

Suddenly all hell broke loose as the challengers flew in; wailing and howling, screaming and cracking their whips. They chased a lap round the pit to announce their arrival, whipping their mounts and the crowd to frenzy. Their piebald pacers eventually reared to a screeching halt, scattering debris and grooving furrows in the sand as they drew up next to their competitors. Two angry figures stood in a fired up red chariot, wearing the same masks and strange demonic patterns but brandished a spiked ball and spears. The crowd settled into the comfort of their plump seats, expectant of a good race. To everyone around the arena, the identity of the challengers was hidden, but all four looked strong and determined and stared at each other menacingly.

'To the death!' the command raged and the flag went down.

Targ and Suma were first off the block as their horses were edgy and pumped up. The black coursers had to hear the crack of the whip to get started. The first spear was thrown at the black charioteer after a few laps, but Ronu managed to swerve out the way as the whispering blade missed him by a breath. The contenders would retrieve it on the way round he thought. Clebe positioned his first arrow and sent it straight back to them; it got stuck in their wheel and unbalanced it but Suma steadied himself and managed to clear it by hanging precariously over the edge of his red chariot. The crowd went wild at this death defying stunt. He dragged himself back and proceeded to load something at the rear of the carrier. The sand, dust and dirt blown up by the charging vehicles obscured the observers view. Then he stood up and started to rotate a lever which spewed out a deadly cargo of rocks, stones, boulders and other hard edged implements, deliberately aimed at the black carriage power source. Ronu had to pull back hard.

'This is despicable and shouldn't be allowed!' a memory of innocence emerged as Ronu blurted out concern for the horses. 'If one of those rocks caught a shin, it would be a disaster.'

'When is anything fair in this forsaken place?' Clebe shouted back, his eyes ignited and furious with hostility. 'Come on, let's show 'em what we're made of.'

But it was too late, a jagged implement struck the black courser hard and it reared up screaming.

'Release the breast strap,' cried out Clebe. 'We shall have to ride with a single horse.'

The injured courser was severed from its harness and tried hard to keep up, but eventually limped its way to the outside of the ring in defeat. The black car surged on over the uneven terrain as the red chariot sped away from them. Suma threw another spear - and missed again. Ronu manoeuvred the single horse powered black chariot round the course as best as he could and drew level as Clebe sent a second arrow that lodged in the other wheel; this one stayed put.

The horses were hurtling round now at top speed covering several laps of the arena and both carriages were thrown about as they hit every part of debris on the track. Clebe aimed his catapult high, it seemed the only way to hit his target from the speeding wooden vehicle, his strong arm pulled the sling back as far as it would go and when it was released a heavy rock was sent soaring through the air and found its target with a thud. The crowd gasped as it knocked Suma out of the chariot, but he was not finished yet and he managed to stumble out of the way and retrieve the misaimed spears and rocks to hurl back at them.

The chariots sped round spraying out particles of sweat, froth, dirt and sand through the air to the applause of the onlookers. The two charioteers both remained focused and determined as they sped round the track littered with fragments of debris.

Targ then started to swing a spiked ball above his head to gain momentum, then he turned for a moment, focused on the unsuspecting rival and let go of the chain. Smack! It sank into Ronu's left shoulder; he crumbled with the pain and gripped his wound. Targ started to celebrate, especially as his nemesis had been demobilised and he watched him slump down awkwardly. Clebe jumped forward to take the reins of the black chariot, just one driver and one horse were in control now.

More laps raced by as Targ's carriage was much lighter now and sped away quickly. The black chariot was behind when Clebe's sword was hurled through the air; it split the back axle in two and the red chariot was thrown in the air as it hit a loose boulder. Targ was flung out of the disintegrating vehicle and as he scrambled for freedom, the galloping black horse and carriage thundered over his neck, killing him instantly.

Suma was waiting on the perimeter and surged towards the black carriage with venom and hatred, wielding a retrieved spear and aiming it at the back of Clebe's head. Ronu could see from his position though and reached for the metal ball at his side and with a mighty force from his right arm sent it back to crush the attacker full on in the pterion bone. Suma sank to the ground, he tried to steal another throw but death was already on his heels.

It was over now and the place erupted with elation. The collapsed red chariot was cleared away; Suma and Targ were thrown over their beaten horses and led unceremoniously out of the arena. The two victorious lads responded to the cheers of an entertained throng and relished in their jubilation. As the applause died down, the closing curtains heralded the end of the battle and the triumphant winners were led back to their rooms.

'I really thought we were a gonna a few times there,' Clebe reported back to the waiting pack.

'They must have taken the stimulant, they were really fired up and brutal,' said Ronu.

'They were so sure they were going to win,' vented Clebe.

'It was all bravado though, hot heads and all that,' continued Ronu.

'You have to believe, you have to stay strong, it's the only way to survive this,' said Namir.

Dainn put an arm round Rufus. 'We all have to believe. Remember that won't you.'

Rufus nodded.

'I told you we would get our revenge,' lamented Clebe.

'Yes you did dear friend, you did say that.' Ronu sighed heavily and put his hand on Clebe's shoulder.

'Their souls had died long ago,' said Lyall. 'You just put them out of their misery.'

Amid the tortured souls, a feeling of redemption and solidarity spiralled round the cold grey walls. 'Hear! Hear! To Ronu and Clebe!' came the raucous tones of brotherhood. And as a triumphant Ronu and Clebe were elevated onto the shoulders of their peers and hugged and embraced by every single one of the boys; somewhere in another locked prison, a heroine was at work.

22

Upstairs in her room Skyrah was nearly ready. She had witnessed the two events and was now fully aware of the sickening plight the boys were in. She had no idea who had been fighting, she couldn't make out their identity, all she saw was the dreadful battles they faced. She prayed that her friends were all right, and as awful as it was to wish death on another innocent boy, she hoped it was they and not her friends who had been slain. She slowly ran her fingers along the line of her totem and silently requested that the great hare in the moon would serve her at this time and honour her in this time of need. With the homage paid she returned to her task. She was confident with the scheme; all the shirts and trousers were made and carefully stowed away. The laburnum pods were fermented and could now do their worst. She had collected a number of glasses and goblets over the preceding months and they would distribute the deadly potion to the intended recipients. She was ready as she ever would be and returned to scanning the map she had painstakingly drawn with Roma, just to be absolutely sure of her route.

That evening Domitrius Corbulo summoned

Skyrah for their third dancing session of the week. She decided to wear her finest indigo gown and wound her hair up into a fashionable chignon complete with a spray of purple aconitum. She sprayed a minimal amount of scent over her skin and then carefully placed the bouquets of white snakeroot and hemlock into her small bag and waited for the General to knock on the door.

He was in an affable mood that night and complimented her all the time. Her dancing pleased him, they partook in conversation now and she always smelt divine.

'You are looking particularly pleased this evening master, are the games going well?'

'As well as to be expected, the Emperor is very happy and that is my main concern, keeping my master content.'

'As is mine my lord, as is mine.'

He smelt her neck. 'Do you not worry about your friends now?'

Her skin prickled with goose bumps as he mentioned the clan and moved closer to her at the same time. She had trained herself not to think of her friends while she was acting, she might expose herself. She smiled at him, a blissful smile. 'Not anymore,' she lied.

He beamed at his beautiful conquest as he took her hand and led her to the centre of the ballroom. She twirled a few times at the request of his fingers until his other hand curved in to her waist and pulled her to a natural pause. He smelled her rich hair with several deep breaths and then the music started. She started to hum in tune to the chords as her feet swept around the floor; spinning, turning, gliding from one foot to the other, holding his gaze and keeping momentum. She arched right back as he supported her and exaggerated her free leg high into the air. She stayed there for a few beats then he pulled her back up before continuing to pirouette around the room.

'I will have to keep it short tonight.'

'Oh why is that my lord?'

'I have to welcome the guests tomorrow and there is much to do in the morning.'

'Of course my lord, whatever you wish.'

'Let me take you to your room now.'

He led her graciously up the ornate staircase. She had to remain calm, she knew what she had to do, for now was the bewitching hour, everything she had worked for rested on this moment.

At the top she recoiled in shock and moved a gloved hand to her mouth. 'My lord, I have been most forgetful, I have left my purse in the ballroom, would you mind if I retrieved it?'

He looked at her trying to find the deception, but he was so tired now and it was very late. She wouldn't do anything foolish at this hour.

'Go on then, I will sit here on this chair, but hurry now, I don't like to be kept waiting.'

'Of course sire, thank you.'

She ran down the stairs and collected her bag. Her heart was pumping uncontrollably. This was it now.

She must not fail. She had scrutinized the route from the map so many times. She could count in her head the amount of footsteps it would take her. She knew it would only take a few minutes.

She craned her neck at the bottom of the stairs to see that the coast was clear and then sprinted towards the kitchen. A moving shadow caught her eye and she stopped still behind a pillar. This was by far the scariest thing she had ever done, one false move and everyone would suffer. She had to remain calm otherwise her own breathing would give her away or her thumping heart would reveal her. The shadow went as quickly as it had arrived. Was it in her mind or was someone really there? Roma had told her that everyone was too busy with the games; surely Roma wouldn't lie to her. She strained her ears, she couldn't fail now, their escape was so close. Everything depended on the success of this night mission. It was deathly quiet.

She looked behind her to check that the General hadn't followed her down the stairs. No one was there. She ran to the next pillar and stopped again. Had she heard something? No, it was in her head again, she searched around with flared eyes and ears peeled back to detect the slightest sound. It seemed as if the shadows were creeping against the walls with her, she immediately thought of Lyall and his harrowing experience in the tunnel. 'That was a lot scarier than this place.' She chastised her weakness. 'Stay strong Skyrah, believe you are as nimble and as silent as a hare, believe you have its speed and agility, believe it girl, believe it.' She felt the tattoo on her arm, she felt the strength and power of her totem. She dropped her head and took some deep breaths. 'Calm down woman, you have time.' She looked up and focused on her task. 'Go, go now.'

She chased the ticking seconds into the kitchen. She heard the faint squeaking of rodents; her presence sent them scurrying away and now the kitchen was empty and deathly quiet. She saw the huge cauldron of porridge that would be served to the guards in the early hours of the morning. She quickly emptied the contents of her bag into the oats and honey and shut it tight. But she was drawn to the kettle of simmering water hanging over the fire. She stopped. She thought quickly. 'What can I use? This is far too good an opportunity to waste. Oh of course. Blessings totem for giving me insight.' She carefully removed the purple aconitum flower from her hair and dropped it in.

Her deed was done. She turned and hurried back to the stairs. She stood behind the pillar again. She tried to calm her pulsating heart. She closed her eyes and slowed her breathing down. She thought of her totem and believed. Slow rhythmic breaths eased through pursed lips and only when her breathing was controlled did she emerge at the bottom of the stairs. The General was waiting at the top with a thunderous look on his face.

'You said you would be quick,' he raged.

'I am sorry my lord, the vocalist was singing my favourite song, I just listened for a little while, please forgive me, I promise it won't happen again.'

'Where is the beautiful flower that you had in your hair?'

She reached up to feel for the missing accessory as if in surprise. 'I don't know my lord, it must have fallen out as I rushed back to you.'

'No matter, I will send you some more. Come, the hour is late, I must retire now.'

23

'Rufus and Wyn!' Barked the order the next day.

'No you can't take them, they are too young,' Lyall sprang to their defence.

'Get back you savage.'

The heavy baton rendered him helpless as it was thrust into the pit of his stomach.

Dainn ran in to help him and punched Scowler full on in the jaw. The huge fat guard sprawled out like a blubbering walrus as knuckles rained down on him. Punch after punch was thrown as Dainn's fists cracked against Scowler's skull. His comrades pulled him off fearing the consequences.

'Let me at him, let me finish him off. The sick low life!'

The two youngest boys were screaming and standing behind Namir.

'Come on Poxface, take me,' Lyall snarled, trying to stifle the stabbing pain in his abdomen. 'We're all going to die anyway, why not give me another chance.'

The guard's right forearm swiped him aside and reached for the youngsters. But Namir wasn't going to give them up either and backed them into a corner.

'You can't take them. I will fight again, put me against the General, I will rip his heart out for you.' Lyall was on his feet again. 'What's wrong with you vicious deviants? You can see they can't fight.' Lyall's rage boiled up and gushed from him in a howl of fury. He threw himself at Poxface and seized him by the throat. His fingers were trying to grip his windpipe but instead just hung on to folds of jowl. Scowler came rushing in and grappled him to the ground and crushed him into submission.

Dainn broke free from his restraint and pulled the guard off of Lyall, throwing him out of the door and hurling obscenities and threats that would terrify the devil himself. He then stood there blocking the entrance. The whelped guard ran away.

Lyall lay there. He thought that Skyrah would have saved them by now; he thought that another day might give Rufus and Wyn a chance. The throttled guard smashed his baton into Lyall's head again and again until he collapsed. He couldn't get up. He was dazed and concussed and the room span round him.

'Don't you get tired of this, answering to a mad Emperor, the gods will pay you back for your sickening crimes?' Lyall was drunk on words as blood poured from his wounds.

More guards had been summoned and lay into Dainn and Lyall. They kicked and beat them senseless.

A wry smile crossed Scowler's face as he took delight in proclaiming their punishment. 'Your stupidity has cost your clans their lives. You two will live to tell the tale and will be forced to watch every second of the flaying. Because, by the orders of the Emperor, tomorrow, instead of the arranged game; the rest of you will be strung up on stilts and burned alive.'

Lyall put his hands over his ears to drown out the sobs of the whimpering children. Six guards dragged the young boys from Namir's grasp. Dainn was beaten over the head until he passed out. The guards spat on them as they dragged away Rufus and Wyn.

*

That morning Roma turned up with Skyrah's breakfast of scrambled eggs on toast and her usual bright frame of mind shimmered around her.

'Good morning Skyrah, it's going to be a strange day today, I can feel it in the air.'

'Well it's my birthday today Roma, so that's special, not strange,' she lied.

'Is it really, well happy birthday Skyrah.'

'Thank you Roma, in fact I was wondering if you could come a little earlier at lunchtime today and maybe partake in a little herbal drink that I have made as a celebration for us.'

'A herbal drink?'

'Yes it's one I have with my mother and sisters every birthday, it's a tradition that has been passed down for centuries; my mother credits it to the beautiful hair and stunning good looks that run in our family.'

'You have made it for me?'

'Yes Roma, you mean a lot to me, we have talked so much over the past few months, you have kept my spirits up when I was so low. We have become very close and I wanted to share this with you.'

Roma looked at the reflection in the mirror and saw a plain girl with thin mousy hair and a pale complexion staring back at her. The thought of taking something to help her look more like Skyrah was just too irresistible to ignore. 'I would love to, I am so excited, thank you so much for sharing your family secret with me,' the maid went to the door and turned around. 'But I don't have a present for you.'

'Don't worry about that, your presence is all I need.'

The young girl smiled back and added. 'There's not many guards and servants about today, they have all gone down with a dreadful sickness, they have been ushered out to the stables away from the guests, but it means I should be able to slip up here early without anyone noticing.' She turned and locked the door as she went out.

Success, that was the first stage of the plan under way. She just had one last thing to do while she waited for the return of Roma. She took the eggs and rubbed them into the bread to make a dough, she then added some camomile herb to make sleep cakes. She rolled them out into several balls and concealed them with the rest of her produce. Her mother had told her often of how parents would sneak them to their children at bed time so they could have a peaceful night's rest.

They were harmful enough, but a quick remedy that worked many times for worn out couples. She changed into the most exquisite gown in her wardrobe, the most recent one from the General, and waited for her unsuspecting accomplice to arrive.

*

The two young boys were sobbing uncontrollably; they had to be trussed up to keep them still. All morning they sat shaking with fear.

'You, young savages, here take this,' a cruel barbarian tried to pour a concoction down their throats.

They spat out the forced contents.

'It's the only thing that will help you now,' goaded the guard. 'Take it.'

The boys were defiant; they had remembered what the older boys had told them, it was bad and made you do things that you didn't really want to. But a fragment lingered on their lips and as they moistened their dry mouths with a cracked tongue, some particles managed to slide down into their small stomachs. Pain jabbed into their heads as the drugs began to work and twisted their rational thoughts into a flurry of the demon kingdom. Everything was distorted, rushing past in a blur of colour. Black, green, grey, brown, congealed in a haze of darkness.

A deathly tone plagued their ears and they held their hands up to stop the sickening sensation. The youngsters tried to fight it, tried to control it and screamed in agony as the stimulant took hold. It was useless though; the powerful drugs were doing their very worst inside the young malnourished bodies. The effects happened so fast. Violent thoughts consumed them, power roared through their veins and stayed there swirling in their tiny cores. By the time the guards came back to start the initiation process the boys were in a traumatic trance consumed by thoughts of killing their opponent.

By midday the sun's ferocious heat had thickened the air in the arena and penetrated harshly into everything around it. Two young boys who didn't recognise each other were standing in front of an audience cooling themselves with arched silk fans and hungry for blood.

They began to move about very slowly, copying each-other's stances. They had been drilled and trained for this; focus, aim and don't delay - for delay means death. Day after day they had practised their moves, but this time they were drugged and not in control as they paced around the arena. Through unfocused eyes they vied each other and toyed with each other, they stumbled as they lurched forward and retreated, spreading themselves like bats with huge wings round the wide open space.

Both boys felt incredibly strong and powerful and it wouldn't be long before one drew blood. Rufus thrashed out first and punched Wyn full on in the face; he was surprised at his own strength and studied his small fist for longer than he should have. Wyn swayed backwards but steadied himself on his right foot and struck out with his left knee. Rufus threw up the entire contents of his stomach on impact and fell down clutching his groin. The shouting around him urged him to get up.

Wyn was still dazed by the strike to the head and toppled ridiculously around the arena. Rufus followed him with unsteady feet and threw himself at his opponent; he wanted to break both of his legs in two. He imagined that he was a giant and that his huge stature would outwit his challenger. He dived at Wyn but the bigger boy was too quick, he retreated quickly and reached for the dagger tied to his calf. Wyn started to thrust and swing at Rufus, desperate to pierce the unprotected skin. Rufus stumbled back, his wild chaotic limbs flew around in defence. He was confused and panicking. He didn't have time or the space to get to his knife. The tip of Wyn's blade edged ever closer to its victim. Suddenly Wyn launched forward like a spring and caught Rufus on the arm, the knife split the skin and blood trickled from the wound. Rufus shrieked. Glory was in sight. Wyn hounded him and drove down on him, he could win this fight, just a few more jabs and victory was his.

The crowd were screaming and bellowing now, holding their hands up to hoarse throats. Rufus looked at them and then back at Wyn in horror and staggered back. He fell on to his rump and began to scramble backwards to the rear of the arena searching for a way out. His frantic legs accidentally kicked sand in Wyn's face; the bigger boy staggered back and dropped his dagger as his hands flew up to his eyes. He was blinded. Rufus realised this was his advantage and grabbed more sand and frantically started throwing handfuls of it to thwart the pursuit of death. Then he saw the knife on the floor, glinting, inviting, beckoning him to take it. This was his opportunity. He would be the victor now and everyone would be scared of him. He didn't see Wyn in front of him anymore, all he saw was the face of the General trying to kill him. He had to slay the General, he had to do it. He stood up and ran to get the knife. He was screaming as he rushed towards Wyn. Through grit covered eyes Wyn saw the figure coming towards him wielding the glint of a blade. He screamed out loud; 'No don't! I beg you. Please don't!'

24

The maid had dutifully turned up as arranged, earlier than her usual time. 'Well here I am as promised, and you look radiant Skyrah, that is such an elegant dress.'

'Thank you, I am so glad you are here, I would be celebrating on my own otherwise. And to be honest Roma, there is no one I would rather be sharing this special drink with than you.'

The maid couldn't take her eyes off the dress or the clan girl who looked particularly exquisite today.

Skyrah offered the drink. 'To us, to beauty, to long life.'

Roma took the offering and they chinked the glasses. 'I echo that Skyrah, thank you and I hope you will have a good day, despite spending most of it on your own.' She knocked back the glassful in a single swallow.

'I will do, thank you,' assured Skyrah. And wanting the moment to last, raised her glass to Roma and gave her a sweet smile. The maid noticed her friend's delay in drinking, but rather than be suspicious she made an impromptu suggestion.

'May I have yours if you are not drinking it?'

'Of course you can, here you are.'

Roma sipped on her second drink more slowly, absorbing the powerful benefits of the herb. She swilled the contents in the glass and smelled the aroma. She took a sip and washed it round her mouth. 'I can feel it working already, this is really very good.'

'I know, it's a wonderful recipe, and it's all thanks to you for bringing me the flowers that I am able to share this with you.'

Skyrah could see Roma swaying, her legs were giving way so she guided her to the bed. 'Maybe it's a little strong for the first time; perhaps you should sit down and drink it.'

'Yes, maybe I should, but it means it's working doesn't it?'

'Yes, you are experiencing the signs,' assured the young clan girl.

The maid's head began to swim, she began to feel faint, she didn't feel very well at all. She reached to her swelling throat, gagging, mouthing to Skyrah for help. It didn't last long; soon she was unconscious and immobile. Skyrah had little time. Nimble fingers undressed her-self and undressed the maid, she exchanged their clothes.

'I am so sorry, but my friends lives mean more to me than yours. I hope the General is lenient with you, for you did nothing to assist me or encourage me. If he is not, then I hope your death is swift. Just as I hope mine will be if I am caught.'

She ran her finger along the energy field on her arm for strength. Nothing could go wrong now. It was imperative that she remained calm. She had rehearsed this so many times in her head, just like the previous night. It would work.

She put her hair up into the braided knot of a maid and hid it under the cap that Roma wore. That would be the certain give-away she thought to herself, long black lustrous hair instead of thin mousy strands, the General would notice straight away. She even whitened her face and hands with the ground egg shells and white paint she had been saving.

She knew the effects of the fermented laburnum would last a long time, the potion was definitely strong enough, she didn't know if it was fatal though. She really didn't care now anyway, the primary concern was her friends who were depending on her.

Skyrah reached into her hiding place in the floor and carefully took the stored glasses out and filled them with the powerful laburnum nectar. She put them on a hidden tray, carefully eased the key from Roma's apron pocket, unlocked the door and slid downstairs. She manoeuvred her way to the front terraces dressed as a kitchen maid. Her powdered face and hands concealed the sticky sweat of excursion and terror. Thank goodness she didn't have to speak to anyone; Roma had always complained that hardly anyone spoke to the female servants. No one would bat an eyelid at a servant girl handing out drinks to everyone on a hot summer day; it would be considered a good idea by those in attendance at the games. The drinks were offered to Poxface and Scowler who were standing at the entrance to the palace; they obviously didn't have porridge or tea that morning. Parched dry mouths took the inviting drink on this stifling afternoon in June. The guards were trying to defeat the tiredness as she collected their empty glasses on her way back. They were slumped down unconscious as she went past them on her second run. Her heart quickened as she pirouetted back along the sun drenched terrace and saw the General sitting there. She remained calm and focused; her head was bowed low the whole time. She didn't make eye contact with anyone as she passed the bright yellow cocktail to the unsuspecting guests. The General was more interested in the sickening torture unfolding in the arena before him than a maid handing out beverages. More thirst quenching drinks were knocked back in appreciation, finally getting to the blissfully unaware Emperor and his General. They weren't distracted as the tray appeared in front of them, they didn't want to miss the crack of a crushed rib or the spine chilling snap of a broken vertebrae.

She had to go back one more time to get the clothes. She glided effortlessly on nimble feet past the slumped guards, taking the haul of keys from them as she did so. She had to thank the gods that those in attendance were a bloodthirsty lot. No one took their eyes off the battle in front of them; two wretched little boys, drugged and fighting for their lives. Not one person noticed or took a double take at the dowdy servant girl moving quickly about the grounds on an important mission.

Most of the staff were in the kitchens preparing the huge supper that would follow the day's games. It was to be served in the grand dining room later. Not many would be attending that celebration she thought to herself. She retrieved the skilfully made clothes and stuffed the cakes into her apron. She then rolled up the map and tucked it down the back of her white blouse. Before she locked the door for the last time she looked at the sleeping girl. 'Thank you for everything, I hope you find love and peace wherever you are.'

She turned the key to continue with her mission and hurriedly trod her well-worn path to the terraced gardens. At the arena's edge, the poison had begun to affect the audience. Some were shouting and screaming, reaching to their throats as their windpipes swelled and broke off the air supply. Others just sat rigid with bulbous eyes protruding from purple sockets as voiceless mouths gagged for oxygen. She didn't show any emotion as she moved swiftly about, instead she smiled as she thought how the women's faces now resembled their puffed up purple dresses, and the crimson britches of the men were the exact shade of their swollen cheeks. She moved hastily past the stricken crowd, avoiding desperate hands reaching out for help and ignoring pitiful groans for assistance. Did they ever think about the plight of those before them who were suffering? No, they didn't, not once. Their mere presence threatened the lives of so many clans as the Emperor strived to amass total rule and power. So with an easy heart she clutched her massive pile of shirts and britches tighter and quickened her pace to stop the murderous boys.

Rufus threw down his weapon as Skyrah approached them. His focus was broken; his aim interrupted, the delay made him think. She picked up the dagger and approached the panic stricken Wyn.

'No don't! I beg you. Please don't!'

'They are hallucinating from extremely powerful herbs.' Her thoughts immediately broke into soothing words of kindness. 'It's all right boys, I have come to help you, I am going to take you home.' She coerced with the youngsters as she put the discarded dagger in to her apron pocket.

The effects were already beginning to wear off now and her tones of comfort gradually brought them out of their trance. She led them to the dormitories, unlocked the doors and fell in. Rufus immediately ran to Dainn for safety. A bleary line of gaunt faces looked up from their desperate thoughts and took a while to register what was going on as Skyrah stood in the open door. A quivering Wyn hung on to her for dear life.

Lyall recognised her straight away under the disguise; nothing could hide that beautiful face. 'Skyrah, you're safe, you're alive. I knew you would come.' He rushed over and grabbed his friend and span her round in the air laughing and crying at the same time. But he winced with pain and gently put her down.

'Your hurt Lyall, what have they done to you?'

'We've all taken a beating today - but you should see the other guys.'

She hugged him, wishing that he really could see the other guys. 'Is everyone here?' her voice was more than anxious as she looked for her clan.

'Yes, we are all here,' he replied. 'Thank the gods you got here before they hoisted us up onto stilts.' Lyall shivered at the thought.

Skyrah looked puzzled.

'I will tell you later,' he assured her. 'But for now let's rejoice.'

She turned to face the captives. Her lifelong friends she saw first. Followed by the ones she recognised from the clan games and some others she couldn't place. But although they looked wretched and pitifully thin, they were all crying with happiness and relief.

'I never gave up hope Skyrah, I knew you would save us.' Namir was next to hug her, rivers of joy streaming down his face.'

'My friends,' she said with whirlpools in her eyes. 'I am so glad you are all safe, I have worried about you day and night.'

They were all standing around her by now.

'I looked up to the window every night,' cried Lyall, 'willing you to save us.'

'I was working on my plan from day one, but it took so much time. I could not risk one mistake, for the slightest whim of impatience would have meant certain death for all of us.'

Clebe held out trembling arms and held her shoulders, 'I will never underestimate the power of a woman again; you have surpassed all expectations when we had all but given up hope.'

'You have shown such strength and resourcefulness,' championed Ronu and kissed her hands.

Her clan clambered round her, hugging her and bestowing all sorts of accolades on her as they held each other close. The words were like music to her ears.

'I want to thank you dear lady from the bottom of my heart and from all of us, we owe you our lives,' intercepted an anxious voice. 'But please, we are not safe yet, we still face certain death while we stay here, we must go now.'

Namir looked round to face a grim looking Dainn holding on to a terrified Rufus.

'Yes, Dainn is right, we must go at once,' agreed Namir breaking up the celebrations. 'We shall share our stories later.'

'I have made these,' said Skyrah refocusing on her mission and putting aside the triumphant accolades. 'Get into them quickly, we have to get through the town without looking out of place, but we must hurry.'

All the boys clambered into the clothes she had made. Dainn and Lyall helped the drug induced youngsters.

'See Rufus, I told you we would get out, but you have to stay brave, we still have mountains to climb.' Dainn wrapped a make shift bandage round his wound.

'I'll stay brave Dainn, I promise,' whimpered the boy clutching his injured arm.

As Dainn slipped the britches onto the drowsy lad he felt the dagger still strapped to Rufus's leg. 'Shall I relieve you of this?' he said kindly.

'Take it away from me, please take it away. I never want to see one of those again.'

He handed it to Lyall who slipped the blade into the waist of his trousers. 'We've got to get past the stables,' he said, clutching the trembling hand of Wyn.

'It's all right, I have made some sleep cakes for the stable boys; let me go first.'

The escapees were led into the sunshine, their heads hung low and they gripped on to each other as if a perilous precipice edged before them. Spots danced dizzily before their eyes as they battled with the glare of the sun. Once the menacing dots had faded they began to look around in earnest, frantic that a guard would appear and bludgeon them senseless. But no one was around. Mouths gasped open and wide eyes rotated as the deathly scene unfolded before them. The whole place was still and eerily quiet. An arm raised for help, a groan could be heard, the sun kissed the skin of dying bodies, it was unlike anything they had ever seen. The boys looked in awe at the total chaos that one girl had managed to create. How had she done it? How was it possible? Any living thing was asleep, dead or dying, they didn't know which and they didn't really care. Even an army would not have been able to enforce such a massacre on this scale with no loss of life to their own men. Not one person suspected her and yet she managed to disarm the whole fortress.

But now wasn't the time to ask questions, this was the day they had all been praying for; their freedom, and they followed their new leader.

As she got to the stables she took her cap off and let her tumbling dark locks fall over her shoulders, she looked back at Lyall and Namir and winked. She looked a total vision of loveliness. She entered the stable block. There were only five stable boys in total.

'Where are the other stable lads?' she asked.

The boy pointed to the rows of bodies. Guards and servants all mixed together; some with horse blankets over them, most just lay where they were put. She couldn't believe it. So many people had been affected by her potions. 'What a good thing I had the purple aconitum, that's what did the most damage,' she thought to herself triumphantly.

The stable boy continued. 'There is a terrible sickness, everyone is dying, the other boys went home, we are all afraid.'

She looked around at the subdued stable that was now a sick bay and slowly a window of opportunity beckoned. 'Yes I came to warn you, something terrible has happened,' she suddenly changed her plan. 'You must get out of here quickly, do not look behind you, just go home to your families and close all the windows and doors when you get in. Whatever you hear, do not go outside.'

'Why? What's happened?' asked a bigger lad.

'Sorcery and black magic. Death is on the heels of everyone, some say it's the heat that has driven people mad, others say it is witchcraft. Whatever it is you must leave, and go quickly.'

'What will you do?' they asked in unison.

'I will follow soon. I will get the rest of the horses out and look for anyone who can still walk. But you must go now.'

'Here,' said the boy picking up some garments hanging from an old meat hook protruding hideously from the wall. 'Take these britches and scout cap, you cannot ride a horse in that flowing skirt.'

'Thank you…?' she waited for his name.

'Macus, my name is Macus.'

'Good luck to you Macus - stay safe.'

'And to you fair lady.' He stared at her for a while until the disturbance behind him broke her spell.

Panic had set in and the other stable lads scurried about frantically getting the horses ready.

'Don't come back,' she urged. 'Now quickly make haste.'

'Thank you,' they said together, and galloped out of the stable yard and off into the distance.

She climbed into the britches and tucked her blouse in. Her hair was scrunched up into the cap. She called the clans in, who were amazed at her transformation so quickly into a boy. But they had little time to gawp. The steeds were quickly tacked up and led outside. Sixteen horses assembled noisily on the cobbled yard; billowing and snorting, grinding the snaffles and chains inside their mouths, shaking their heads and swishing their tails. Dainn and Lyall took the drug induced boys in pillion. Siri lifted his brother in front of him.

Skyrah in her more comfortable attire jumped on hers swiftly. 'Let's go!'

But Lyall wavered and held back.

'What's the matter brother?' called out Namir.

'I can't go, it's too good an opportunity.'

'What are you talking about we have to go?'

'But can't you see, the whole palace is asleep or dead, I can cut the heart out of the General, slay the Emperor and retrieve the Seal of Kings.'

'You can do what? That's far too risky!' exclaimed Clebe.

'He's right Lyall, it's not safe. I don't fully know the potency of the potions,' called out Skyrah.

'But look at that lot in there, they're not going anywhere soon, look at them, they're half dead.'

'But I don't know about the others, or how much they drank; besides I do not know where the Royal Seal is kept. It would be far too dangerous,' urged Skyrah again.

'If we acted quickly then we could do it, I know we could,' he persisted.

'But what if we can't Lyall, what if Skyrah is right and the General and his guards wake up, we won't be able to take them all on,' said Namir.

'But I have this,' and Lyall produced the dagger that Dainn had taken from Rufus.

'Have you forgotten the weapons that they have between them and the rest of us have nothing?' cried out Dainn.

'Keep that for hunting Lyall, some of us still have injuries from the last few days and you took a another beating this morning. None of us are fit enough.'

'Ronu is right, we are half starved with no energy, that's why the soldiers have to get the stimulant in us,' urged Norg.

'They would kill us all,' said Bagwa.

'We have to go now,' stepped in Dainn. 'It is unsafe here, we will get an army like we planned. It's the only way.'

Namir rode up to Lyall and put his arm around him. 'We have to go now; it is too unsafe, look at Rufus, look at Wyn. What about Zeno? Can they fight? No they can't. Their lives are in danger if we stay. We will get them home now. Then we will get strong, and then we will get our revenge. I promise brother, I promise you just like we promised our father.'

'Please Lyall,' begged Zeno.

Lyall looked at the wretched crew of starving boys, the pitiful looks from Rufus and Wyn in front of him, barely hanging on as it was. All the hard work that Skyrah had gone through would be for nothing. He put his dagger back in the waist of his trousers and nodded to his brother, he then addressed the clans. 'I'm sorry comrades, I guess I am just getting too impatient. I thought we could do it without any more bloodshed to our people. But you are right, let's do it properly, let's go and get an army.'

25

The Emperor opened his eyes and lay back as comfortably as he could. Most of the pain had abated and now he merely felt deathly tired. The view around him was grim. As far as he could see, dead and sick people lay where they had fallen, though over the last few hours most of the moaning had faded away and only the flap and squawks of corvids disturbed the quiet. He began to feel light headed again and his eyesight was definitely ebbing away. On the very edge of his fading eyesight many figures appeared to be moving about, they were grimacing and stooped in pain. He had never felt this bad before and had certainly never felt this close to death.

As the ruler of the Empire of Ataxata and with the Seal of Kings in his possession he had been privy to the best treatment and the greatest care with honourable and trustworthy people around him. But these events were unfathomable and could possibly be treason. He needed to find out the source. The thought of severe retribution ignited him; he tried to sit up but was beaten back again with the pain.

The General turned to him. He wiped the froth from his mouth as he opened his swollen lips to speak.

A frail whisper emerged. 'Thank the gods you are alive my lord. The Teacher is lying next to me quite dead.'

'What happened Corbulo, does anyone know?' the Emperor groaned with exhaustion.

'No, the last thing I remember was the most excruciating pain in my abdomen and my throat swelling so much that I couldn't breathe; but I don't know why it happened or what caused it.'

'We need the physician, he will know the cause.'

The General struggled forward to obey the command, but the movement made his head swim so much that he was forced to sink back again beaten by the powerful poisons in his body. He feebly waved his arms about to get the attention from someone, anyone. He didn't have the strength to shout. A younger guard staggered over.

'It is chaotic master, everyone is in a bad way. The physician has been summoned.'

'Good, good,' said the General meekly.

'What about the captives, where are they?' spluttered the Emperor.

'I don't know my lord, there are terrible scenes out here, maybe they are in the dormitories consumed by the sickness themselves, no one has been spared.'

The Emperor nodded a few times, relieved that the captives were still there. He closed his eyes. The General threw concern at the guard.

'Help get the Emperor into the shade man, this heat will only make things worse.'

'Of course master.'

The young guard wrapped the royal arm around his neck and heaved the Emperor to his feet. The guard weak with fatigue himself was only just able to move him. He signalled to a comrade by way of a faint whistle, to get a chair ready in the shade. Even though the sun was still intense and burning brutally, the four o' clock shadows gave some protection.

'I will leave you here my lord, the physician will be here soon.'

The Emperor waved him off and closed his eyes again.

Corbulo sat waiting for his sickness to subside. He slowly rotated his head to observe the scene. Some people were dead, that he was sure of, others were coming round, albeit slowly, but they would be all right. He craned his neck to look into the arena, no one was there. No prostrate bodies, no blood, no sign of death. The guard must be right he thought, they were all quivering in fear inside their dormitories. Wretched cowards, pathetic savages, they should have helped the dignitaries; they should have called for assistance. No matter, they would all burn at the stake now anyway, every one of them; and he would gladly light the fire. But more importantly, what had caused this mass destruction? It had to be something that had been consumed in the palace that morning. If it was anything else then the bodies of the two savage boys would be in front of him right now.

Absent minded foolhardy cooks, they too would be burned alive for their actions. The conundrum tired him; he would launch a thorough investigation later. He retreated back into his chair again tipped his head back and with closed eyes faced the turquoise sky above him.

The physician lived outside the royal residence on the other side of the town. The soldier approached by way of a pebbled path that widened in front of a viewing platform that also served as a step up to the house. Two carved doors stood wide open, allowing a view of floor to ceiling of leather books; a rosewood drinks cabinet displaying a decanter and drinking bowls, and a dark mahogany sideboard with a bowl full of dried dandelion heads. The middle aged physician sat in a large green leather armchair in front of a desk, his head bent over a scroll, a cup of dandelion tea at his side. He responded to the knock by putting down his quill and adjusting his maroon physicians cap.

'Enter,' a kind voice greeted his visitor.

The soldier saw a man in his mid thirties of slim build and neat appearance. The room's ambience suggested that the man lived by himself; simple and sparse with muted colours. The characteristic elegance of a woman's touch was not evident. Maybe there was a house servant to assist him, but certainly no one permanent.

'Please sir, you must help us.' The poor man collapsed, the physician went to his aid but a raised hand yielded him. 'There is no time, I will be all right, but please sir, make haste to the palace.'

'I must tend to you, what good are you to the Emperor if you are dead?'

'But I fear the Emperor will be dead unless we go right now.'

Without any further questions he retrieved his apothecary bag, went round to the back yard to saddle up his tethered mare and followed the ailing soldier to the palace. The chaperone was extremely ill and could barely hang on to the reins while his gelding was doing its best to keep to a steady trot and not unseat his mount. The hot afternoon was a disadvantage to them both and the court physician couldn't get any more information out of his aide at all.

A buckled road weaved past the sun baked meadows and adjoining wilting farms, through the quaint villages and jostling buildings and into the royal borough. The physician noticed how quiet the villages were and how all the shutters were pulled together. An eerie silence floated like a heavy storm cloud and not one person was outside to witness him pass through.

The roadside had been staked with long poles complete with the palace flag secured to them and every door had a spray of harvested wheat tacked onto it. Not that he made this journey very often, but he was sure he hadn't noticed such behaviour at any time before. Those at the palace were a healthy bunch; even the Emperor in his old age needed very little in the way of remedies and potions; but on the occasions that he was needed, many a boy would run out at the sound of his horse's hooves and appeal to the royal visitor for a tossed coin of the realm, which he duly obliged. Then there were the burly women getting on with their chores or gossiping over the hedge and clipping the rascal who had just retrieved a coin. But today was very different. Today it was dead.

He couldn't ask the guide what was wrong, he had little energy to ride his horse let alone talk. But he would find out soon enough he thought and continued the race against time in absolute fear of what would greet him round the corner.

The late afternoon sun was falling now and out of the pink tinged sky rose the palace. He combed his way round the outside courts and alongside the palace walls into the stable block. The horses were led away and another escort guided the healer to the Emperor. He followed the usher's lead down the path trying to speed up the pace - but it was futile - everyone was affected.

He past rows of rigid contorted bodies, disfigured faces strewn with bile and froth, their stone cold glassy eyes were still; they lay there unmoving, lifeless; all lined up in the shade of the grass topped terraces. The immaculately manicured garden was blanched with the squawks of fighting corvids and the sounds of people struggling to stay alive. Among them was the Ruler of the Ataxatan Empire.

The healer fell at his side. 'My lord, it is I, Meric the physician.'

The Emperor slowly opened one eye, his face was pale and disfigured, his breathing slow. He trembled as he spoke. 'Oh Meric, thank the gods, but I fear it is too late for me, something quite bad has happened here.'

The physician looked inside his mouth and took note of the frothy saliva, he then felt his pulse, it was very weak. His skin felt clammy despite the heat of the sun. The whites of his eyes were almost yellow with dilated pupils and he couldn't focus at all. The Emperor was slipping into a coma. 'Someone help me!' he called out urgently. 'I need to get Gnaeus into his room.'

Five once strong guards rushed over and with the feebleness of young infants lifted the Emperor to his feet. The General became aware of the commotion and staggered over.

'What is it Meric, what's the matter?'

'He has been poisoned Domitrius.'

'What! How?'

'I have my suspicions, but will need to investigate the kitchens first.'

'What can I do?'

'Bring my bag and I will try and treat him, but I fear it is too late. The powerful sleeping sickness of the poisons that everyone succumbed to has prevented immediate attention.'

'And we were all out in the midday sun for such a long time.'

'Exactly, dehydration and poison is a death curse.'

More guards came over to seek orders.

'Is everyone in the same state Domitrius?' asked Meric.

'We all have varying forms, some are already dead; others are extremely ill and probably won't make it. Those that are bearing up tend to be younger and healthier.'

'You will need to burn the dead. The heat will cause all sorts of diseases that will spread quickly amongst the palace. If the poisons don't kill you then the contaminations will. Those that survive will be very weak for some time yet.'

'You heard the physician, gather the dead and prepare to burn them.'

The General led the remaining party into the palace. Two guards lay prostrate across his path. 'Get those two dead bodies out of the way quickly, burn them or bury them, I don't care which.'

Scowler and Poxface were hauled unceremoniously away to their final resting place while the party headed for the staircase that led to the upper levels. The Emperor was weakening with every step. The physician was the only one with any strength now. Somehow, from somewhere the General and the guards dragged the patient through the vestibule and stopped for a breath at the base of the stairs.

'Not much further men, do it for your Emperor.'

The instructions from the physician ignited them into action and they hauled with every last drop of energy that they had. They ascended the stairs slowly, carefully and desperately. Heaving, groaning and panting with every step along the corridor. The Emperor worsened. At last they entered the wide, bright royal apartments and the huge wooden doors opened to the regal bed chamber. Solid mahogany posts with pure gold inlays supported the mammoth bed. Yellow and crimson tapestries concealed the crisp white bed linen underneath and an oval window threw a dusty myriad of summer rays over the giant family portraits. The Emperor winced in the light. The curtains were drawn at once sending the dust particles in all directions; the room instantly became sombre and dull and the faces stared out of their frames in solemn disapproval. Gnaeus stumbled, weak with fatigue. He was laid out on the bed while the physician took out bottles and herbs and plant remedies from his bag.

'Send someone to get foxgloves and feed it to the patients, I am not sure if they will work at this stage, but it's worth a go.'

'I will go now,' said the General. He turned slowly and gripped his side; he stifled a bolt of pain that shot through his stomach and made him retch.

'Are you all right?' threw a concerned Meric.

'I will be, take care of the Emperor, there is someone I have to see first.'

The General edged his way along the corridor, holding on to the wall as he went. Several times he collapsed but hauled himself up again. He coughed and spluttered; a guard came out to help him. 'I'm fine, go and get the foxglove like the physician said and give it to those that need it.'

'All right master, if you are sure.'

The General nodded and the guard limped off.

He continued to drag himself along the landing as the wall supported him. The pain was intense again; he gripped his side and bit down on his bottom lip. 'No more dancing for a while,' he grimaced. 'I must tell Skyrah what is going on.'

The route to her room took him ages. His muscles would not respond to the urgent messages his brain was sending. Gripping on for dear life; each frustrated, slow, awkward step took him that bit closer to her. At last he stood outside the room. It was locked.

'Thank the gods she is safe,' he said. He reached for the key. He fumbled and trembled. He dropped it on the floor. 'Damn it man, get a grip.' He seethed between his teeth. He rocked forward and reached to his full extent and with clammy fingers retrieved the key. His shaking touch tried to find the lock. His dilating eyes tried to focus. They wouldn't work together. He shook his head and concentrated. So very close. He wiped the sweat from his brow and tried again. At last the key went in and he moved it anti clockwise. The movement flipped the catch with a soft click. The lock freed itself and he opened the door.

'Skyrah it's me, are you all right?'

There was no answer.

'Skyrah where are you?'

The glistening jewels on a brand new gown caught his eye. He staggered over to the bed. He saw a sleeping figure wearing it.

'Wake up Skyrah.'

His voice was gentle.

228

The figure lay still and quiet. He squinted his eyes and tried to focus. He couldn't see very well. He got closer to the unmoving frame.

'Skyrah.'

There was still no life. He slid his arms underneath the body and lifted it up. He smelt the hair, he breathed in the aroma of its neck. His arms spread out wide as he recoiled in horror. The body fell back into its dent on the bed.

'Who are you? What have you done with my Skyrah?'

He touched the cold hand. He picked at the limp hair.

'What have you done with her?' he screamed at the body. 'Tell me now, tell me, where is she?' A piercing cry echoed round the room out of the door and into the corridor. It filtered into the room where the Emperor lay dying.

A fragile finger pointed to an impressive oak chest. Meric stood up to follow the appendage and touched a drawer. The Emperor blinked once. The drawer was sensitively opened where a red lacquered box and a richly embroidered red pouch was retrieved. Again Meric sought a sign that he was following the correct procedure as he took ownership of the treasures. He held the pouch carefully, its heavy circular shape settled comfortably in his hand. The long ornate box was trimmed in gold with the Emperor's seal pressed into the lid; a delicately curved leverage was clasped securely to conceal the contents. The box and the pouch were taken to the Emperor. Gnaeus had very little time left and summoned Meric closer. The physician leaned into the lifeless man who could barely whisper now. With a long broken sentence he gave his final orders: 'Give these to Domitrius for me, he will need them.' The Emperor sunk deeper into the bed and let out his last breath.

Meric sat forlorn for a while immersed in prayers and his own thoughts. He then passed his hand over the deceased Ruler's face and closed the frozen eyes. Two guards had already flown to help Corbulo in his frantic state of mind. The other two were instructed to stay with the Emperor.

Inside Skyrah's room they found Corbulo on the floor with his head in his hands. The curtains were ripped from their poles. The wardrobe doors were torn from their hinges, the beautiful dresses had been disembowelled and discarded in rage. The dressing table drawers and their contents were emptied and scattered all over the floor. Precious porcelain, broken cups, saucers, plates and bowls lying in pieces around him. He didn't look up once, his knees were drawn up to his chest and his back was pressed up hard against a wall. 'Go and check the dormitories,' he ordered. 'And take that imposter with you and burn it.'

26

The group had reached the main entrance and slipped through easily without the regular posting of a palace guard. They clattered through the approach road and stopped briefly as they looked out at a land of freedom beyond the city walls. Before them lay the Empire of Ataxata; silent and brooding under the heat of the sun. The air still hung heavily over the royal borough and the town seemed even hotter with its warmed masonry walls and even hotter flag stones. In the distance a number of carrion birds drifted overhead, lured by the smell of death and the easy pickings of decay. The shackles on Lyall's neck rose and he shuddered as he thought of the hungry flock. With everyone together now Namir led the boys through the ghost of a town. Few stalls remained opened, and those stragglers that still littered the streets were engrossed in the news of the recent malady at the palace.

Out of the town they opened up into a canter. Skyrah urged her horse forward past the farms and open fields of wheat and barley. The same lads who had fled the scene earlier were now busy putting up stakes and flags as a possible warning to those entering the royal borough. The shutters in the cottages were being closed. Protective shards of wheat were being secured to doors. Other than the grooms, no evidence of life abounded.

When she reached level ground she discarded her cap, shook the reins and her horse leaped forward. She crouched down and looked straight between the stallion's ears and thundered across the plain. Behind her the boys kept pace, shrieking wildly and excitedly.

'You go girl, you have earned this freedom!'

She wanted to create as much distance between them and their captors as she could; for eight long months in brutal conditions was enough to test the resolve of the bravest soul, so she galloped across the land with the wind in her face, and her hair streaming behind like billowing waves of taffeta silk.

She reined back to a canter and laughed out loud from the exhilaration of the gallop, or was it the run for liberty, her feelings were mixed. The boys caught up and whooped alongside her as they too relished in their new found freedom. Entering the eaves of a forest she slowed to a stop, breathed in the air and slid off her mount's back as he came to a halt. She lifted the drooping muzzle with both hands and laid her cheek on the animals nose, then she tucked the stallions head under her arm in a gesture of affection. 'Thank you,' she whispered. 'Thank you for getting me away so quickly; I think I shall name you Meteor.'

The horse tossed his head up and down as if to acknowledge her embrace and his new name.

'Shall we rest here a while?' she called out to the

clan.

'I think that's a good idea Skyrah, we don't want to exhaust the horses too much,' agreed Lyall. 'My mount has got a bit more weight to carry as well.' He looked at Wyn hanging on in front.

'Yes, it's tricky galloping with sleepy boys,' said Dainn reining his horse to a stop.

The herd rattled their bridles and chains as they tossed their heads and swished their tails in excitement. They too seemed to enjoy the race.

'I'm sure there is a stream close by, if my memory serves me right,' said Ronu.

'Let's go and check,' chipped in Clebe.

'I'll come too,' said Bagwa.

'I'll help with the younger boys.'

Skyrah carefully lifted the youngsters down and settled them by a tree. She would go off to gather for a meal and make a temporary bed for herself and the youngsters soon. The lower branches of the pine tree were the driest and the easiest to get to and there was plenty of dry tinder around; she would look for a firestone and flint to get a small fire going later. There would be plenty of roots and greens around the forest plus a gourmet of herbs and leaves; and she still had her cakes. They would be safe for the young boys to have. Help them sleep better as well, ahead of the long ride the next day.

'Good thing I kept the dagger, said Lyall. 'We will need this tonight.'

'Yes and I have one too, I retrieved it from the

arena earlier.'

They shared a smile together.

'You don't know how many times I sat looking up at the palace,' he continued, smoothing the soft muzzle of his mount and feeling safe at last.

'I did too Lyall, every day I looked out from my prison.'

'Did he hurt you? Did that bastard do anything, because if he did, I swear I'll...' His voice trailed off as Skyrah interrupted him.

'He didn't hurt me Lyall, I swear,' she stroked Meteor.

'So what did he want you for?' asked Namir coming into the conversation after settling his horse.

'To dance,' she said truthfully.

'What?' the brothers said in unison.

'That's all I did, I danced with him. He gave me fancy clothes and lovely jewellery. I had a very nice room. But I was a prisoner there. I went out of the room three times a week; only for an hour or two, sometimes even less, and I had to be escorted by him on each occasion. But it gave me the time that I needed to perfect my plan.'

'Oh my,' groaned Lyall. 'We were all slaves in one way or another.'

'They're monsters! I'm going to kill them all,' murmured Siri as he rested by a tree with Zeno.

'We will, Siri. We will destroy them all,' crowed Lyall reassuringly.

'And we will, because now we are free and can

summon an army and get our revenge,' cheered Norg. 'It feels so good to be out here in the fresh air, I feel revived and strong again and can take on anyone now.' And he breathed in the scent of the forest and lifted his face to the sky.

'I have something of interest to show everyone though.'

But Norg's moment of bliss and Skyrah's attempt to share the details of her map were interrupted by a loud shriek from behind.

'We have found water, come quickly.' It was Clebe staggering back up an incline dripping wet from head to foot. 'It's clear and cool and clean, come bring the horses.'

'Show us later Skyrah, and tell us how you massacred an army all by yourself, we all want to know,' Namir's excited voice trailed behind him as he ran down the hill.

She smiled proudly; there would be plenty of time to show them the diagram and tell the tale of her successful escape. She untethered Meteor and with the rest of the boys led the herd down the sloping path. They heard the noise first, the laughing and shouting, the splashing and excitement, the playfulness of unleashed young men. Brutality and cruelty had invaded their tortured souls for too long now, so this amount of frivolity was good to see. Meteor edged away nervously as a barrage of water came his way.

'Steady boy,' she stroked his muzzle. 'It's only Dainn and Bagwa having a water fight.'

As she guided the horse to the cool inviting ripples the others followed his lead and drank from the stream. The boys threw off their clothes and ran in, nothing could stop them submerging themselves and throwing the free flowing water at each other now. Skyrah watched them and smiled, then she started to snigger through her nose, it was the funniest sight she had ever seen, eighteen young men in their underpants playing in the water like children. She laughed until she collapsed against a tree, holding on to her stomach. She couldn't stop. Her laughter became infectious and the boys started having spasms of laughter with her. It made them feel so good; it was so easy. They hadn't laughed like that for months.

'Hey, there's a fish,' called out Lyall amongst the raucous behaviour, and speared it with his dagger.

'And another,' yelled Namir, and skilfully plucked the weapon from the air that Skyrah had thrown.

'There's loads,' cried all the boys scrambling together to secure a feast.

Skyrah went back to the camp and dug a hole and lined it with rocks. She made a fire with her firestone and flint and left it to heat up for a while. She then searched up and down the water's edge for the right combination of greens and herbs and added them to the stone oven. She collected a concoction of coltsfoot for its salty taste, nettles for a tangy flavour, pigweed and wild sorrel. The stones sizzled perfectly with the wet fish on them when they arrived. She piled on the pine leaves and pine nuts, then a layer of smaller stones and finally covered it all with dirt. The lads put their clothes back on, settled the horses and returned to the makeshift dining area.

'Food fit for a king,' said Lyall smelling the aromatic meal and taking his seat next to her.

'And a queen,' she laughed back nudging him.

'Reminds me of the Clan,' said Namir.

'Reminds me of freedom,' echoed Ronu.

'To home,' called out Skyrah as she passed round the cooked fish to the boys.

'To Skyrah, our saviour,' they all cried out together.'

'Now tell us Skyrah, how did you do it?'

27

Meric decided to leave the lacquered box and pouch till later. The General would have to view the deceased Emperor and get sworn declarations from the witnesses that he died from his afflictions. Then he would have to make the final decision about the Emperor's funeral arrangements. For now the Emperor would lay in the State Room, it was cool and dark enough in there. Besides, Corbulo was in no condition to do anything so important at the moment, he would approach him about those things on the morrow. Instead the physician went down into the scullery to start his investigations; because the only way to get this much poison into a palace household could only have come from the cookhouse and that's where he made for.

By now, the palace was like a morgue; cold, dark and inert. The kitchen was empty, devoid of any pulse. The dead and nearly dead had been taken outside in a hurry; no one had survived this.

Carcasses of unprepared meat were seared and strewn over the worktops, paralysed vegetables waiting to be severed remained in their rows. Ageing feathered fowl and different sized rabbits dangled from bound legs in the pantry awaiting the chef's knife. The air was clotted with trapped heat and the smell of burnt embers engulfed the room.

He sidestepped the spilled pans and broken crockery scattered all over the floor. Drawers were pulled out and cutlery was abandoned. Somewhere in the room echoed the sound of dripping, he couldn't make out the source. He trod his path carefully through the chaos and turned things up-right where he could. He wandered about lifting things up and smelling them, rubbing his fingers over surfaces and analysing the aroma, he had a nose for toxins and deadly assassins, he would soon know what caused this mass extinction.

He opened the lid of the cauldron and peered inside; but reeled back with the waft of steam that tried to choke him and found himself gagging with the smell. He grabbed a cloth and pulled it off its heat source, it clattered to the floor with a din that could raise the dead and rolled over the flag stones cooling itself down. He watched and waited as it writhed around on the stone floor, eventually putting out a leather covered toe to slow it down. It came to a standstill and he craned into its core. The remains of the breakfast dish were stuck like glue to the base of its massive container and acted like a compost bed to its parasite. He flicked something out of his pocket, reached in and pulled the deadly assassin out with the handkerchief. He blew on it and wiped away the debris with dextrous fingers. It was still hot. He lay it down on the kitchen table. He recognised the distinctive shape of the white snakeroot, its small snowflake heads would have gone unnoticed in a cauldron of oats and water. Wicked and powerful, a plant so poisonous it could kill a human who had drunk the milk of a goat fed on the stuff.

On closer inspection Meric noticed something else. Imbedded in the gruel was the limp remains of hemlock, small white lacy umbels which would be so cleverly disguised in the grains and as so expertly intended, would also have gone unnoticed. This deadly stalker affected the lungs so acutely it would eventually cause suffocation by drowning; a very slow and agonising death indeed.

He was intrigued and almost in awe of the perpetrator's knowledge; not many would know how to administer this, certainly no one at the palace would be privy to such information, it was only the Apothecarist or Physician who would know such things. His mind was in a quandary as he went over to the cauldron to investigate further. The contents had evaporated away to nothing but a thimble full. And there was another killer; aconitum, the beautiful purple flower known as Wolfsbane and Leopardsbane, the Queen of all poisons. He had the culprits and how they were administered, now he had to find the killer and why they did it. He made his way back to the gallery and knocked on the door.

'It's me Domitrius, Meric.'

'Come in Meric, and please excuse the mess, there has been a bit of an accident here.'

The first thing Meric saw was Corbulo slumped against a wall, his confused head in bloodied hands. He then looked about the room at the smashed up furniture.

'Are you all right, Domitrius?'

'Yes, I am, I have had a bit of a shock that's all.'

'Your hands, let me look at them for you.'

'No, we don't have time, I will be all right.'

'If you are sure. But I am sorry to inform you that the Emperor has passed away, he was not strong enough to fight the poison.'

The General hung his head again. 'I think I know who did this to us.'

'Oh good, that saves me the task of finding out, so who did it?'

'The maid, she did it, the unthoughtful, unappreciative wretch.'

'How do you know it was her?'

'Because when I came in here the girl who I was looking for had gone and the imposter was in her clothes on this very bed.'

'So where is the girl and where is the imposter?'

'I don't know, Meric, I don't know where the girl is. The imposter has been taken away to be burnt.'

'I take it that the imposter was already dead.'

The General looked at the physician with a glare that took umbrage at the question.

'I'm sorry Domitrius, I had to ask.'

The General continued to stare ahead.

'Would you know where the maid's room is, I would like to look around?'

He suddenly made the connection. 'Of course!' The General stood up and wobbled, Meric went to help him but was pushed away. 'That's where she has hidden the girl, come with me.'

The General wasn't thinking straight, Meric knew that. Nothing at this stage meant any sense at all.

'It's this way Meric.'

The physician followed the distraught man back down the staircase, back through the kitchens and down further into the basement. Eventually they came to a row of stone storerooms; the type of room that was cool in the torturous summer months, but in the winter it would be worse than freezing.

'I think it's this one,' and the General slowly opened the door hopeful of seeing Skyrah waiting for him on the other side. He was sadly disappointed. They looked around the cramped room that was barely six foot square. Just about big enough for a bed, a chest of drawers and a small earthenware brazier with a pan on top. 'It's not this one, it must be the next room.' He tried all six rooms, frantically searching in all of them until he reached the last one. 'This is it,' he called out to the physician who was still rummaging in the first room.

'How do you know, have you found the girl?' Meric sprinted to the last dwelling.

'No, but I recognise these.'

And stuck to the stone clad wall were eight paintings of flowers, beautifully executed with copious amounts of attention to detail.

'Did the maid paint these?'

'No she didn't, I have a number of paintings done by the same artist.'

'And who might that be?'

'The girl, my friend, she did them.'

'And who is this girl you call a friend?'

'A savage, but unlike any savage I have seen before, she is my muse, my property, my dancing companion in the evening.'

Meric raised an eyebrow. 'If it's alright with you Domitrius I would like a thorough search of both rooms.'

'Both?'

'The maid's and the girl's, I don't want to leave any stone unturned, or any floorboard untouched.'

'But it can't be the girl, she was shut in her room all the time, and the only time she came out was with me. The maid had access to everything and look how close she is to the kitchen.'

'I'm not convinced Domitrius, I need further proof.'

'As you wish, just find the girl for me.'

The men climbed back up the stairs and exited through the kitchen. Meric stopped at the large wooden table and invited Domitrius to see what he had discovered.

'This is what I found in the cooking pots.'

The General peered at the unlikely suspects; a spew of pitifully limp and faded plants.

'These are what killed most of the people in the palace,' Meric declared.

'Weeds!' Domitrius scoffed. 'I have never heard such nonsense.'

'They are very poisonous plants Domitrius, extremely powerful and deadly.'

'But I didn't have anything from the kitchens this morning, I didn't have time.'

'Which makes it all the more important to search the rooms. Something other than these poisonous plants affected you Domitrius.'

The bristling General and mystified physician went quickly in search of some guards who could ransack the rooms. Most of them were outside disposing of the bodies.

But then two anxious figures ran up. 'Master, the boys have gone!'

'What!' Domitrius bellowed so loudly that even the physician cowered. The back of his hand cracked across the informant's ear, slamming him to the ground. 'You wait till now to tell me!'

The soldier reached up to his head and hunched around trying to dodge the General's fist. The punches hammered hard into his chest, shoulders and back.

The physician winced and turned away.

'We tried to find you master,' stuttered the other guard, giving the reason for the delay but tensing his body for a vicious attack. He closed his eyes and hunched his neck. His body went into spasms as he waited for the blow. But it didn't come. He opened his eyes. He searched for the fist. The General was not there. He was halfway on route to the dormitories.

'I have a job for you though.' And the physician sent the soldiers off to ransack the girl's rooms.

28

There were soldiers moving about everywhere; searching the barns, the stables, the hedgerows, anywhere that a savage could hide. The depleted force of the palace worked tirelessly. Most of them were barely fit to search, but they had already been at the end of the General's sadistic fist so carried on regardless. The remainder were stacking firewood in the wagons and shuddered at the consequences.

'May the gods have mercy on them should they be discovered,' said one grim soldier.

'And us if they aren't,' said another.

The General was beside himself when he found out that all the horses were gone as well. 'Where is my horse, where is she? If they have taken her I will round up all the stable lads and burn them in those wagons, then I will burn their families on top of their disfigured bodies and then burn one guard a day until I get her back.'

'The soldier's horses are safe in the meadow master, yours is with them.'

'Are you sure?'

'Yes I have checked myself,' said the guard. 'I had to get one from the field when I went to get the physician.'

'Was it you who got Meric?'

'Yes sir, it was sir.'

'Good man, good man, but I still want to question the head stable boy.'

More soldiers were deployed to track down the head stable lad. It wasn't difficult. Everyone knew that he lived in the village outside of the town.

'Where are you taking him?' cried his mother.

'I'm sorry ma'am, we're under orders.'

'It's that General isn't it? That evil man, he's a curse on the palace,' wailed the boy's mother crying into her apron.

'It's all right mother, I shall just tell the truth.'

'When has that ever saved anybody Macus? You know as well as I do that anyone who crosses him doesn't survive his brutal fist and the burning wagon. I still remember that awful day, it's imprinted in my memory, the awfulness of it all. His own men and their families burned alive because his fancy girl escaped.' She shook her head into her apron again.

'But I haven't crossed him have I?' her son comforted.

The two soldiers looked at each other, not daring to utter what they were really thinking.

'We have to go Macus, we are sorry. The General is in a foul temper and we can't provoke him any further.'

The General was waiting and seized him by the throat,

half throttling him with one hand and with the other drove three sharp blows into his belly. Macus closed his eyes and doubled over in pain. The deranged man seethed within a hair's breadth of the groom's face. 'Now listen very carefully boy, unless you want to die right here right now and never see your family again, you will answer my questions.'

'Yes master,' he groaned.

'Some time today the horses were taken from the stables, who took them?'

'It was a girl.'

The General punched him again in the pit of his stomach. 'Stop lying boy otherwise I will burn your family to a cinder and have your head severed from its neck and secured to a post.'

'I'm not lying master, she was beautiful with long dark hair, she had a lovely voice and seemed so kind. She looked like a maid.'

'Why did you think she was a maid?'

'She was wearing a maid's dress.'

'Was she with any boys?'

'I didn't see any at first. She said everyone was dying because of a curse, because of witchcraft. She told me to go, she told me that she would look after the horses.'

'When did you see the boys?'

'When I was putting out the warning signs to traders and travellers, I didn't want any more people getting hurt.'

The General spat through his teeth as he

punched him again. 'So why didn't you come and tell me?'

'The boys were stable lads like me. She said she would look out for survivors and take them to safety - I thought that's who they were...' his voice trailed off.

'Well you thought wrong, you imbecile, you half wit, I should feed you to the pigs...' The General fumed and went to raise his hand again - but Meric stopped him.

'Enough Domitrius, he's had enough, he's told you the truth. You know what happened now.'

The two soldiers ordered to ransack the rooms came running up to the physician. 'Sir, you need to see this.'

The General let Macus drop instantly and followed Meric and the soldiers upstairs back into Skyrah's room. They stood at the doorway gawping, amazed, hardly believing what was in front of them. It was in a worse mess than before. All the furniture was precariously balanced in an uneven stack. Women's clothes were strewn on top of the mound. The carpet was pulled right back to the window and all the floorboards were up. Meric followed his nose to his left and looked down. A graveyard of laburnum and azaleas greeted him, their coffin still wet from the soaking. Poppies, aconitum, white snakeroot and hemlock lay in their regiments; and in nice neat piles alongside the official ranks were the offcuts from the clothes she had made.

'Did you have a drink at any time today

Domitrius?'

'Yes I did, we all did, all of us, we all needed a drink and it was so refreshing.'

He stopped short. He now realised. The paintings. The request for flowers. The dead maid. The empty dormitories. But how had she done it? Then he remembered Meric showing him the plants in the kitchen. 'She ran back to get her bag on our dancing evening last night. I remember that she took ages and I was angry with her. How stupid of me, how could I have trusted her?'

'You were lucky not to have had anything from the kitchen today. I suspect all the dead had consumed both.'

'How though?'

'The palace guards and maids would have been hit first and that was the main part of her plan. Last night on your dancing evening she ran back to get her bag but she also ran to the kitchen and left the toxins to fester in the cauldrons. First thing this morning half the workforce was dead or dying after consuming their oatmeal and drinking water from the pan. With them out of the way she could go on to phase two. She got her maid to drink the laburnum and azalea concoction, by a means we do not know, but she managed it and changed clothes with her as well, even putting her hair up so as not to be recognised by you. The maid had a key to this door which she took and went about unnoticed as she slipped round the guards and guests with a tray of poisoned drinks. She got the dormitory keys from a dead guard, let out the boys and you know the rest from the stable lad. Quite clever really.'

'What about these?' and the General grabbed handfuls of material from its lair.

'She made clothes that would make the prisoners look like stable lads. Macus has already told you that he thought she had rounded up the grooms.'

'But she's a savage Meric, a stupid savage, how would a stupid savage know how to do all of that?'

'A good head and a good heart are always a formidable combination. But when you add to that the knowledge of a clan woman then you have something extraordinarily unique.'

'What are you talking about man?' seethed the General.

'I suspect she had planned this for months Domitrius. She is a clan girl, not a savage girl and she's a very clever woman, not stupid at all. She had you fooled and the maid fooled. She has been trained from a young age to recognise plants. She has been taught to sew and paint using earth's apothecary. They live by the land. They know the soil and every fibre in it. They feel its beating heart and how it breathes.'

'How do you know all of this Meric?' the General's eyes narrowed.

'I just know. I recognised the style of paintings and the type of flowers that she chose. She probably doesn't even realise that she's killed more than half the palace. They kill carnivores that attack their livestock and vermin that spread diseases, they don't have the need to kill people. But there are many types of plants out there and they need to know which are poisonous and which are not.'

'I gave her everything Meric, everything she wanted, she only had to ask.'

'Except her freedom. The two most important things in her life are her freedom and her clan. You took them both Domitrius.'

But Corbulo had switched off and was thinking about Skyrah. How could he hate her? There was something so very special about her. Of course she was beautiful; she radiated charm and was exceptionally sophisticated for a savage. She excited him. And she was clever, so very clever and that excited him even more. She had brought a whole palace to its knees and killed so many people; men and women, guards and soldiers, servants and maids. She even killed the Teacher and the Emperor. How very devious and cunning. He liked that. He imagined her smile and that softened him. He caressed his bruised knuckles and widened them as if holding her close to him. He could still smell her, and she smelt so divine. He imagined her lips forming into a kiss. He closed his eyes and remembered their last dance. He began to sway with the imaginary music in his head.

'You must rest now Domitrius, it's been a very tiring day and you are still unwell,' urged the physician bringing the General out of his moment. 'Tomorrow we have to deal with the Emperor's assets and make arrangements for the funeral.'

But the General was planning how to get Skyrah back, and to do that he would have to get rid of those clan scum once and for all.

29

There were many stories shared that night; spectacular tales of bravery and courage but mostly despicable tales of depravity and despair. Everyone now hoped that Skyrah's concoctions were strong enough to fatally poison the guards, all the palace officials, but especially the Emperor and the General. She felt a pang of sadness for Roma though. If she was dead, she hadn't meant to do that; for she had no way of knowing the levels of toxins she was administering. But the boys were her main concern now though and she shared out the cakes that she still had on her person, to be sure they had a good night's sleep.

'Do you ever remember falling asleep?' Lyall remembered Lord Tanner saying. 'You never do because the night air is mysterious like that. It descends on you like a heavy shroud, its long black fingers slowly concealing everything in its path. Mist and darkness hover like a hideous veil, bewitching its prey and stripping it bare of energy and life.' He would dramatize his voice and curl his tongue around every word. 'Sneaking up and sucking the life from the victim who is unaware and unprepared. It's impossible to fight back the aroma and stifling effects of dusk and nightfall. Leaves shake and whisper to each other as the cold night air descends. Branches creak and crane and twigs seem to snap unprovoked.' Wild searching eyes added to the terrifying rendition. 'Who knows what goings on occur under this engulfing spell, who knows what tricks are played and acted out when the eyelids drop so heavily over tired eyes. Who knows what demons come out to play under the blanket of the night?' The voice in his tired head trailed off as Lyall fell asleep and began to dream of Canagan, the King of Durundal.

'Son, you have shown such strength and such courage, you took it upon yourself to destroy the enemy and in so doing have secured the future of Durundal and the safety of the Seal of Kings. And to you brave soldiers of the realm, I thank you from the bottom of my heart for your allegiance and bravery. My son, it is time you took the crown and led these people into a safe future. I hereby renounce my claim to the throne and proclaim you, Lyall, king of Durundal.'

Lyall kissed his father's hand and stood by the dead General. He picked up the discarded war flag of the deposed Ataxatan army and broke the standard in two across his thigh. The raven embroidered white silk totem, now stained with the blood of a thousand men was unceremoniously discarded on top of the deceased General's body. He then drew out his sword and shredded the bloodied material into several pieces before he delivered his message to his people. 'This is the end of the Emperor's rule, this is the end of the

General's domination, and this is the end of fear and retribution. No longer will our clans, tribes and villages be persecuted; no longer will our people live their lives in terror.'

'Hear, hear! Hear, hear!' Came the collective response and he found himself lifting his eyes to a brand new day and the welcome sound of a dawn chorus.

A mist settled round the dense forest and weaved its way round the massive oaks. The low rays of the sun exposed freshly spun cobwebs glistening with dew and the ground was covered in patches of nature's jewels. In the distance a few twigs snapped, some leaves rustled but the horses were settled, so he lay back with hands behind his head and allowed himself time to breathe.

Skyrah had woken earlier to find some birds eggs for breakfast. The remains of the chargrilled pit were still smouldering contently. She liked to wrap wood sorrel around her eggs before they were lowered into the pit so she went in search of some. No one was up; even the earth was still and sleepy. The fingers of the day were just beginning to stretch out and creak. The sun was feeding life back into the veins of the soil. But she needed to freshen up first, before the boys woke up and disturbed her moment of tranquillity and peace.

The cool water felt so good against her naked skin. It had been such a long time since she had lay in the calm ripples of a gentle flowing stream and felt that sense of floating and total abandonment. She waded in slowly, and carefully gripped the slimy base with her toes and felt the silt ooze between them; she giggled with the thrill. A few small fish were brave enough to nibble her submerged feet and she gasped with the surprise. She splashed herself gently and washed her face; the grime and sweat disappeared with each shower and then she lay down in the water and let it spill over her entire body. She stayed there, experiencing the magical moment as the trees loomed over her and in the distance she saw the snow tipped mountains. Even in the summer they were covered in a white sheen. How did that happen she wondered? A flock of birds gracefully flew overhead. She stood up to embrace the morning and held her arms out wide. She held her gaze to the morning sky, squeezed the excess water from her hair and thanked her totem for bringing her good fortune and keeping her safe. She thought she was alone. But someone was watching.

Namir had got up even earlier to find the right path out of the forest. He had seen the mountain range in the distance and wondered if that would be a safer way home. He recognised it as the Giant's Claw and skimmed up a tree to steal a better look, because if they could get through that, he knew it would lead to home.

But he had heard a sound and camouflaged himself behind the branches. He stayed incredibly still and quiet as a cat. He felt like he was hunting again and dared not breathe. And then he saw his visitor. He looked away as she disrobed, but temptation beckoned and he watched her step into the water; a siren, a mermaid, beautiful and captivating. She was the strongest woman he had ever known, no wonder she was able to massacre a fortress, save eighteen boys, feed them all and learn to ride a horse, all in one day. She had always been a fighter he knew that. Even from his earliest memories he had known her strength and fortitude but this went beyond anything he had ever known before.

There was something different about the way she looked as well; she wasn't a young girl anymore; her waist had narrowed and her hips were more rounded. Her legs were long and toned and her hands elegantly stroked the water. She was a most desirable woman with her tall, perfectly sculpted body, her long dark hair and smooth olive complexion. Though not only did she have these physical attributes; she was also smart, strong, resourceful, and a fiercely protective female. This was a sign. He knew it was their destiny to be together as husband and wife and he knew what he had to do when they got back home.

Climbing down from the tree with the grace of a leopard, he left her cocooned in the tranquil peace and serenity. He knew she wouldn't want to be disturbed.

'I think the best way home is through the mountains,' he informed the yawning boys as he made his way back into camp.

'Isn't that a little tricky?' gasped an astonished Lyall stretching himself upright. 'I mean, we are riding horses not mountain goats.'

'I know Lyall, I know, but they won't be steep glaciers all the way through.'

'So we won't go careering down a precipice then?'

'No we won't brother,' he smiled.

'Namir is right,' said Siri rubbing his teeth with a roll of bark. 'I know these mountains well, my people have lived there for centuries.'

'But we didn't come that way with the General,' said Zeno with a yawn.

'That's because some paths are very narrow with steep inclines, treacherous and in some parts impassable for a wagon and a heavy load, but a horse can do it, even if we have to get off and lead them.'

'Can you lead the way?' asked an anxious Rufus, hardly believing that his family was so close.

'Of course I can,' assured Siri. 'As soon as I am in those mountains the fragrance will take me home.'

'The rivers will take us to our clans,' said Dainn. 'They will get you home much quicker Rufus, you'll be reunited with your mother and father in a few days.'

'And you'll be reunited with Ajeya.'

Dainn and Rufus started to dance about together, linking arms and shrieking with delight. To be this close to home had been a long time coming. Zeno and Wyn joined them.

'I think we should pack up camp as soon as possible, clear everything away; tracks, debris, anything that suggests we were here,' said Ronu earnestly.

'Not before breakfast,' said Skyrah, coming into the conversation. 'I have found these eggs, it would be a shame to waste them.'

'Of course Skyrah, we will have time,' said Namir. 'I'll give you a hand.'.

'Let's take the horses down to the stream while Skyrah and Namir prepare breakfast,' suggested Lyall. 'They will need a drink before we start and we don't know how long the journey will take us.'

30

The next morning the General was woken from his slumber by Meric pulling back the bedchamber curtains. 'Good morning Domitrius and how are we today?'

'Well I don't know about you but I'm feeling terrible.' He tried to prize his eyes open as the bright morning sunlight made the room a landscape of dancing shadows. He sat up and blinked away the blur of sleep. His head ached, his body screamed, and his mouth was so very dry.

'I have made you a herbal concoction Domitrius, it will help to rehydrate you.'

Domitrius looked at the physician with a hint of hesitation; he was a little wary about taking herbal remedies in the wake of the most recent disaster.

'Come now Domitrius, please don't hurt my feelings by airing the guise of mistrust.'

Domitrius stretched out his arms and legs, pushing past the sharp pain still lingering in his gut. He took the offering and thanked his friend. 'I am still perplexed as to why you know so much about the savages Meric.' He smacked his lips with the refreshing cordial relieving his parched mouth.

'Clan, Domitrius, not savages.'

'All right, clan then.'

'I was a pilgrim once and lost my way. I was alone, cold and hungry. A clan tribe took me in and gave me shelter. They also opened my eyes to the kingdom out there.'

'And what kingdom is that Meric?'

'Well what I told you yesterday; that the earth is a living breathing organism full of life giving nectar. The clan taught me that, and I'm the man I am today because of them.'

The General looked at him witheringly. 'Hmmm,' he eventually said and knocked back the potion.

'We have a big day today Domitrius, we must lay the Emperor to rest.' Meric was keen to move on as he could see the air of contempt in the General's eyes. 'The soldiers are out there stacking the pyre and I have sent word round the town and villages that the funeral is at six o clock this evening; the same time as his death last night. So come, we must prepare as there is still so much to do.'

The arena would take the funeral pyre, a configuration using thick stakes of oak, beech and ash; stacked together to form a raised platform. It was now the centre stage for his final curtain; a theatre that had witnessed the final moments for many a boy, and now it was the Emperor's turn. Though in an ironical twist of fate he was the one killed by a savage and an audience would be seated to witness his departure.

The grounds were lined with a litter of people; the ones that had survived the poisoning, the ones that felt compelled to pay their final respects because the kind physician had asked them to.

The stable boys turned up, but only because their mothers had told them to.

'That General will haul all of us up into one of those wagons if you don't go.'

'We don't want to give him any reason to vent his wrath.'

'You still need a job son, those horses will still need looking after.'

The stable lads only went to see him go up in flames, they didn't much like the way he had treated boys in all the years they had known him. Even his own son had been sent to a hostile land that was full of ogres and undesirables.

'What a fitting end for the monster of all monsters,' Macus thought as he took his place at the back. 'I would love to personally thank that beautiful girl. Perhaps she could do the same to the General one day.'

Soldiers positioned two oil drenched burning stakes at either end of the pyre with the Emperor's flag and coat of arms displayed behind it. The sky cast a dull backdrop as the audience faced the heavy overhang of the arena; a cruel place that witnessed such despicable acts of death, cruelty and misery. Many thought that the whole place should be torched now.

Suddenly a lone trumpet sounded and the audience shook away their private thoughts and every head turned to see the procession coming through. A wide bier was being carried by the General, the physician and six soldiers. A silence descended broken only by the slow scuffling of leather soles.

None of the people wept, it was evident most were only there because they were required to; even the atmosphere was chilled on this muggy day. As the bier passed the audience, they craned to see the body. He looked like he was sleeping, draped in his royal colours and robes; it looked like a bed was passing through.

The Emperor's body was lifted onto the pyre and his banners were laid on top of him. All the soldiers exited in a curve round the sides and took their place on the seats. Only the General and the physician were left to ignite the pyre. They each took a burning stake and jabbed at the mound as they walked around feeding it with the oil and flames. They stopped at the port and starboard and lanced their stakes into the belly of the beast. The pyre immediately sucked them in and the flames began to grow. The shoots got higher, gaining more strength and momentum as the fuel propelled them. It looked like his poisonous pit of snakes had come alive and were slithering and weaving around him. The wood cracked in many places and splinters were spat out to the crowd. Everyone recoiled in disgust; no one wanted to be tarnished with his ashes. The smoke collected in the roof of the arena and settled there like a heavy raincloud about to burst at any moment. And as the wood disintegrated and the body was consumed, the fire eventually died down and all that was left was a simmering pile of embers.

The crowd dispersed quickly and quietly, the soldiers put away the chairs and the physician found the General inside the ballroom.

He poured them both a drink. 'To the Emperor.'

'May he find peace wherever he is,' toasted Meric in return.

'May we all find what we are looking for my friend.' And the General raised his glass again.

'Well, I have something that may go half way to provide that for you,' began Meric. 'The Emperor was keen for me to give this to you. I received it just before he died.'

The General looked at him with raised eyebrows, eager to see what he had been bequeathed.

Meric first of all handed him the red lacquered box. Domitrius carefully inspected it, looked at it from all angles and stroked the exquisite craftsmanship. Only when he had thoroughly investigated the size and shape did he release the gold clasp that secured the lid. The inside was polished smooth and gleamed at him. It shielded a roll of parchment sealed with wax and tied with a silk cord. He took it out and looked around, he was unsure whether to read it in Meric's presence or leave it till later, but decided it would be best to have a witness. He quickly pulled apart the knot and broke the seal, spreading the scroll open. It was a proclamation by the Emperor that was signed on the very day that he had safely delivered to him the Seal of Kings. He scanned it quickly and looked shocked. He scanned it again and cast a thoughtful expression. A more thorough read made him smile. He put down the parchment, took his ceremonial coat off and walked over to the double doors. He looked down to the arena and laughed to himself. He breathed in a lungful of fresh air and let it out with a joyous sigh. He then began to dance with an imaginary partner all around the ballroom, completely oblivious to Meric's gaze. Meric took the parchment and read it out loud.

'On this day of November in the twenty fifth year of my reign; I, Emperor Gnaeus III of Ataxata make provisions for my Will and Final Testament. In the event of my death, my loyal servant and honourable companion; General Domitrius Corbulo will become the new Emperor of Ataxata. He will also take the titles of Governor of the province of Ataxata, Supreme Commander of the Colonies, Lord Protector of the Ataxatan Empire, Soldier of the Realm and Master of the Ataxatan Army. I bequeath everything that goes with the title of Emperor including all my personal wealth in properties and estates, my belongings and antiquities. My only son and heir, Cornelius Gnaues 1V, has renounced his claim to the throne by dishonouring me and remains in exile. Therefore with no other living dependent, I give everything to my General. This Will is made in my own hand. I am of sound mind and body and this is my final request.'

The physician looked shocked. 'Many congratulations General, I am your humble servant.'

Domitrius stopped his dance and swivelled round to face him. 'I am not a mere General Meric, I am an Emperor in waiting now and you are my witness. Gnaeus gave his instructions and you served the proclamation with your own hand so you will address me as such.'

'Yes my lord, apologies my lord.' And he bowed very low. 'But you must be sworn in to make it legal, otherwise it's not binding.' The General was taken aback. He was not expecting that. He perused a while and then a snigger escaped his lips.

'Who's going to swear me in Meric, look about you, who is left, who can do it?' He paced around the room, laughing at the preposterous idea. He then snatched the paper from Meric. 'As far as I can see, this proclamation and you as my witness are all that I need to make it binding.'

'The proclamation has to be circulated my lord, in case of an uprising or a challenger later on. You don't want to be seen to have not followed procedure and protocol.' Meric backed away and averted his eyes; he could see the General losing what little patience he had.

Domitrius marched about with the paper flapping wildly behind him; grumbling and complaining, muttering and blaspheming from his puffed up red face. 'Procedure, protocol. Who's going to challenge me then Meric? That half breed son of his? The one we had to send away because he wasn't man enough to face his duties. Couldn't witness any torture while we all searched for miles and miles and turned everything over to secure his future.'

Meric raised an eyebrow which didn't go unnoticed.

'Goodness knows where he is now anyway. Idling his time away writing poetry or playing a worn out psaltery is my guess.'

'That's as may be, but you can't leave anything to chance.'

'All right, all right, have it your way. It will be arranged by my captains. Besides, I have some important things to do before I can finally celebrate my good fortune.'

'Errm, my lord, there is one more thing.'

'What now Meric, I really am tiring of you.'

'It's this.' And he gave him the red pouch.

Domitrius opened it carefully and slowly. The sun caught its edge as he pulled it from its protective casing. He held the disc up to the sunlight and then kissed it. He remembered the day he took it from the king in Castle Dru and he knew that one day it would yield the greatest prize. A sinister grin spread across his face as he placed the Seal of Kings over his neck and took ownership. 'This Meric, will never leave my body and unlike Gnaeus, this will stay round my neck and I will sever the head from anyone who tries to take it from me.'

'That is a good idea my lord, keep it safe.'

'Now I have everything; the land, the palace, the

people, the guards, the soldiers. Now I will take even more land and make this empire the greatest empire of all. And it will be mine, all of it, every last corner and every last grain.' And then he looked the physician straight in the eye. 'And I will get my Skyrah back and wipe the rest of those grubby little savages off the face of the kingdoms.'

The physician recoiled in horror.

The General returned to look out of the window.

'Your work is done here now physician. Please leave me. I have a battle to prepare and soldiers to enlist. I bid you good day.'

Meric left, his work was indeed done. He was terrified for the clans of the lands, he feared for their safety. Everyone's lives were at risk now. He bade farewell and left the palace for the very last time.

31

The horses shook noisily and snorted out the last remnants of darkness. After a much welcomed drink from the stream and a snatched mouthful of watery grass they too were ready for the next stage of their journey. A hearty breakfast was enjoyed by all and the debris was buried and brushed over with fresh earth. With full bellies and a goal in sight, the clans returned to their mounts.

'Good morning Meteor, I hope you slept well,' Skyrah kissed the stallion's soft velvet muzzle. He nodded his head up and down to acknowledge her gentle touch. 'Just a couple more days then you can have a lovely long rest,' she stroked the protective hair inside his ears. The horse swished his tail in eager anticipation. 'You understand everything I say don't you?' Meteor responded with a nicker and she hugged the long muscular neck.

She watched as Namir checked his mount's legs by running a firm hand down the full length of each limb. He then checked for any hard debris lodged within the hooves and picked away at the stubborn flints that would cause injury. With that process done he gave a pat to his steed and began to saddle up. She noticed how each boy in turn did exactly the same thing; so not wishing to be different, she checked Meteor's legs and hooves.

'We head north to the mountain,' signalled Namir as he mounted his ride. 'Just follow the summit.'

A cacophony of heaving bodies pushing up from lengthened stirrups and weighted down horses finding their balance preceded the rattle of movement.

The second stage was under way but it seemed to take forever to work their way through the enormous dense forest. It was a vast maze of narrow tracks and passageways hindered by corridors of bracken and brambles.

'I didn't think it would be this difficult getting through,' shouted out Lyall pulling a hogweed from his boot.

'Just keep your eyes on the summit,' urged Namir.

'But it keeps disappearing behind the trees,' yelled out Rufus craning from his front position.

'Follow the largest birds then,' suggested Siri. 'They circle high in the sky.'

'That's my totem,' the youngster shouted back. 'The falcon, she looks after me.'

'Then look out for her little one and she will lead you home.'

The train pushed through the matted undergrowth brushing away the thicket with purposeful steps. Every now and then a small creature skittered away as the procession disturbed them. The horses spooked. A wood pigeon or grouse was panicked into flight, that made them sidle. For extraordinarily strong animals, they were extremely skittish, but the boys were getting edgy as well. The glade was becoming all too familiar at every turn. Trees, boulders, bushes, they all bore the same resemblance and the clan started to panic. The horses felt their fear, they responded to the twitchy nervous muscles from their pillions, all except Meteor. His rider had every trust in their leader. She didn't once doubt Namir or his navigational skills and her horse never flinched or felt unsettled, he carried his warrior like a war horse; she patted him, encouraged him, guided him and soothed him and they both felt at ease. Finally the trees and vegetation began to thin out and the welcome sight of the wide plains opened up before them.

'At last,' cried out Lyall. 'I thought we were going round in circles.'

'What! With me at the helm brother?' called back Namir. 'Never!'

The clans howled with laughter, but most of it was relief. Bagwa had spent a good deal of the journey telling anyone who would listen of hunters getting lost and going round in circles. 'When you are lost, the tendency is to go right all the time,' he had said.

But now, with home in sight they found extra vigour and the horses responded to the sight of the sweeping wilderness by charging into a gallop.

'Now we can fly.' Skyrah's voice echoed as it was caught in the flying tendrils of Meteor's mane and

271

she looked back to see the other boys leaping with great strides into the thrill of the ride.

As the clans surged forward, the rattle of hooves echoed in the canyon, eating up the ground and spraying out debris of grit and sand. It was a good surface for the horses and gave them a welcome stretch, but this would be the last time they could gallop for a while; the ground would now become treacherous and uneven. It would have been impassable for the General and his entourage of wagons, but the boys could do it easily with their horses and light load.

The boys steadied to a trot and at the entrance of the pass they halted.

'Look!' Cried out Rufus with excitement.

They all looked up to see a peregrine falcon swooping down from the top of the mountain range and hovered in the air, looking for prey.

'The lord of the skies,' he acknowledged with admiration.

'The horses have uncovered their lunch I do believe,' said Norg from the back.

'Yes lots of small rodents for them to gorge on,' replied Ronu. 'The best hunters in the skies they are.'

'This is why it's called the Giant's Claw, just look at the size of those talons,' called out Siri.

'I think it's because of the Mountain Lions that once lived here,' replied Namir turning round on his mount.

'No mountain lions have ever lived here, it's always been falcons and eagles.'

'Not so Siri' responded Namir. 'My father has always told us the story of a traveller who was chased into our settlement by a mountain lion.'

'Really?' cried out Rufus who was now more impressed with the story of the lion.

'They don't live here anymore though,' intercepted Dainn.

'Of course they don't, that was the last one. Just eagles and falcons live here now,' smiled Namir, appeasing Dainn's concern.

'Tell us the story then,' urged everyone.

So as the horses jostled for position, Namir entertained the boys with the story of the traveller who encountered a ferocious mountain lion and lived to tell the tale.

The posse continued their journey through the canyon and witnessed the raw beauty unfolding before them. Miles upon miles of rolling hills and wooded river valleys scattered themselves along the fringe of the mountain and allowed respite and cover for small rodents and birds. Natural caves and waterfalls had been gouged out of the mountain with centuries of battling weather providing feeding grounds and homes for larger mammals. Their route into the gorge exposed three rivers; each one was fed from rainwater that forged down the rocky glacier and kept the rivers clear and flowing. One river would take the Hill Fort Tribe home, the other would lead the Clan of the Giant's Claw back to safety and the longest route of the outside river would take Namir and his people back to the Clan of the Mountain Lion.

The daylight hours had brought an abundance of sunshine with a crisp air and a slight breeze which kept the temperature calm and pleasant. Soft winds cradled worn faces and as they stood in the estuary that divided the river source, the coolness of the water was a much needed break that refreshed the boys and the horses.

'This is where we split up men,' Namir stood tall in his saddle. 'This is where this particular journey ends.'

'I know the way from here,' said Siri. 'I can guide Dainn and his clan back to the Hill Fort.'

'Thanks Siri, safety in numbers,' nodded Dainn.

'Thank you for saving us Skyrah, I will never forget you.' Rufus was humbled.

'That's from all of us,' declared Dainn. 'We are all indebted to you brave lady.'

'To Skyrah.' The spasm echoed round the crest of the mountain and alerted the birds of prey into flight again.

She beamed at the accolade.

'We all know what we must do, we get the youngsters back to their mothers and we get an army,' began Namir. 'We don't know what size legion the General will be left with, but we must be prepared for an onslaught.'

'We will send out messengers to collect information and inform all of you,' said Lyall with strength.

Skyrah felt a chill run down her spine.

'We wait to hear from you. All of you, may the gods protect you,' said Dainn. 'Let's get these young ones back home and gather our supporters.'

'We shall meet again, and when we do, vengeance will be ours,' triumphed Siri.

All arms were raised in a triumphant salute and the boys parted. Namir's words stayed with them as they ventured back to their homesteads. 'Go and find your armies men, take care as you go and when we meet again, we will get our revenge for all those stolen boys.'

The clan of the Mountain Lion started upstream along the watercourse that flowed near a ravine, then they began ascending the mountain along a tributary creek forcing their way through heavy underbrush. They stopped by a steep rock wall over which the creek spilled in a cascading spray. The wall presented a barrier that ran parallel to the gorge. They followed the course of the gorge and began to follow it upstream again. They began their ascent up the challenging stocky glacier. Home wasn't far away now, but the only way was up and over the rocky edged perimeter; an arduous course which required the skill of the horsemen to guide their animals round to the other side in safety. As they edged forwards and round to the other side, an expanse of land unfolded and the party remained speechless as they absorbed the spectacular vision.

Pine and spruce dominated the higher elevation

and was home to a range of squirrels, birds and pine martens. The boys embraced the smell of freedom as the wind picked up and the trees thinned out to a familiar sight. Miles upon miles of grassy foothills were exposed where the trees clustered in sheltered valleys. An expanse of land whose far end terminated in the grey brown rock of the mountain, sparsely covered with clinging growth, soared into the mouth of a cave. This was easily recognisable, this was Lyall's cave.

The stream they were following gushed into a river and beyond that was their camp. A falcon had followed them, like a personal guard heralding their return with a haunting cry and saluting her thanks for uncovering a sleepy vole.

Specks of light, born from dusk, bounced off the rock formations and lit the way for the weary troops; while a blanket of dazzling dew remained sentinel and highlighted the colours of their clan's peace and tranquillity.

At last they were home. They looked at each other. They were safe. And for the last time on that particular journey, the ten jubilant lads galloped home for a clan's welcoming.

'I can smell the dinner cooking,' cried out Ronu. 'I hope they've got enough for all of us.'

'The odour is reviving every part of me,' said Clebe galloping even faster towards the camp with Norg close on his heels.

'Come on you lot, me and Wyn will race you back,' and Lyall dug his heels in to his mount.

But as they entered the safety of their homestead a stranger was coming into the enormous dense forest. He was on a mission. He wore a grey cloak with a hood and was almost concealed amongst the vegetation. He and his horse could follow the clans; he was an expert in his field and he could seek them out. The Master had a nose that could track anything that he wanted and some of them had been a little careless in tidying up and covering their tracks. The Master got off his horse and pulled back his hood, he wanted to hear the forest talking. He pushed back his cape and touched the ground to feel their path. He closed his eyes and plied the soil between his fingers; he held a sample up to his nostrils and breathed in the aroma. 'They came this way,' he assured himself.

He brushed the ground again and carefully destroyed any evidence. He pulled his cape around him and covered his head with the hood.

'I must warn them,' said Meric. 'There is no way that the General or anyone else will hurt my friends again.'

He got back on his horse and continued the journey that would take him back to the Clan of the Mountain Lion.

32

He remembered it well. He was en route from his home in the city of Ataxata to find his vocation north of the borders and had been travelling for most of the short winter day in the freezing cold.

His decision to cut through the mountain pass had proved to be a hazardous one. The skies were clear allowing the temperatures to drop so far below freezing that his horse's breath settled about her muzzle in a delicate web of frozen lace. By mid-afternoon the mountain top was spraying small particles of such fine ice that made it seem like he was journeying through a kingdom of polished crystal; and as the sun went down the crystal glacier became treacherous.

'Easy girl, easy, just take it slow.' He remembered saying.

Up hill and down dale they went, over ridges and steep tracks. She seemed to slide most of the way and was getting skittish and fractious. A pack of howling wolves were following him but a roar from somewhere out yonder made them scatter. He crouched down low behind his filly's neck and pulled his cloak over him. She was uneasy and whinnied. Her ears rotated constantly and her nostrils flared wide with fear.

He urged her on convinced that something quite dangerous was following them. A dark shadow moved around the boulders and the crevasses, a creature that was used to this terrain and slid around with ease. They were nearly at the end of the precipice, not too far to go now and the open expanse of land could be seen.

'Come on girl, you see that, we will be safely out there soon.'

But something unsettled her and she skidded. He drove his legs in to her sides as he tried to steady her. He was nearly unseated as she reared up and broke into a gallop that took them out of the pass and onto the plain. Faster and faster they went, thankful for the solid ground. The panting horse created some distance, but a mountain lion was in hot pursuit. With white eyes glaring and flared nostrils snorting, the filly's endurance was tested to the limit as she increased her stride. But the giant had claws which added momentum by gripping its surface and soon it was catching up.

A village loomed and they made for that, hoping that a man made civilization would deter the beast. But it didn't. It had food in sight and gained on the stricken filly. As they swung round into the camp the stampeding aroused an alarm. The frigid icicles trembled in fear and the ground shook in response. People looked out of their doors in horror, children were ushered frantically inside.

He remembered hanging on tightly, absolutely rigid and petrified. He felt the carnivore's breath as it gashed his leg. He screamed in agony. The lion wouldn't yield and leapt again, this time it gripped onto the hind quarters of the exhausted horse. Savage claws ripped into the muscular flesh and the filly kicked out with her rear legs. Blood oozed from the wounds and filtered into the ground. The smell intensified the grip of the lion and it sank its hungry incisors into the mature flanks. The horse screeched in pain and reared up. The ice couldn't support her and she fell. He remembered being thrown and recoiling in terror as the beast wrapped its gigantic jaws around her throat. He couldn't do anything. The wound to his right leg was so deep that it rendered him helpless. Both his arms were gashed from the fall and he thought his right wrist might be fractured. The petrified animal wouldn't give up and fought for her life with the little energy she had left against the unrelenting hunter.

But instead of hiding away, the villagers came out. The beast was too engrossed with its primal instinct to notice them. They hammered it with spears, knives, catapults, sling shots and anything else that they could find. They did this again and again until the monster released its grip and let go of the horse. One brave soul took close aim with a spear, lunged towards its heart and secured its fate. The lion slumped onto its frozen grave, dead.

The distressed horse was on the ground, exhausted and wounded. She tried to get up but couldn't. Everyone was out of their huts, anxious to find out what had disrupted the onset of eventide. Even the pack dogs had left their warm hearths and now barking and racing around charging up to the deceased lion and retreating just as quickly. The quiet time of day was now in chaos as never before had anything like this been witnessed. A bustle of anxious faces expressed their concerns.

'Coming into civilisation like that is unheard of, they never leave the mountains. The gods must have sent it to test us.'

'Our clan totem has come to seek out the weak and infirm.'

'No, it sacrificed its life for us to give added strength for the winter months.'

'The horse knew this was her salvation.'

'Comrades, comrades,' came a voice of authority moving everyone aside. 'Let us have some room to give this poor lad and his horse some attention.'

'Yes, they are safe now,' another voice spoke.

'Come men, let's move the carcass and can someone please control those dogs.'

'My horse please someone tend to my horse!'

'Your horse will be fine, we will help her,' came the gentle voice of a young woman.

Meric watched as four or five clan females began administering potions and soothing the poor filly. The frightened horse became aware that they were trying to save her and stopped yanking her head up and flashing the whites of her terrified eyes. Horizontal ears now pricked up. Flared nostrils calmed. She lay her head calmly and let the women do their work.

He heard a voice amongst the chaos and lifted

his eyes.

'You see, your horse is in good hands. Please come with me.'

That was fourteen years ago when he was a lad of twenty. He remembered a beautiful woman taking him into a hut and dressing his wounds. She bathed his leg with a piece of soft rabbit skin then applied a pulp of iris root, spinach and radish leaves to the deepest incisions. Strips of willow bark and cherry wood were wrapped in a secure bandage around his fractured wrist. Another concoction of clover and alder bark was simmering on the hearth. She turned away to mix the brew as he shyly exchanged his ripped trousers for a simple tunic top. The poultice was left in place to aid recovery on his arms and legs and his feet were bound with warm sheepskin boots to protect them. Finally she fitted him with the fleece from a boar and gave the soothing potion to relax him.

'You have been through a terrible ordeal,' she said kindly, putting his cloak back over him.

'I have never been so frightened,' he said, grateful for her compassion.

'Your horse will be all right,' she continued, her brilliant blue eyes shining with affection.

'Yes I will pray for her. He sipped slowly from the drink she had made him and never took his eyes off her as she busied herself sorting out her pharmacopeia and humming a beautiful tune that rested him.

'The wild wind blows through valleys my love,
The wild wind blows through the trees,
The wild wind blows o'er the rivers my love,
But will n'er get closer to thee.
The wild rain storms through the valleys my
love,
The wild rain storms through the trees,
The wild rain storms o'er the rivers my love,
But none will get closer to thee.'

She was enchanting with a natural shyness oppressed beneath an exterior that was both charming and intelligent. She had a graceful long neck that supported a defined jaw. Her lips were full under a straight narrow nose, high cheekbones, and huge whirlpool eyes were framed by deep dark eyebrows that matched her tumbling waves of ebony hair.

'Skyrah, stay with the young man and make another mixture of iris root and spinach for him, I will take this solution to his horse.'

The toddler did as she was told and sat with Meric, chewing the root between her teeth and then spitting it out into the shredded spinach and mashed radish. The mother soon came back to tell him that the horse had been taken to a stable to rest and the same poultice was healing her wounds. 'She has had a shock but she will be fine in a few days.'

A man joined them with a very young boy, the same man who had fatally speared the beast. The youngster went and sat with Skyrah and shredded the leaves in the same way.

'Good evening young man, my name is Laith and I trust you are feeling better.'

'I am sir, thank you sir, my name is Meric and I am forever in your debt. I fear I can never repay you for saving my life and for all your kindness.'

'We always help those in need where we can.'

'Thank you, for I would have died out there had it not been for you and your brave people.'

'You are welcome young man, but tell me, what brings you to these parts in such treacherous weather?'

'I am on a journey kind sir, to seek my vocation in life.'

'Well you won't be going anywhere soon, I suggest you stay here with us until the spring, when you and your horse are fully recovered and the weather is warmer.'

'I don't want to be any bother.'

'You will be no bother, we welcome you to our village. Chay will look after you.' He looked at the little girl making the medicine. 'With the help of her daughter Skyrah.' Then the boy looked at his father. He didn't have to say anything, his question was in the eyes. 'And maybe Namir can stay for a little while.'

'Of course, I would be delighted to have them sit here with me, they seem delightful.'

'Only for a little while Namir, it's your bedtime soon and Meric needs his rest.'

The two children smiled at each other.

'But we will celebrate tomorrow and I hope you

will join us. Only if you are able to of course, I realise that your wounds are deep.' He looked at the gooey poultice covering Meric's swollen leg.

'Of course, what are we celebrating?'

'The gods have sent the clan totem to us and we must give thanks.'

'The mountain lion is your totem?'

'Yes we are the Clan of the Mountain Lion and we see this as a sign that our clan will continue to grow and you have brought it to us.'

'I was beginning to think the short cut through the mountains was a mistake, but maybe it wasn't.'

'No it certainly wasn't. You will always bear the marks of this journey, and the meat from the mountain lion will give us strength to see out this harshest of winters. But most importantly its spirit will give us the power to survive and the gods will look down on us favourably.'

'The hide will make many warm clothes,' added Chay.

'Those teeth will make good weapons,' said young Namir.

'Its claws will make fine jewellery,' said Skyrah.

Laith smiled. 'I will see you again tomorrow, until then get some rest; and Namir, I want you back before dark.'

The next day the mountain lion was skilfully butchered with the liver saved for Laith and Meric. Just like the stag ritual, this was considered the most important part of the animal and shared between the man who killed it and his chosen aide. The blood was collected carefully and distributed around the outside the circle of stones, to keep its strength in and the bad omens out. The heart was sacred and buried at the centre of the standing stones. It beat out loud to the gods while the spirit of the lion defended the homeland. For this was the Clan of the Mountain Lion and this was their ceremony of honour; a whole community coming together to pay their respects to the sacrificed beast.

At the celebration, great praise was lavished on the gods for sending them the lion. Tributes were given to the stranger and to the leader that would forge a lifelong connection. The final thanks were bestowed on the spirits for bringing Meric and his horse safely to the clan.

He stayed with Chay and Skyrah till late in the spring. He had recurring nightmares and had to be treated with kindness and sympathy. For weeks his wounds needed constant changing and he needed extra warmth in the torturous winter months. Chay was the gentlest woman he had ever met. She had lost her husband to a fatal disease when Skyrah was still small and blamed herself for not being able to successfully treat him. So she made it her duty to become even more proficient and knowledgeable with the fruits of the earth, and she honoured that vow. Every spring and summer she would search and cut down, mash and boil, ferment and harvest; and then test to see the effects of a variety of plants, roots, leaves and bark.

With his stay she became close to Meric and thought that he had been sent to her by the gods to demonstrate her unrivalled skills.

He remembered that memorable day going out with Chay and Skyrah to look for nature's apothecary. With spring came the new shoots and an array of healthy nutritional vegetables, herbs and plants; and of these, Chay knew them all. She knew the medicinal content of every single one. She could identify those which could heal wounds and those which could cure ailments and those which could kill pain. She knew the poisonous ones, the ones that could cause a mere tummy upset and those that could be fatal, and it was time for Skyrah to learn about nature's harvest from her mother.

'Meric, would you like to come out with me and Skyrah, we are going to identify some plants today.'

'I would love to.'

'I am going to give her a little tuition in herbal medicine. It's part of a clan girl's life journey.'

'It would do me good to learn as well. Thank you for inviting me.'

Chay arched a smile. 'Come on then little one, let's show Meric how much you know.' Her mother's gentle command encouraged the youngster to follow.

The three of them walked alongside the river edge and into the burgeoning meadow with the older woman pointing out and explaining the properties of the new life she found along the way. 'I want to find lots of plants today, especially spinach and radishes because they calm inflammations and viral infections, we have run low on these so I need Skyrah to seek them out for me.'

Nimble fingers and observant eyes sought out the hidden apothecary amongst the vegetation; naked to the ordinary man, but a life support to the ardent explorer, and as if conjured up by magic a blanket of herbaceous flowers waved their vibrant blooms urgently in the south westerly breeze.

'Which plants heal?' asked the young girl running ahead, hungry for knowledge and new skills.

'Yarrow is the most valuable healing remedy and we need a lot of those, so look for its feathery leaves, strong stems and broad white flower heads.'

'What is this one?' the young voice asked again, foraging amongst the stalks and colours.

'That's oregano, it's a very good aid against poisonous insect bites - and this one is thyme which is excellent for tummy aches.'

The barrage of questions continued from the junior chemist. 'What about these pretty yellow flowers?'

'Those are marigolds and can heal burns and this is mint and is very good for digestion.' She saw Meric whispering to Skyrah and her heart warmed at her daughter's smiling face.

'I know these ones,' called out the little girl, picking at something. 'Meric calls it teeth of the mountain lion, and look what I can do.' She secured a stalk in her hand and scattered the tiny parachutes with her breath.

Chay laughed at the name Meric gave them.

'You are extremely clever, and those lion's teeth are very powerful plants,' said her mother noticing the similarity between the shape of the dandelion leaves and the teeth of the mountain lion. She then offered a popular culinary delight. 'Catch these plants early when they have yellow blooms Meric, and you can make very good tea with them.'

He watched as Chay picked a dandelion and blew on her own white gossamer ball. He saw the air born seeds being whisked away on the breeze and disappear over the meadow to a new pasture, a new settlement, a new life.

It was a sign. It was time for him to go. He knew his vocation in life now. He knew his calling. He wanted to be a healer.

33

The clan were out preparing dinner when the first sightings were made.

'Chay, come quick, it's Skyrah, she has returned to us.'

'Thank the gods, thank the gods.' And she crumpled on to her knees to give thanks to her hare totem. She wailed into the sky and wept tears of joy.

And gradually as each mother saw her child, when each wife recognised her husband, and lovers felt the cord tighten; they fell on their knees and gave thanks to the great gods in the sky. The fathers and siblings followed the howls and when they saw the reason for the excited screams, ran towards the galloping racers. There were cheers and jubilations amongst all, and a frail Laith was assisted by an even frailer Zoraster as he staggered forward to greet his sons.

The arrivals skidded to a halt, jumped down from their mounts and rushed over to their waiting loved ones.

Skyrah saw her weeping mother and her heart melted; she leaned forward and whispered into the soft twitching ear of her stallion. 'Wait here for me Meteor, I have to go and see someone very special.' With that assurance she jumped down from her horse and ran into the loving embrace.

Laith stood proud with an arm round his two sons. Husbands and wives embraced. The younger boys were scooped up by worried fathers and carried aloft on broad shoulders with frantic mothers running behind them hardly daring to believe that this magical day had come.

'Praise be to the gods,' hailed Laith. 'And praise be to our clan totem, the powerful mountain lion who has protected our boys.' He released his embrace and stood before both of them, a hand was placed on each shoulder and he studied their faces.

Namir looked tearful. 'Oh father, how glad we are to see you.'

'You looked out for each other boys?'

'Yes we did father,' said an equally emotional Lyall. 'We all looked out for each other, all the boys did.'

'And Skyrah, is she safe, is she well, is she all right?'

'Father, Skyrah is without doubt the strongest, bravest woman I have ever known,' exclaimed Namir and looked her way.

'We wouldn't be here now without her,' said Lyall. 'We all owe our lives to her.'

Laith followed Namir's gaze towards the brave young woman still wrapped in her mother's arms and smiled before escorting his sons away. 'Come my boys, let's eat; you look half-starved to me and far too pale. Dinner is ready. The clan will eat together tonight and give thanks for your safe return.'

'Father we have to get an army, we know where the General is, he may be quite ill so we have to make haste, we don't have much time,' began Namir.

'Whoa there son, slow down, all in good time; for now I want to enjoy you being back safely with me, then we will talk of armies and revenge.'

Chay was with her daughter. 'Are you sure you are all right?'

'Yes I am fine mother, truly, I am well.'

Chay still couldn't stop stroking her hair and kissing her fingers.

'I saved the boys using the poisons that you taught me.'

'Oh Skyrah, my brave girl.'

'I don't know the full extent of their injuries, but it knocked out the guards, the soldiers; even the Emperor and the General were unconscious long enough for us to escape.'

'Laburnum and aconitum?'

'And hemlock, white snakeroot and azalea, I used them all.'

'And you always thought what a waste of time it was and wanted to go out hunting with the boys.'

'I know mother, I was wrong and you were right. That knowledge saved all of us; I can't bear to think what would have become of us otherwise.'

Chay kissed her daughter's forehead lovingly.

'You are here now and you are safe, that is all that matters. Come let's eat, you look thin and far too pale.'

Jubilant faces and chattering voices made their way to the feasting area. Parents who had never given up hope gripped on to their sons as the harrowing stories of their ordeal were described in fastidious detail. Shock after shock was revealed as the true extent of their plight was shared. Shaking heads swayed in disbelief amid voices stunned into a traumatic silence.

But the shining star and the true heroine of the entire evening was Skyrah. The one who had saved all of them with her careful planning and faked allegiance to the General and she spoke in depth about her planning. Though the real beneficiaries of her detailed discussion were the young girls of the clan; for now they would appreciate the true value of their mother's teaching and never underestimate the power of nature's harvest.

The food revived them and the full moon dripped her light on the clan people throughout the night. And as she did, the women looked up to the face of the sphere and saw the image of the hare looking back at them.

'That's my totem Lyall, can you see how brightly she shines down on us.'

'I can Skyrah, and she looks very beautiful.' He smiled fondly at her. 'And do you hear my totem in the distance welcoming us home?'

'Yes I do.' And she craned her ear to listen to the

haunting sound of the wolf as it looked up to the same moon to sing its soulful tune.

And somewhere in the distance the leopard sat camouflaged in a tree, looking down on everything, surveying its domain and planning its next move.

Skyrah went off early to settle Meteor in his new home, Namir was already there making sure the horses had hay and water and were content in their new environment.

'Sorry Namir, I should have come in earlier to help you.'

'You were busy talking to the girls,' he said kindly.

'I wanted to say goodnight to Meteor, he is such a fine animal,' and she nuzzled into his soft muzzle.

Namir stopped putting out the straw and came and stood beside her. 'Skyrah, there is something I want to ask you.'

'Of course, what is it?' she looked puzzled as he anxiously searched for the right words.

'I've been meaning to ask you for a while now,' he looked nervously to the floor. 'But the moment has never been right.'

'Oh?'

'Would you...' The words froze on his tongue. In his head he wanted to pick her up and hold her tight and ask her to marry him. And in his head she would say yes and they would fall into the fresh new straw that he had just laid and hold each other tightly all through the night. And the hare goddess in the blistering full moon would gaze down on them with love and give them her blessing. They would wake up late in the morning and surprise everyone with their news.

But conscience strangled his desire and reality took precedence. He knew that they still had unfinished business. They had a war ahead of them. They wouldn't be able to prepare for a wedding with everything else they had to do - and there was so much to do now. It was such a fraught time in the camp. So he stopped. Now wasn't the right time. He would do it after the battle. There would be lots of celebrating then. That would be a much better option. He stumbled and stammered in his panic. He had to think of something else quickly. 'Would you teach me about the plants and the flowers? I remember I used to ground them up with you when we were small, but I never knew what they were for; maybe you could show me now.'

Her voice was slightly reticent. She thought he was going to ask her something else, something that would unite them forever. 'Yes, of course I will Namir, I would be happy to.'

'That's good then, that's really good, thanks Skyrah, um, shall I take you back to your mother?' He knew he had disappointed her.

'No Namir it's all right, I will stay with Meteor for a while.' And when he had gone she buried her head into her stallion's mane, whilst outside the stable Namir chastised himself for being so weak and making an utter fool of himself.

The next morning there was much work to be done and the clan arranged a meeting in the large communal hut. They had to work fast and time was of the essence.

'I have a map here,' said Skyrah.

The boys looked at her in a stunned silence, was there no end to this girl's talents?

'I tried to show you the other day in the forest, but the fervour for freedom was too distracting,' she smiled. 'So here it is now.'

'What map is that ?' asked Lyall.

'I drew a plan of the palace with the help of my maid, it's really detailed and shows where everything is; the rooms, the passageways, the armoury and where the Seal of Kings will be.' She carefully rolled out the parchment and held her hands on two corners as the boys looked at her in disbelief with wide open eyes and even wider mouths. Namir was still chastising himself for his wasted opportunity.

'I'm sorry but I don't think you will be needing that Skyrah.'

The congregation span round to see Laith enter the room with a stranger.

'This is my dear friend, and he has come with some very interesting news for us.'

A middle aged man with a kind face under a maroon hat stepped forward and the parchment sprang back into its neat little roll.

34

The General had enlisted the help of his captains.

'I need to raise an army and I need to get one fast. I have a very important mission for everyone and I want to complete it before the cold weather sets in.' His captains listened intently. 'With Gnaeus gone and his death witnessed by so many citizens, I wish for a copy of this proclamation to be circulated around the city and its borders so everyone knows that I am now the Emperor in waiting. The proclamation has to be seen by the nobles and gentry of the lands before I can be sworn in... something about challengers and other such nonsense, but I have to follow protocol.'

'Of course my lord, consider it done.' The six captains bowed together after acknowledging Corbulo's sneering final remark.

'I also want you to enlist as many rogues and thieves as you can, give them a few shillings to tempt them for now. But say there are several bags of gold in it for them if they do a good job. Go to the ends of the kingdom captains, look down alleyways and look in caves, search in grottos and under glens to seek out the lowest life and those that would kill their own mother for a piece of silver.'

'Of course my liege,' came the response.

'I will get the remaining soldiers to collect all armouries from the basement and give it an overhaul, plus I will personally visit the farmers to replace the stolen horses.'

'If that is all, we shall go at once my lord.'

They saluted their General and disappeared into the shadows.

With his men gone the General ventured down below the main living quarters into the dark vaults and into the basement that housed the armoury. He passed through ornate corridors where whispering galleries held a thousand secrets and preying portraits followed him with inquisitive eyes. Several mahogany doors and a squadron of stairs led to a winding staircase that took him deeper into the bowels of the castle.

The dripping sound of water indicated how far down he was descending and the damp chill curled round his face. He reached the side of a locked gate and a burning torch threw a dim light. He unlocked the gate with a key secured to his belt and he went into a long rectangular prison. Straight away his senses were heightened and alerted, he walked amongst the cold metal statues and felt a shiver run down his spine and recoiled as they rang out with the ghostly screams of a thousand men still trapped inside their metal skin. He could hear the thunderous roar of stampeding horses and foot soldiers full of fear charging into the depths of the unknown. The smell of alloys, wood and ivory saturated the air and seeped into the porous walls of this timeless capsule. He could even taste the spilled blood from terrified souls that would consecrate the ground forever and nurture the next crop of wheat.

He thought of all the battles that he had fought, all the soldiers that he had taken the life from, all the women who had lost a lover, all the children that had lost a father. He ran his finger along the blades of iron ore and around the gold hilts that stood bravely supporting the metal. Bows and arrows were made from the finest wood, bronze was moulded into protective headwear and shaped into thick impenetrable body armour.

He walked about the museum for a long time, playing out and reliving all the battles that he had won, witnessing the death that he had been a part of, glorifying in the depravation and loss of life. The hunger in him rose like a fury. The furore of total control ignited him and he revelled in the taste for more slaughter. He was fired up for a massacre once again. His veins pumped round nefarious blood, and glory was in his sight. This victory would give him absolute power, and now, finally, he would wipe out all that wretched vermin from civilization forever.

35

'Please Meric, tell my people what you told me.'

The physician took his maroon hat off and clutched it between his hands as he stepped forward. He bowed to Laith to acknowledge the request and smiled at Chay who had come in with them.

'My name is Meric, I am an old friend of a lot of people here,' and he looked around at the familiar faces. 'There are also two people sitting here who won't remember me, but I remember them fondly.' He looked at Namir and Skyrah. 'These two were so small when I first came here. It was Laith and Chay who looked after me, but it was a whole clan that saved my life.' He disappeared into his hat and crumpled it up nervously as he remembered. He looked up at Chay again and smiled. Laith's expression encouraged him to carry on.

'Many years ago I was a traveller who ventured through the mountains in search of my destiny. I was attacked by a mountain lion on the way and survived to tell the tale because this most honourable man took me in and this respected woman showed me my vocation,' he nodded humbly towards Laith and Chay.

They both bowed graciously to the accolade.

'See I told you it was true,' Namir nudged Lyall

Lyall as Meric continued.

'And now I stand here amongst all of you, as your humble servant, and am now able to repay that unrivalled act of kindness.'

What could it be they all wondered? A range of bewildered expressions, raised eyebrows and shrugged shoulders were exchanged amongst the audience.

'I have come from the Palace in Ataxata.'

Gasps and swivelling shocked faces expressed a renewed interest in the man standing before them.

'I am the court physician and was summoned there a few days ago.'

Wide flared eyes hungry for knowledge pierced his own.

'What I found there shocked me.'

Skyrah swallowed hard.

'Nearly the whole palace was dead or dying. Not many survived I can tell you.'

The clan leaned forward hanging on his every word and gasped. Lyall cracked a smile and pulled Skyrah towards him in a triumphant embrace.

'The Emperor is dead. The Teacher is dead. Most of the guards are dead.'

The boys stood up and cheered, the roof of the hut nearly came off with the jubilation. They were dancing and swirling Skyrah around with such vigour and excitement the leader had to step in.

'Calm down boys there is so much more. Please, let Meric finish.'

The clan sat down again and waves of mumbled

excitement rumbled along the rows.

'The General survived, he tried to put the blame on the maid at first. She was found in Skyrah's room wearing fine clothes, but stone cold dead. He ransacked the room in a fit of rage looking for you Skyrah.'

Skyrah winced and said a silent prayer for the young girl.

'But when I looked in the kitchens I recognised the poisonous apothecary used in the oatmeal and the hot water.'

Chay looked at her daughter with pride.

'We ordered the rooms to be searched and that's where we found more evidence of the plants used. I knew it had to be a clan girl. No one else has that sort of knowledge; there is not a living soul who knows so much about plants.'

Skyrah looked to her mother again and smiled.

'We burned the dead, the guards, the soldiers, the servants. We burned the Emperor.'

Cheers and applause rang through the hut and out into the camp.

'But the General has now been made Emperor in Waiting. With the Emperor's son missing; General Domitrius Corbulo has been bequeathed the title. When he is sworn in he will have control of the palace, all the estates and all the kingdoms that go with the title.'

'May the gods help us,' Jonha's chilling tone came from the back of the room.

'He also has the Seal of Kings and wears it round his neck,' continued Meric.

Lyall sat up rigid, his eyes fixed on the physician. 'What? He wears it?'

'Yes Lyall, I am afraid he does, he has sworn to wear it at all times, and I know from your father here, the despicable and murderous way it was taken.'

'He will pay with his life; I will not rest until he is dead.'

'That is why I am here Lyall, that is why I want to help all of you.'

The clan hushed as Namir instructed: 'Please go on.'

'The General is summoning an army. He is going to attack this clan first; he will take Skyrah back with him as his prisoner and massacre the rest of you. He will then take down all the clans and all the people in them; men, women, children and babes in arms. He is mad, quite mad.'

'How long have we got?' Clebe's voice was thick.

'I don't know, maybe a few weeks, a month at the most. He is still quite ill from the poisoning, so he will want to get fitter. He needs to recruit a new army as the rest are dead and that will take time.' Meric's voice grew anxious now. 'But you must get supplies in the way of armour, and you must enlist a lot more men.'

'How are we going to do that?' said Silva.

'I will put myself forward,' said Kal. 'My son is nearly three years old now; he displays the eagle totem that represents freedom. We are expecting another child soon. I have to protect my family so my children can live their life to the full, so they do not grow up in fear. Their freedom is their right.'

'I will join you,' pledged Jonha the blacksmith. 'My Arneb is fifteen years old, I do not want her to become a slave to this barbarian, or die at his blood stained hands. By the grace of the gods I give you my word.'

Godan the carpenter was next to pledge. 'I will join as well.'

'And me,' shouted Nemi the herdsman.

'Count me in,' voiced Sable, one of the fletchers.

And one by one, all the fathers of all the young children followed Kal's stance and pledged allegiance to the clan and their freedom.

'I shall go and warn the others, and get word to the clans that we need more men. Who's coming with me?' heralded Kal in a strong stoic voice.

'I will,' said Jonha punching his fist in the air.

'And me,' voiced Nemi wrapping an arm round Jonha.

'Let's go right now,' urged Godan scrambling to his feet followed by Bray, his apprentice.

'We need a lookout as well, to track the General and his men; otherwise we have no way of knowing when they have assembled,' Laith's voice was grim.

'I will warn the other clans,' hailed Jonha. 'Then I will camp in the forest with these men for as long as it takes. We will get word to everyone when the General is on the move.'

'Good man Jonha, your daughter will be proud

of you, and all you men who have put yourselves forward, may your totems protect you.'

'It is an honour Laith.'

The troop of fathers saluted to their leader and made haste to saddle the horses and onwards to their call of duty.

'What about armour though? We can't get our hands on any,' cried out Clebe.

'Oh yes we can,' said Lyall with a thin smile. 'It's in the castle.'

'Castle Dru, of course,' Laith's look was chilled.

'Yes, it's all kept in the basement.'

'We will have to go through the cave in that case,' said Namir. 'It's the only way. Are you all right with that Lyall?'

'Of course I am. I want the sharpest sword and the most lethal dagger and I personally want to plunge them into the heart of that depraved General.'

'Then you can take back The Seal of Kings, Lyall, the legacy that is rightfully yours,' roared Laith finding his triumphant voice. 'Come let us go to the stone circles, we must pray to our gods and totems for added strength. We need help and guidance now. This is our darkest hour comrades.'

36

The General had decided to spend the next few weeks getting himself fit and battle prepared. He would eat a rich and varied diet, take lots of rest and look after himself well. There would be no more wine, spirits and overindulging, he would lock away the expensive cigars that he and Gnaeus used to share. He would begin training straight away with his array of deadly weapons and perfect his sword fighting skills with both left and right hands. He would call on his captains to train with him throughout the day until his arms fatigued from the motion and his hands and fingers bled from the grip. He would challenge himself to be the Master of the Sword, the bow, the dagger, and the spear. The thought of charging alongside the cavalry with all of those weapons on his person delighted him; mounts were always guided by the rider's legs and an armoured shield would be more than enough protection against a bunch of pitiful untrained savages.

Nevertheless, he would still need to go out on training runs to become proficient and expert in all those disciplines. He rose at five in the morning and trained hard until nine. Then he took a light breakfast followed by rest and caught up with his paperwork.

Lunch at one would be followed by an afternoon of heavy training again. He would take supper at six, followed by battle strategies with his captains at dusk, then retire to his chambers at nine. This gruelling regime continued for weeks, until he looked strong and muscular, with an insatiable hunger for blood.

The weather had turned when the first of the recruits had arrived, and Vortim Vontiger had been appointed the new General in waiting.

'Give them the dormitories Vortim,' said Corbulo with a cruel smile. 'They are better than anything they've had before.'

His successor rasped a throaty chuckle.

'And supply them with lots of liquor so they don't feel too deprived.'

'Do you want me to lock them in? After all, they are unpredictable barbarians, who knows what they will do?'

'No Vortim, we don't want any complaints like last time.'

Vortim Vontiger laughed out loud and strode out of the room leaving a smirking Domitrius Corbulo to go over his plans.

A few more days would allow the other recruits to arrive and then he would be ready to train them. He had enlisted a thousand troops by way of posters and leaflets, talks and recruitment, where each one had been promised riches beyond their wildest dreams. A few were the soldiers and captains who had survived the poisoning, many were rogues who had nothing better to do, mostly they were thieves and barbarians who had nothing to lose. The soldiers would train the rogues and the thieves in the arena. He had offered farmers huge amounts of money for their horses, to replace the ones that the clans had stolen, but never intended to pay them.

His army would be a magnificent collection, an awesome spectacle and a force that would be far too superior to take on. He would crush the life out of those savages, starting with the Clan of the Mountain Lion. He would take Skyrah back with him to remain as his muse, his prisoner, his dalliance; she would pay for the rest of her life for what she did. And then he would begin another offensive and another until all the clans and all the savages were either dead, imprisoned or his slaves. Soon, he would be the greatest ruler the kingdoms had ever seen. His eyes glistened and his lips moistened, and he began to dance as he conjured up the vision.

37

The initial ripples of fear had been replaced by stoic shards of vigour. Words of determination had rumbled through the camp, and while Namir and Lyall were preparing to go back through the tunnel everyone else was preparing in their own way.

Mothers and wives began foraging and preparing vast amounts of wholesome food. The totems were blessed, the tattoos were defined, and the elders sang in ancient tongues and chanted over simmering pans. Girls were carving a range of protective talismans. Destriers were out training during the day and brought back to the stables to have oil soaked liniment rubbed into their legs at night. Men and boys had begun basic weapon training, the blacksmith was forging his steel, older children made flights and arrows for the archers, and younger ones made pictures for their fathers.

'Your husband is a brave man,' said Laith catching Orla hanging clothes out on her line.

'I know he is Laith, he really wants to show everyone that he can make a difference.'

'And he will Orla, our children will grow up in peace.'

Four year old Arran came running out, the eagle totem highly visible on his arm. 'Where's father, where is he, I want to give him my drawing.'

Laith scooped him up. 'Well that is a fine drawing Arran, did you do that all by yourself?'

'Yes I did,' cooed the youngster. 'It's my eagle helping father. I want to give it to him.'

'He left while you were sleeping big man, he didn't want to wake you. He is out in the mountains now protecting you, protecting all of us.'

Arran looked out towards the Claw. 'He won't be safe without my eagle drawing.'

'Arran, he will be safe. He has many comrades with him. He has his totem looking after him. All of us have prayed for his safety. He has your eagle protecting him right now; he has all of our totems with him. But keep that drawing by your bedside and when you sleep at night, the eagle will fly with you in your dreams, soaring into the sky, watching and protecting. Then you will know he is extra safe.'

The boy reached out for his mother. 'I'm going to put it by my bed right now.'

'Will you look after your mother for me while your father is away?' Laith said kindly handing him over to Orla.

Arran hugged his mother tightly and sealed a wet kiss on her cheek. 'Yes.'

'That's good, I knew I could rely on you big man.'

Orla smiled and settled her son down, the

blooming pregnancy tired her.

'After you have put your drawing by your bed, rest a while with your mother and tell her how your eagle will help everyone.'

He ruffled the lad's hair as he turned and saw Jonha's wife chatting with their young daughter. He remembered choosing her name for her fifteen years ago. They were in such a turmoil deciding on a name. Wife didn't like what Jonha liked and Jonha didn't like what wife liked; so they came to him in all his wisdom. He remembered reading somewhere in his distant past that Arneb was an ancient word for hare; and since all the girls bore the hare symbol on their arms, he deemed it a most suitable name. He smiled at the young girl, full of innocence and vulnerability. 'Arneb, such a lovely name and such a delightful girl.'

They saw him and waved.

'Where does the time go?' he asked himself. He waved back and carried on with his walk and left them to talk in the glorious sunlight.

Close by, Ronu was coiled in a loving embrace with his spouse and Clebe was in deep conversation with the bride he had recently wed. Bagwa was playing peekaboo with his baby daughter as his young wife looked on adoringly. And two old friends walked past them all and smiled at the signs of affection.

'It's so good to see you again Meric,' said Chay.

'And it's good to see you again as well. Where have all those years gone?'

'It seems like only yesterday I was showing you

the plants in the meadow.'

'And what a difference that day made to two people,' began Meric. 'It gave me my calling, and Skyrah's knowledge most definitely saved all those young men's lives.'

'It's a lifetimes work,' began Chay. 'All the girls are showing such an interest now.'

'And some of the boys I expect. We all owe so much to you.'

Chay tried to hide a blush as she dropped her chin but recovered sufficiently to ask his plans. 'Will you be staying with us a bit longer this time?'

'Well that's my intention if it's all right with everyone. I don't plan on going back to Ataxata for a while.'

'I am pleased to hear that Meric, I do enjoy your company.'

'And I enjoy yours too Chay.'

'Would you come to dinner this evening with me and Skyrah, I am sure she has lots of questions to ask you?'

'That would be most kind gracious lady; I am keen to find out the intricacies of Skyrah's deception.' A genuine smile and a crooked elbow invited Chay to be escorted down to the river's edge. 'We have much to catch up on my dear.'

Admiring eyes hovered over the kind face and her chin dropped once more to spare her rising blush.

Back in the village the boys were preparing to leave.

'Are you sure you want to come with us Lyall? We all understand if you don't.'

'You won't know where to go if I don't come.'

'We can find it brother, you could draw us a map.'

'No, I have to come, it was my home for fourteen years, it would be wrong of me not to.'

'Well only if you are sure, but we do need that armour and fast.'

'I know, it will save so many lives. Such a shame my castle family couldn't get to it in time.'

'But we can brother, and we will execute their revenge.'

'That's what will keep me going and drive me on through the cave.'

'Good man, come on, let's go.'

Lyall followed the rest of the lads through the camp taking solace that there were six of them this time. They crossed the open space between the village and the cave in jovial spirits. But by the time they reached the entrance and saw evidence of animal fur and fish skeletons littering the opening, that laughter had disappeared and it suddenly became very serious.

Lyall's nostrils flared as he went back in the tunnel for the first time in nearly four years. Namir wrinkled his against the smell of stagnant water and damp walls.

'I can't believe you went through here, and I am astonished that our mother did as well, it's like your worst nightmare.'

'I know,' replied Lyall, his voice was tight.

'I suppose mother had already been through with father, so knew what to expect,' surmised Namir. 'Maybe she had a torch like we have. But you Lyall; I just cannot imagine how scared you must have been.'

Lyall was already feeling the adrenaline running through his veins. 'The cave and tunnel seem so much smaller now. But I guess I have grown a lot more and I can see where I am going this time.' He shook away the memory.

But the further they went in, the more cold, damp and suffocating it became. The sinister experience of light depravation was overwhelming.

'I thought there were all sorts of creatures around me, I was almost making myself believe there were devils lurking in the dark.'

'Thank goodness we have these grease lit lamps otherwise we would all be terrified.'

'Just use one lamp at a time though otherwise we will use up all the fuel.'

They kept walking, they kept talking, reliving tales of bravery, hope and courage, tackling every subject they knew to stop their agitated minds creating distorted visions of terror.

The softened floor suddenly became rough stone and the walls folded in on them. The earth shivered beneath Lyall's feet and he picked up the pace.

'Hurry up,' he quailed. 'I am feeling anxious now.' He felt a hot tingling sensation in his spine and that beaded sweat of fear collect at the back of his neck.

The helpless feelings he experienced as a child rose up without combat and settled with a knot at the back of his throat. And now with his companions around him, swirling their lanterns in the darkness, his kingdom became a tunnel of wandering wraiths.

Bending low beneath the timid light, the boys trod the path that Lyall had carved all those years ago. The muffled sound of leather soles and rasping breaths echoed in the chill of the passage as hurried feet broke into a slow trot, eager to get out of the ghostly dark.

'There will be a door up here soon,' he called out trying to stifle his panic.

It would seem that a barrage of chests and bales blocked the door when they arrived. Ronu and Clebe pushed their backs into it, alternating with Namir and Lyall laying down and pushing with their feet. Bagwa and Norg pummelled with their fists. And ever so gradually the solid fused door began to edge open and the group were able to crawl through.

At once a squadron of nesting birds took flight noisily, they had got used to not being disturbed for years now. With pumping hearts and shots of adrenaline pumping round their flurried bodies, the boys recovered enough to brush away the dust ridden cobwebs and look around at the devastation.

Then a gentle touch caressed Namir's face and Lyall felt a kiss on his forehead. They were instantly at ease.

'This is where our mother died isn't it?'
Lyall nodded.

Namir reached up to the caress and held it there. Lyall could still feel the chill of the kiss. The boys stood dazed and disbelieving at what was before them. The windows and doors were charred beyond recognition, years of torrential rain and harsh weather had bruised it beyond repair. The ghostly echoes of people moved through the cold stone walls, their voices hushed in respect for the living. Namir put an arm round his brother, he couldn't find the words to say; instead they all paid a silent vigil.

For Lyall, the castle was a stranger now, a hushed place full of grey dust and empty shadows. There was no feeling, no warmth, no echo of laughter and love; the General had torn the very heart from it the day he murdered his parents.

He broke the deadly silence and focused on the task. 'Come, we have work to do.'

Namir agreed. 'Yes let's finish what we came here for quickly.'

'You will find everything you need in the basement, all the chainmail coifs and hauberks, plus the leggings and gauntlets and all the weapons that we need will be there. You will also find some wooden carts to transport it all.'

'Are you not coming with us brother?'

'No Namir, I'm going to stay here for a while and pray. I didn't know what had happened to my family back then - but I do now. I have some grieving to do and pay my respects. There a lot of friends here who I didn't say goodbye to.'

'If you are sure brother, I don't like leaving you alone.'

'I am not alone, I can feel their presence around me. And for you too Namir, this is as close to our mother as you will get - take time on your own to imagine what it was like in its day.'

Namir looked humbled and choked back a hard swallow. 'I won't be long, I promise. I just hope we can get through safely, the castle is quite unstable.'

'It will be fine, you have your leopard totem and our mother guiding you.'

Namir went one way and Lyall went the other. The timber roof had given way and exposed the wrath of unforgiving elements throughout most of the castle. Many rooms were inaccessible now. Corridors and floorboards had gone up in flames or just deteriorated over time. Wooden stairwells and bannisters lay rotting in their graves. The mortar structure gave some stability to the withered remains draped over it like the body of a decomposing crow. The boys followed the stone passageway downwards, clinging on to a range of charred irregular shapes that creaked and groaned, and they passed teetering slabs that were about to perish and join the other black ashes on the ground. As per Lyall's instructions they entered a tunnel that fed into a long chamber, and at the end of the chamber was the armoury room. The boys worked quickly and quietly, it felt almost sacrilege disturbing the tomb of the brave. It was cold and dim and every so often a whisper would curl affectionately round a neck or a cheek. Again Lyall was right, the amount of body armour was extraordinary and they stacked up high with everything they could.

'We'll take this lot out now,' said Bagwa. 'But I'm not sure these three rickety wooden trolleys will manage the load.'

'I think I saw some upturned crates outside that we could use,' said Clebe. 'Perhaps we should go and get them.'

'Good idea. We'll leave these upstairs and then go and get the metal ones,' said Norg.

But something else had caught Namir's eye. 'Wait a minute,' he said cautiously. 'There's something here.'

'What is it?' Ronu turned as the others disappeared.

Namir moved carefully, his soft shoes almost whispered on the stone floor as he approached the structure. 'I don't know yet, shine the torch over here.'

Ronu projected the flickering light onto Namir. The monster was draped in fine cobwebs and a mist of dust clung desperately to each thread. The particles made him cough as he sent them flying through the air. The fragile web clung to his fingers.

'That's the size of a small tree,' gasped Ronu with his heart racing.

'It's a sword,' Namir exclaimed. 'It's massive, bring the light over will you.'

The scabbard was of thick dark leather with a pure gold chape and locket at either end. The hilt was pure obsidian stone which morphed into a leopard's head with detailed snarling teeth and chips of emerald set into the eyes. The cross guard had an inscription along the ridge that he couldn't quite make out. He looked at Ronu as he removed the scabbard. 'It's not as heavy as it looks.' he chimed as the silver blade sang out to him and revealed a triple fullered sword that looked as if it had never been used. It glimmered in the light as Ronu held the torch closer.

'Look at the beveled grooves Ronu, look how perfectly they have been made. Only an expert in his craft could have made something like this.'

'There's an inscription on the cross guard Namir, can you read it?'

'Just about Ronu... hang on a minute... bring the torch closer... '

Namir wiped away the ingrained dust with the corner of his sleeve and blew the inscription clear. He looked closer and squinted. 'I don't believe it...'

'What does it say Namir?'

'You really won't believe this...'

'What?'

'It says Laith.'

Up above them Lyall walked through the ravaged ruin of the Great Hall and remembered those joyful occasions. He stopped where the royal dais once stood, but nothing remained of it apart from a pile of ashes and some burned out charcoal embers. The empty fireplace looked cold and forlorn, the disfigured candlesticks on the mantle wept tears of molten wax and had solidified where they fell. Lyall continued round and back upstairs. He prodded the edge of an open door into his mother's chamber, he had always felt so safe there, but this time he quickly recoiled as he felt the wind pushing against it from the other side. A sentinel of surveillance doves took flight in response and the noise made him jump. He stepped back and something moved beneath his feet. He looked down and saw the tattered fragments of one of his mother's books. He bent down to pick it up and it fell apart in his hands. 'She's not here anymore,' he cried aloud, and the walls groaned a weary response. Memories flooded through his mind as he held the fragile pages to his heart. The days of jewels, furs and bright fabrics were a distant past. Feathers, plumage and crystal crowns all but a memory. He knelt on the soiled rug outside her room and vowed his revenge. 'It won't be long now mother, I promise.'

In King Canagan's chambers he saw the remains of an oak table where the king dealt with matters of the realm; a debris of strewn ashen papers were evidence of the sudden attack. Tapestries and portraits hung unrecognisable from their once enviable positions whilst the threads of rich velvet curtains clung in shreds to blackened charcoaled poles.

Everywhere was decomposing. It was nothing but a carcass now where a hideous savage attack had ripped out the heart and soul and left behind a lifeless corpse.

But in the corner, something was still breathing, something was unsoiled and alive, its beating heart summoned him. It was the royal box of coin, it had been left untouched, it was as though the torturous fingers of fire couldn't devour it. Indeed the General and his hands couldn't move it. Perhaps they hadn't even tried though; everyone knew they were after a greater prize.

A deep gold chest, inlaid with golden scrollwork and detailed ornamentation was the only object in the whole castle that hadn't been destroyed. The Durundal coat of arms adorned the heavy lid while the huge lock and key were still intact. He didn't resist the urge to unlock it and peer inside. A treasure trove of silver and gold blurred his eyes and as he sifted the wealth through his fingers, something caught on them. He lifted it out to see more clearly and at once an aura of rainbows fired through the air and sent spectrums of light around the dead and decaying room; it was the chain of the Queen's own blue diamond pendant. He gasped as the memories resurfaced and let the pendant fall back into its resting place. He shut the lid in an instant, afraid to let out any more of the precious cargo. Too much had escaped already. He turned the lock and patted the lid. He sat on the box with his head in his hands; thinking, contemplating, analysing his future.

Eventually he stood up to leave, but turned to speak to his parents memory. 'Mother, father, I will use this one day to restore the castle to its former glory. My new wife will wear the Queen's Blue Diamond Pendant on our wedding day. Happiness and gaiety will abound once more. Riches and opulence will herald the Lords of Durundal again; but until that day - my heart is yours - and I will avenge your death - and I will take back the Seal of Kings.'

The day was still young when Ronu and Namir found a tear drenched Lyall with his back pressed up against the torched door and knees held tight against his chest.

'At least I'm the other side now,' he croaked.

'Dear brother,' Namir wrapped his arms around him.

Lyall sniffed back his runny nose and wiped it clean with his sleeve. 'Everything all right?' he patted his wet eyes with the back of his hands.

'Yes brother, everything is fine. But you are not going to believe this Lyall, look what we found.' And Namir presented him with the magnificent sword. 'Can you read the inscription?'

In the daylight it was easier to read and Lyall choked back his tears and braced a smile. 'My goodness, I never knew. Father, I mean Canagan never told me. This is just amazing. Thank the gods you found it. Laith will be overcome with joy to be reunited.'

'I know, come on Lyall, thanks to you we have what we need.'

'Where are the others?' he asked.

'They're just outside in the grounds, getting together a couple of the metal carts; we saw some upturned ones through an opening, the timber ones are too fragile and won't carry the weight,' said Ronu humbly.

'All right, that's good, let's go now, I've seen enough.'

Outside, the years of savage weather and unhealed battle wounds had beaten the sumptuous castle into retreat. Trailing branches that once stood tall and erect, limped lifelessly in an attempt to hang on to something more solid. Stone walls bore the scars of fire damage and resembled a beast that was all but dead. A weathered portcullis hung like a fragile web of aching limbs and the magnificent drawbridge that was once the stronghold was now permanently disfigured where it bore ragged edges and was transparent in places. It was a dismal end to a once fine landmark.

'Bastards,' seethed Norg. 'What makes a man turn into a vile monster that could do this?'

'I don't know Norg, but this place is giving me the creeps.'

'Yes, it's a sad ruin now, come on let's get these carts back on their wheels and be on our way.'

The boys had what they needed and carefully weaved their way through the mounded clumps of tufted grass. Their path then guided them through the castle remains into the room that would lead them back into the cave. They put most of the armoury into the three huge metal trolleys which eased the load on the three wooden ones and pushed their precious cargo into the tunnel entrance.

'Are you all right Lyall?' asked Bagwa kindly when he joined them.

'I will be,' he said. 'It just makes me more determined to watch that low life die and see his army suffer.'

'That goes for all of us Lyall, we all want to be the one that puts the dagger through the General's heart and carve out the demise of the Ataxatan Empire.'

'I am just glad that the weapons we use will have come from the Castle and that the General's soldiers will die at the hands of Canagan's blades. But look what Namir found,' he added proudly. 'It's Laith's sword.'

'What, really? let's see the beauty.'

'Where did you find that Namir?' asked Norg.

'It was in the armoury propped up against a wall.'

'That must have a name,' said Bagwa inspecting the glistening weapon. 'All swords that magnificent have a name, I wonder what it is?'

'Lucky the General didn't see it.'

'He was after something else though Clebe, he didn't even make it that far,' bristled Lyall.

'I know,' Clebe's heart sank with the recollection, and a sympathetic arm touched the boy's shoulder. 'Come on, let's get you out of here.'

38

'This is remarkable,' Laith trembled with emotion. 'I never even dreamed I would see her again.' He held up the sword to the light and a spectrum of colour bounced off her body as he kissed the triple fullered blade.

'We all wondered if it has a name?' asked Lyall.

'She, not 'it' Lyall. Can't you tell by her beautiful pommel?' Laith corrected him as he admired the beauty.

'She then, does she have a name?'

'She certainly does son,' he looked at her proudly. 'You all have had the pleasure to meet Leopardsbane.'

The boys smiled.

'Of course it is,' said Namir. 'It couldn't be anything else could it? And that's why I have the leopard as my totem.'

Laith was waiting for the correction.

'I mean 'she', sorry father.'

'Of course this beautiful creature is a 'she', just like the leopard on your arm is a female. Have you ever seen how a female protects the ones she loves. And I'm not just talking about in the animal kingdom that a female will fight to the death or put her own life in danger to save her young. Look how Skyrah risked everything to save all of you boys, and Lyall, your own mother, she gave her life so that you would survive.'

All three of them swallowed the emotion at the accolade.

Laith continued his tribute. 'Females nurture and protect, they are fiercely strong willed and should not be undervalued. Everyone thinks it is the man at the helm, that the male is the strength as he wields his way through life. But do not under estimate the power of a woman boys; never underestimate her power.'

The boys were humbled and remembered Clebe's emotional tribute to Skyrah back in Ataxata, and they reflected on the bravery and act of love that their mother had shown in the face of extreme danger. They felt proud to have such women in their lives, and gave the silence time to catch up until a faint whisper reached out.

'Who gave her to you?'

'My father gave her to me,' the quiver in his voice struggled. 'He had her specially made by a master craftsman.' He stopped and looked up. 'But Canagan has one also - was that one not there?'

'No father, just this one,' Namir's response was thoughtful.

'Perhaps the king took his to use in the battle,' suggested Lyall.

'He must have done,' agreed Laith. 'They are very special.'

'But maybe the General stole his sword as well as the Seal,' lamented Namir.

'Undoubtedly,' agreed Laith. 'And if he did, then he will be using her, as she's pure silver and gold.'

'How will I know if she's the king's sword?' asked Lyall.

'Because she's exactly the same as this - except she has a wolf on her hilt.'

The settlement rang to the sound of steel. Skilled metal workers forged even more swords and lances while the women weaved protective garments and made shields out of layered animal hides. Day after day the clan trained hard, practising tight phalanxes and forming shield walls whilst attacking each other with blunt wooden swords. The noise was a swelling tide with weapon training, war games and strategic exercises. Horses galloped as weapons were deployed around them. Then there was the rotating wooden octopus with hanging sandbags and the destriers charged into those as well. This exercise had been executed with such force that if the practice dummies had been real Ataxatan troops, then they would have been depleted in an instance by the spitted lances and curved sabres.

Lyall had led a regiment of archers and spent most of the daylight hours practising on a prepared shooting field. The butts used mounds of earth for targets and the archers sent wave after wave of arrows to stand like flags of honour in the dug up ground. Farmers, gardeners, shepherds, unused to the cutting materials, trained so hard that their fingers bled; so as well as the cloaks and shield defences, the women made leather finger guards for their protection. Nothing was left to chance and anything that could strike a devastating blow was excavated and lined up with the ballistas for the greatest impact. Weapons used for hunting the stag and the boar now became even longer and more powerful with razor sharp edges and toughened welded shafts. And when the last of the light had drained from the sky and a half moon rose over the horizon, the earth stopped moving for a moment and gave them time to breathe.

39

The General and his men clattered their way along the palace roads and out of the city at dusk. Lights were on in the small pink houses and curtains twitched nervously as the entourage rode out of town. The hard stone road that gave away the cavalry, morphed into soft green verges and a light summer breeze pushed small dark clouds to shower and bring the scent of primroses from grassy mounds.

Compounds of condensation billowed from wide nostrils. Rustling armour and chain mail signalled a dense layer of bodies and beasts. Each soldier and captain strode forward, navigating the others uniformly; they were focused, anxious, silently praying and preparing for the discipline of battle.

The General's party had a two day ride. He had decided to go through the pass of the Giant's Claw which took them past rivers, ravines and mountains on their course back to the borders. This was Clan domain and it had to be taken at all costs, for this would form part of his growing Empire. All subjects would be massacred, not one infant would be left alive to come looking for him in years to come. He didn't want to spend the rest of his life looking over his shoulder.

No, they all had to go.

With the army behind him immersed in their own thoughts, the General reined his horse to a halt.

'We rest here,' he said, finding a dense area of forest with the mountain range on the horizon. 'We must collect our thoughts and remind ourselves why we are here. Remember no man, woman or child must be left alive and the girl called Skyrah will be taken as my prisoner. Do you all understand that?' He looked at them severely as a thousand faces nodded to him. 'If anyone harms that girl I will personally disembowel them.' He feasted on the element of fear with a hunger in his eyes. 'We will leave at first light. Anyone found sleeping in and holding up the proceedings will never see the sun rise again.'

'When do we attack the clan my lord?' asked a rogue dweller, eager for his first taste of blood.

'We attack at dusk. That is always the best hour in my experience. They are seldom prepared and never expect a twilight raid. So rest now, for tomorrow will be a long day, but it will yield the greatest prize.'

The group dismounted and loosely tied their horses to the branches. The soldiers and captains assisted with the weapons and removed their cumbersome armour. The down and outs, rogues and thieves lounged about in soft leather hides, cackling and jabbering throughout the night; they didn't care what lay ahead or who they killed, they just wanted to sever some limbs and be paid handsomely for it. But the soldiers and captains who had sworn allegiance to the Emperor in waiting, knew that those men would not be paid at all and most would not return home anyway.

As the General's army settled down for the night, a group of six clan men went unnoticed as they slid down the trees and made their way to a concealed river. They took delivery of their horses and split into three directions.

'May the gods be with you,' Kal whispered. 'I will go to the Clan of the Giant's Claw with Jonha and then on to the Marshland tribe. Sable and Godan go to the Hill Fort. Nemi and Bray go back and tell Laith. The General is on the move and will attack at dusk tomorrow.'

'To Freedom!'

They raised their arms in a salute and disappeared into the night to deliver their news.

40

Skyrah was proudly grooming Meteor and rubbing wax into his fetlocks and hooves.

'What are you doing?' quizzed Namir as he walked past her with his comrades.

'Getting Meteor ready for battle of course.'

'Why, who's going to ride him?'

'Namir, stop with all the questions, I'm going to ride him.' And she continued shining his coat with a fist of wool soaked liniment.'

'I don't think so Skyrah, fighting is men's work.'

She stopped abruptly and faced him. 'Namir how can you say that to me, and how can you lot stand by and let him?' She burrowed all of them with fire in her eyes. 'I have done so much to secure your freedom. I have shown unrivalled bravery and skills. I have trained with you and stood by you. My charger is the finest stallion on the field and he will protect me. You must let me come too.'

'This is too dangerous, way too dangerous for a girl, we are fighting grown men now with superior weapons, you are no match for them, I am sorry Skyrah, they will kill you.'

'The General is coming to take you back again,

we cannot risk that,' said Lyall supporting his brother's decision.

She cried out in defiance: 'You, Clebe, didn't you say; never underestimate the power of a woman.'

He looked like a startled mountain goat caught off guard. 'Yes I did Skyrah, I did say that and I meant every word.'

'And you Ronu, didn't you pay tribute to my strength and resourcefulness?'

'Yes I did.' He looked to the floor thankful that this wasn't his decision to make.

'All of you know that I am strong enough and skilled enough in the use of weapons. You know I am, you know how strong I am, and that I have the heart and soul of a warrior.'

She saw Namir thinking about it. She tried again with another approach. 'If I am hiding with the women and children when the General comes looking for me, then their lives will be at risk, you know what Meric said, he will spare no one in his pursuit.'

'She's right brother,' said Lyall. 'You know what that sick bastard is capable of. At least with Skyrah on the battle field with us we will know where the General is.'

'I don't like it either,' said Ronu. 'But we can protect Skyrah if she stays close to us, there is no one to protect our families in the camp if he goes looking for her there and we don't see him.'

'I agree with Ronu and Lyall,' said Clebe. 'We have to keep the General away from those in the camp because he won't care who he slaughters, be it a babe in arms or the mother who is nursing.'

Her eyes pleaded with Namir, her very being reached out to him and gradually she saw the defiant frown soften.

'I'm not happy about this Skyrah, you know I am not, but a valid point has been raised in keeping the General away from the camp and keeping you in our sights.'

She started to stroke Meteor again but looked directly at Namir.

'...all right - I agree, but only if you promise that you stay close to me or Lyall, Ronu, Clebe or any one of the clan soldiers. You must promise me that.'

'I will Namir, I promise.'

The boys smiled at her and went to join the others and collect their armour. It was only Namir who stifled his true feelings of deep concern. But his angst was replaced with pride when he saw how splendid each man looked in their protective chainmail hauberks and coifs, with equally protective chainmail leggings and gauntlets, with a sword and mace secured safely in a leather scabbard on their right side, and a battle axe fixed firmly into a belt on their left side with a dagger in their right boot. Some had poles and lances, Lyall had asked for a crossbow, and Namir had a spear.

Skyrah strode Meteor out and placed a hand crafted metal flanchard around his flanks and a jacked leather shaffron over his head. All the women and children had painstakingly and arduously spent hours upon hours making protective battle garments for the horses so they were all attired in the same barding. And now, for the first time, the riders sat high in the saddle feeling like powerful knights and lord protectors.

'You look like a warrior,' said Namir smiling under his tight fitting skullcap.

'That's the desired effect,' and Lyall paraded round the camp practising his aim.

Skyrah was adorned in similar battle dress with a detailed chain mail protective tunic and leggings, rich woven gauntlets and a thick woollen cloak. She wore a linen shirt and a woollen garment under the tunic to protect her small frame. She was armed with a magnificent mahogany cross bow studded with nuggets of coral and turquoise, and a set of highly polished arrows with extraordinary ivory flights with the smoothest steel tips were secured in a fur sheath. She took out her dagger and added a final sheen as she wiped the blade across her thigh. It flashed against the sun's rays and made her squint for a second. 'I shall call you heart-breaker.' A kiss sealed its baptism and heart-breaker was placed carefully inside her leather boot.

'You take care daughter, I want you to come home safely.'

'I will mother, I have promised Namir and Lyall that I will stay close to them.'

'The plants won't help you now my beautiful girl, you have to pray to your totem to protect you.'

'I have done that mother, but I also have my valiant steed, look how strong he is.'

'Yes he is a magnificent horse,' and Chay whispered into Meteor's soft ears. 'Please bring my precious child back to me safely.'

He nodded his head up and down with assurance.

'See I told you he understands every word you say to him.'

'If only men were that easy to make understand,' she teased and threw Skyrah a knowing glance.

'Come now my dear,' said Meric comfortingly. 'She is in good hands, she is a brave warrior. Her totem has looked after her so far, let her go now and fulfil her final call of duty then we can all celebrate and welcome peace back to the clan.'

'My dear Meric, what would I do without you?'

And this time it was Skyrah who threw her mother a knowing glance.

41

The Ataxatan foot soldiers and archers had already taken their positions. Their battle formation was a massive phalanx of shielded soldiers, six ranks deep. The better armoured men were positioned at the front and locked shields in the same manner as the back ranks. The front line of soldiers had the point of their spear aimed at their victim's chests and those behind had their weapons levelled at the horses. Their elite band of archers would give close support to the hand to hand fighters. These were men who marched into battle bearing no fear for they believed that in death the Ataxatan chariots would take them to the imperial kingdom to sit with their god Ataxa for eternity.

The rest of the Ataxatan army saddled up and remounted and the immense cavalry rolled across the land in a north easterly direction. The forest opened up into far reaching views of the plains, and the Clan of the Mountain Lion was looming over the horizon. The General and his men plundered through this opening, riding furiously, their horses drenched with sweat and frothing at their mouths. There wasn't much further to go now and the General ordered his men to be alert and ready as they raced onwards into ambush territory.

At last they could see it. They saw the banners and the lanterns, they heard the horns and the drums, they felt the fear and the panic. They could smell the blood. Vortim Vontiger was the second in command and he brought his mount to a twisted rearing halt beside the smirking General. As his horse frothed and sweated profusely he shouted out over the pulsating bodies. 'This is it men, form up deep and narrow and keep a tight formation. We are going to smash their ranks with our mass.'

A mile or so away, Namir spoke like he had never spoken before as he felt the strength of honour and duty running through his veins. 'Let us go now as warriors and those who give their lives for the clan, may your resting place be divine and may you be richly rewarded in your next life.' He bowed his head solemnly and prayed to the gods and spirit guides for strength and fortitude. 'Fill your souls with fire! Fill your lungs with determination! Fill your hearts with passion and together we will be victorious!'

As they looked out across the plains, they all felt an odd mixing of elation and fear. How long would they have to wait before the other clans arrived? They were desperate for their support.

Namir shot a look over to Skyrah and saw that she was flanked by four men. He didn't care that she was not happy about it, he was not entirely happy about her being on the battlefield anyway, regardless of what everyone had said, she shouldn't be here. Right now, he couldn't wait for this day to be over, because there was something even more pressing at the back of his mind.

But then his thoughts turned to something other than Skyrah as he felt the flats tremble beneath him and the horses began to fidget nervously. His palms moistened as noises were heard in the distance. The dark shadows slid away and the wind picked up pace as a drum beat crept under his skin. And there they were, boiling through the mountain pass and beating the path to destruction.

'Dear mother of gods, it's him,' quailed Lyall. His gaze was on the General clad in red robes, a gold helmet and riding his black charger.

The General surged forward leading the cavalry into battle. They fired their arrows into the air and a war horn blew. Lyall pushed the knot of fear to the pit of his stomach and stood up tall in his saddle. He was looking for the allies. They should be here by now. He should be seeing a storm of dust to announce their arrival. And then he spied the bobbing rows of moving lanterns. It was the torches from the other clans flowing like molten lava round the sides of the mountain.

'Thank the gods,' he exclaimed. 'They are here, and look how many men they have gathered.'

There were thousands of them. The Clan of the Mountain Lion whooped and yelled in absolute elation.

'There's Tore waving the banner leading his troops, look how tall he sits.' shouted Namir.

'And look who sits alongside him,' yelled out Skyrah seeing Lace.

This formidable woman bore the tattooed insignia of a female emperor moth which covered the whole of her back. The four wings spread across each shoulder blade and lower back with four large vacuoles that became her rear eyes. The body of the Saturniidae ran down the whole of her spine and the antenna reached towards her shoulders. This was her metamorphism, this was her power, this was her strength and her extraordinary beauty.

'Look at Siri and Dainn, they are coming from the other side, look at the masses they have with them. And there is another woman that rides alongside Dainn who looks strong and valiant.'

They all stared at the vision before them, their spears a hedge and their shields a wall, and then the tumultuous shouting and yelling began with the banging of shields and the army moved forward.

The General wouldn't have seen the joyful faces in front of him and he wouldn't have seen the sheer mass of young men filing in from the flanks. His army was still charging through the very centre of the pass. The clan's torches kept on coming baring flags and banners of power. The drums were beating, the horns blew out loud. The Ataxatan army looked beaten already. From that moment they knew that the clan's soldiers could outdo the General's and that they could slay twice as many as their own number. That's what gave them unfathomable strength and determination as they stood their ground defiantly. Namir breathed in the enormous power from the generating wind and bellowed out his order to move in. Three hundred blades left their scabbards in flight and the entire force of the clans leaped to the attack storming over the battle field towards the General who was rushing in towards them.

The ground shook with the stampeding sound of hooves thumping rhythmically into the grass lined plain and the earth trembled as a thousand foot soldiers ran in to support them. They didn't have time to panic; adrenalin and a much greater force took over and carried them along with a concoction of excitement and fear. Skyrah's voice rose in power above the din of the galloping cavalry, shouting out her warrior's cry, getting energy from Meteor. He thundered in like a war horse, a valiant charger showing no fear. She leaned in to the animal's quickening pace tightening her grip on to her reins as she urged him on. Foot soldiers with spears and daggers ran in first to cause as much chaos and slaughter as they could.

Dainn reached for his weapon whilst in a gallop and swiftly fixed a bow to the string of his crossbow and sent it flying through the air into the jugular of his first victim. Another arrow was taken that followed the first into the heart of another assailant. Siri came in with the advance and sent in a squadron of archers to deploy their weapons. Skyrah went with Ronu and Norg, firing their arrows and catapults as they moved in.

Clebe and Bagwa displayed strength that had no boundaries; they were still in fighting mode from their

341

days in the arena and remembered the brutality of that harsh regime. Clebe bludgeoned his mace into a soldier who was hanging onto an injured leg, the soldier fell and Bagwa watched his chest cave in under the weight of his horse. Kal had cut down one opponent and was now hacking a pathway through the soldiers for Tore to execute his unfathomable power. The mighty Tore continued to slay men with an agility that belied his heavy build. He was fighting supremely, swinging his sword in tremendous strokes and even though he was surrounded by the enemy forces, no one seemed able to touch him. The men with spears and lances followed Tore, while Siri and his archers stacked arrows in their sheaths and followed Lace.

Many of the enemy were quick to notice the master with his sword and his accomplices. Some men tried to run, others tried to hide, some fought back, but each was swiftly disposed of. The noise of smashing metal on metal reeled through the battlefield. Razor sharp swords sang out the sound of death as they slashed and sliced through the air, carving the blade into anything that got too close to the proximity of the unforgiving edge. The smell of fear hung heavily as the perpetrators were stripped of flesh and bone in seconds.

The smell of blood was worse.

Out on the plain the fighting went on, as soon as they came within range, the deep vibration of the ballista's released bow strings was followed by the smooth hiss of the darts as they flew towards their targets. And further behind the lines a range of catapults launched a shower of boulders against the advancing horde. Longbows began to whisper all along the defences as flights of arrows were shot into the sky and curved in flight to unseat the enemy.

The demons ran in all directions like headless chickens looking for a way through. For an hour the struggle continued with neither side giving ground, but then the Ataxatan army began to yield.

The General yelled out foul mouthed obscenities as he watched the massacre of his men. Under the grip of panic many vomited in the soil, it was like watching day old lambs attacked by a pack of wolves. Those that were left were surrounded on all sides and suffered further casualties in their masses.

The General called for the cavalry to regroup but they were further beleaguered having fallen into an explosion of flailing limbs and weapons. It was difficult to keep a steady stance on a patchwork of crumpled corpses. Dainn was locked in a battle with a captain, they leaned on one another for support as they parried each blow. Both were tiring. Vortim Vontiger saw his opportunity and took aim with a spear.

Hali spotted the impending assault and shouted. 'Dainn, look out!' But he had little fight left in him now.

Silva saw the minefield unfold in front of him and ran towards the second in command but something hard hit him on the head and he slumped to the ground pitifully waving in a frugal attempt to stop the events. Vortim's spear realigned its destination and the weapon left his grasp. It cruised through the air like a missile and hit its target. Dainn collapsed.

Out on the plain next to Silva, an arrow left the bow of a warrior and hit Vortim full on in the chest. He dropped down on the spot clutching the shaft that was rooted to his heart and searched with narrow eyes for where the arrow had come. A tall strong woman stood there, ready to fire again if the first had not been fatal. Kal ran in and plunged his dagger into the captain and rushed to Dainn's side, he was injured and battle weary but he would survive. Enraged, Kal stormed towards the General's men coming in to finish his comrade off. He swung his sabre into a vicious arc taking a man's head clean from his shoulders, he then went on to decapitate half a dozen others with the force of his blade. As Vortim Vontiger and the captain died, the strong woman saluted to Kal and Dainn. She turned and carried on with her mission, but Kal had spotted a fallen hero. Amongst the blood and gore he saw a face that wore the gauze of death. He fell at his side and wept.

Namir saw their comrade fall and felt Kal's pain. He was one of their own clan; Kal's closest friend. He immediately thought of Skyrah. He needed to find her. He came out of his vantage point but through the battle mist and swirling debris he couldn't make out very much at all. Dust had obscured the sun and turned the air a putrid brown. Looking around him all he could see were piles of bodies and severed body parts. The fallen lay sprawled across one another, their red stained weapons abandoned around them. The reek of blood and gashed corpses had encouraged the carrion birds to start their feasting and they got in his line of vision as well. Sweat and dirt ran down his face and collected in wells in the rim of his eyes. Rubbing and blinking made them worse.

Only a few figures were stumbling around in the battle field now, abandoned screaming horses were fleeing the flats, others waited on the perimeter.

He was using up precious minutes observing the scene and was relying on his leopard spirit to guard him but he still needed to know where Skyrah was. Had the General taken her already? The blood curdling thought horrified him. Please no, not again. That madman would surely not be so forgiving this time. Her life was in absolute danger. A silence descended as he looked through the haze for the General and for Skyrah.

But time stands still for no one. The General had spotted the stillness of his prey. 'Now that's what I have been waiting for, an error of judgement. Their leader, and object of Skyrah's desire, is so engrossed elsewhere that he can't even see me standing here.'

Namir's frantic eyes were avoiding the General's direction and did not notice him getting ready for the assault. The General prepared for an ambush, it was now predator and prey, he was going to take this opportunity. The hunter slowly reached for his axe, eyes locked on the vulnerable unsuspecting victim. With cunning perseverance and without arousing suspicion, he withdrew his weapon. Calmly and carefully he raised the murderous blade. The victim was the perfect target, the eyes were focused elsewhere. The predator kept the prey in sight and with acute precision took aim with the hatchet. He exerted a force so strong and sent it flying through the air towards the heart of its intended victim.

The axe penetrated through the brume with a mission to sever its target in two. The momentum of the flying weapon was caught in Namir's peripheral vision but it was too late. The axe was faster than his reflexes. His life flashed before him and everything that might have been. Everything that his father had taught him, everything that he had been through, everything that Norg and Ronu had drummed into him, never become a target, never take your mind off the task. Think, feel and survive. He knew that he had let them all down, he had let himself down, but mostly, he had let Skyrah down. The guilt handle of the axe was all that could be seen as it impaled him on the unforgiving steel and he sank to the ground.

42

She had taken Meteor to safety with the other horses and came back on the field to see Namir fall. She ran to him, frantic, crying and screaming out loud.

'No!' She heard her own voice ringing in the mayhem, the haunting sound trailing off into the distance. The mist and silence hung over him and slowly wrapped itself around the guilt handle. Her own heart was aching. She felt his pain. The fighting was over. A few enemy soldiers remained stumbling in the background, but the rest had been slaughtered. She fell to his side and her tears mixed with the sweat that saturated his broken body. His red stained hauberk and blood splattered weapons were evidence of the battle he had fought. He was pale and weak and dying. Now the silence had gone and instead a voice was in the air, as clear as glass, as bodiless as an echo.

She cried out. 'I'm so sorry Namir - I let you down. It is my fault that you lay here like this. I have killed you because I didn't stay in your sight.'

He looked at the beautiful face that he had loved for so many years. 'At least it's your face that I see before I die.' He groaned in agony and arched his back.

'I love you Namir, I have always loved you.'

And she sobbed onto the mail shirt covering his chest. 'From the days you sat helping me tearing up leaves and plants for my mother, I loved you then.'

His eyes were closed but he managed a smile as he recollected those days; those carefree moments when they had so much fun and couldn't imagine the many battles and challenges that lay ahead of them. He drifted off into another place where he had his imaginary conversation with her.

'When faced with so much despair and destruction, it's only then that you realise what is really important.'

'And what is really important to you?'

'You are Skyrah, you are the most important entity in my life, the thought of you kept me strong for all those months in the dormitory. And amongst all the brutality and butchering you were my shining star, you were my hope, my reason to live. But my biggest fear was not the battles or the monsters I faced - I feared that you would never know how I felt about you, that I love you so very much and I want to be yours forever.'

He drifted in and out of consciousness, he could feel her holding his hand, he could hear her telling him that she loved him, he could even smell her sweet aroma amongst all the blood and death. He saw another place where a fresh new sheet was draped over a peaceful land, where pockets of plants gleamed like jewels on green silk. Amethyst lavender, emerald ferns, ruby roses and sapphire bluebells were bathed in the brilliant sunlight. The sun kissed a brook and the gilded water danced with a thousand diamonds scattered on its shimmering outer dermis.

He saw a pair of eagles come into view turning on seraph wings. He flew to join them. It felt good to be with them, to be free and unleashed, to peel back the tired look from his beaten face. And as his spirit awoke, his soul became alive. His exhausted body felt uplifted and a gentle breeze brushed his face. It stroked his torso and curled around him, he felt strong again in its grasp. It began to pick up pace, it was getting stronger and harder, he was getting colder, so terribly cold, the wind was taking him away, the eagles were carrying him but he now felt as if he was drowning. He couldn't hear her anymore, he couldn't breathe, he had no control over his soul now, he was screaming in his head. 'No, I am not ready to go yet, I don't want to leave her. I can't leave her. Please not now!' His breathing was getting more laboured. He was struggling.

She was holding his hand, willing the life he so desperately needed. 'Don't leave me Namir, please don't leave me. You are strong, you are the leopard, you are my leopard.' She cried into his saturated hair. But the wound was too great. All she could do was hold him as his life ebbed away.

The pointed summit of a shadow edged towards them and slowly covered them until the huge towering figure of death hung over their sanctuary casting a sinister dark eclipse. A gloved hand reached down for her and yanked her off her beloved.

'Lovers always make mistakes,' the General

hissed into her ear. 'I saw him looking for you and as he went down in death I knew you would run to him; the handsome young man with the kingdom at his feet. But alas, look at him now, not much good to anyone is he?' He curved a sinister smile and licked her face. 'Still taste nice, even though you are a filthy savage covered in his blood.'

'Get off me you monster.' She struggled to get away.

'Now now, I thought we were friends.'

'Never!' And she bit into his arm.

The General looked at his bleeding limb in disbelief and hoisted the kicking screaming girl over his shoulder. But Lyall came out of nowhere, charging and howling like a wolf. The General dropped Skyrah to the ground. A trickle of blood ran down her head as she hit the hilt of the axe that protruded like a hideous flag of honour from Namir's corpse. The General didn't have time to check on her lifeless body. His attention was on Lyall. 'Now here comes the other one, this won't take me long either.'

'You bastard, you absolute bastard,' yelled Lyall running in with his sword. He was beyond contempt, he was beyond reasoning. Roaring his rage and his grief, Lyall drove forward sweeping aside all before him with the swinging arc of the sword he'd taken from Dainn's injured side.

The last Ataxatan soldiers fought with ferocity but fell to Lyall's weapon until at last he was fighting hand to hand with the General; the only man standing of the entire invading army and the man he despised most in the whole subject kingdoms. The mighty wolf inside him howled and launched in again and again for the attack. 'You killed my mother and my father and now you've killed my brother and the girl he loved.'

'What are you talking about you demented savage?' The General swept back his red cloak to reveal the Seal of Kings. He adjusted his gold helmet and held aloft a razor sharp sword that was bloodied with the deaths of many young men. And then Lyall saw it, the wolf's head on the hilt; he could even see the words 'Canagan' inscribed on the cross guard.

'You thieving, murdering bastard, you absolute scum of the earth. I am not a savage. You are the only deviant here. I am King Lyall of Durundal and I have been waiting a long time for this day.' He ripped open his shirt to reveal his scar. 'Remember this? You did this to me when I was fourteen years old. But now I am a man and I will get my revenge.'

The General felt the scar on his temple. 'Yes, I remember you, the frightened boy in pyjamas and a shawl; I thought you were dead, alongside that wretched mother of yours, but now I can finish what I started.' He raised his sword to take off Lyall's head. But the boy crouched low and narrowly avoided the brutal blade.

'The Seal that you wear is not yours; it was not the Emperor's to give away. And that sword...'

The General cut short his words. 'Well whose is it then?'

The ogre was tiring of the boy's voice and continued to cut the air near his neck to end the ranting. A sweep nicked Lyall's ear. The boy parried with his nemeses, locking the fiend's blade into his own hilt, then he threw back his head and gave a long howl that stirred all his pent up emotions.

'They both belonged to my father, the king you massacred at Castle Dru four years ago. They belonged to the people who you burned and hacked to death, and now they belong to me, the rightful heir and lord of Castle Dru and all it surrounds.'

'Is that so?' seethed the maniac, lowering his face until he was eye to eye with Lyall and spitting with venom. 'Well let me tell you this young man; your father screamed like a girl when I plunged my dagger into his heart and ripped the Seal from his neck, and now I'm going to relish on your screams for mercy.'

The General snarled and smirked as Lyall flew into a rage and danced around him; attacking and thrusting desperate to get an advantage, trying to get his blade somewhere, anywhere into the devil's putrid skin.

'And if you really are a king then there's no room for both of us in my kingdom now is there?'

Lyall was too wound up to focus now, he was not engaging accurately, his rage had rendered him weak and with all that energy being wasted, he was waning.

The General's fighting skills were superb and he tired of the inexperienced lad. He found an open channel and thrust the hilt of the sword into Lyall's head. The boy dropped his weapon and felt something warm running down his face. He looked at his bloodied hands and as he fell onto his knees he looked in disbelief at his attacker. 'How has this happened?' he thought. 'How on earth can this have happened? I am about to die at this monster's hand with my father's sword.'

The General threw back his head and laughed. 'You were never a match for me boy, king or no king, and the Seal will stay with me forever and give me protection as I slaughter the rest of your people with this rather magnificent sword.'

Lyall slumped, he had failed, he had let everyone down. He dropped to the ground. His body rolled over.

'And do you know what is so ironic little boy?' The General goaded as he licked the blade. 'You are right, this sword is the one I stole from your father and now it will send you to join him.'

A sickening smirk spread across his face as he raised the weapon.

But behind him a figure stirred.

Skyrah opened her eyes to see Lyall fall. Her hare totem called out to her. 'Get up Skyrah, get up now, you have to save Lyall.' She reached out to Namir's lifeless body and with a force that came from her totem sucked the axe from its resting place. There was a fine spray of red dust around her, a remnant of the wrath that had preceded it. She had to keep shifting her weight to steady herself. Bloodied and weak she dragged herself up and called out to the General. 'Oh Domitrius, I have something for you.'

He turned awkwardly, hardly believing what he had heard behind him. He thought she was a ghostly apparition standing there before him. He dropped the sword in shock. The surprise rendered him stationary. She had her one and only chance now. Without thinking of the danger she charged towards him and plunged the blade into his chest.

He grasped it with both hands. 'I was trying to help you,' he cried out piteously.

'Help me?' her eyes narrowed.

'I am the angel of the gods, sent to cleanse and rid the kingdoms of savages and scum.'

She looked at him in disbelief - a madman deranged with greed and power.

'Skyrah help me please. It will be just you and me and we can leave all these worthless souls behind us. You are not like them.' He staggered back, losing blood, holding onto the weapon as Namir's blood mixed with his own.

'What? do you really think I would abandon my family, my lifeblood, those I love, for a madman like you?'

'Skyrah, I am not a madman. I do not kill for pleasure. There is a higher purpose at play, I am the tool to bring justice to our kingdoms.'

'No, Domitrius, I am the tool to bring justice to our kingdoms.' She took the dagger from her boot and thrust it deeper into his heart.

Within seconds, a cavalry sent from the jaws of hell raged around him in a frenzied feast; pawing at him, tugging at him, ripping the life from his core and shredding it before his very eyes. The chaos and torment was thrice the scale of any battle he had fought and it seemed that every tortured soul he had ever taken was clawing at him. Skyrah put her hands up to block the screams. Lyall shielded the glare. The General reached out with frantic arms, his eyes wild with panic and fear. It was a pitiful last attempt for redemption. But no one came. He had sealed his fate long ago. The screams eventually died down. The cavalry dispersed. No one would mourn this tyrant.

Lyall shuddered as the lifeless body fell next to him. He looked up at Skyrah. She had broken the General's heart in two. He ripped the Seal from the perpetrator and clasped it to his heart. They had done it. They had killed the General and secured peace. He had the Seal and he had Wolfsbane. He had his revenge. But at what cost?

He looked towards his brother and his own heart ripped in two. He let out a deep wail and clawed at the bloodied soil. Skyrah dropped down with him and they sobbed together in a subdued embrace. They turned to look at Namir's body. He lay face up. He was a true hero and a true leader. He was her soul mate. He was Lyall's long lost brother and his greatest friend. Skyrah pressed herself into Lyall's arms and wept again.

As the dust began to settle, the clans made their way towards them, united in numbers with a strength that defied their young years. They were all too weary and grief stricken for jubilation, but in their hearts they cheered.

Lyall brushed Skyrah's blood stained hair from her splattered face and took a moment to look over her shoulder to his fallen twin.

But he saw a movement. He watched as his brother struggled to motion a sign; he saw Namir raise his arm for help.

'He's alive Skyrah! Thank the gods - he's still alive!'

To be continued in - 'A Leopard in the Mist.'

On the other side of the world, some ten thousand miles away, a lone man sat in a small tavern at a candlelit table surrounded by darkness and drunken strangers. Golden streaks of tangled limp hair reached his shoulders while a heavy woollen cloak hung almost to the ground covering a torn grey shirt and very worn britches. A paralytic lout on the street had lost his shoes to him, plus a handful of loose change. Under the growth of a few days stubble a handsome face was etched, though some would argue it didn't exist at all. The saturated straw didn't bother him either as he supped on his ale and he barely noticed the pungent aroma of body odour and stale beer. Outside was a maze of twisting alleyways and hidden corners - best to keep away from those places people would tell him - but he wasn't scared of those places, nothing scared him anymore.

www.kingdomofdurundal.com

Printed in Poland
by Amazon Fulfillment
Poland Sp. z o.o., Wrocław